PAST THE
BLEACHERS

ALSO BY CHRISTOPHER A. BOHJALIAN

Hangman
A Killing in the Real World

PAST THE BLEACHERS

A NOVEL BY THE AUTHOR OF **HANGMAN**

CHRISTOPHER A. BOHJALIAN

Carroll & Graf Publishers, Inc.
New York

First Carroll & Graf edition 1992

Carroll & Graf Publishers, Inc.
260 Fifth Avenue
New York, NY 10001

Library of Congress Cataloging-in-Publication Data is available.
Manufactured in the United States of America

Portions of this novel appeared in the *Boston Globe Magazine*.

for Andy, my brother,
and—this book and every book—
for Victoria, my wife

. . . for baseball is continuous, like nothing else among American things, an endless game of repeated summers, joining the long generations of all the fathers and all the sons.

Donald Hall

I.

Chapter 1

I used to lie to my father about Little League. I told him I was a pitcher. I may even have told him that I was the best pitcher on the team.

I was neither. I played—when I played—right field. I played usually one inning per game, usually when we were winning or losing (and more often losing) by a dozen runs.

A pitchers' duel is rare in Little League.

I had my lie down to a science. I told my father I was superstitious, and I was afraid to pitch when he was watching me. I told him I was afraid that he would bring me bad luck, so he could never, not under any circumstances, come to those games in which I was the starting pitcher. He had to be happy coming only to those games in which I had, so to speak, the day off.

My father therefore came to perhaps every other game. At those games he was allowed to attend, he would appear suddenly around the third or the fourth inning, sitting in the top row of the small wooden bleachers, eating a hot dog. I never saw him actually arriving at the Little League field, or making his obligatory pit stop at the concession stand. He would just appear.

In all of the games he watched, he saw me keep score, he saw me drink Gatorade, and he saw me shout at the opposing team. "No batter, no batter, no batter!" "Choosy mothers choose Jif!" "We want a pitcher, not a belly-itcher!" He saw me play right field, and once—but only once—he saw me play third base.

I had always wanted to try playing the infield. I thought that I might be better at stopping baseballs that scooted along the ground than I was at catching them as they fell from the sky. So when the last inning finally arrived and our coach, Mr. Tibideau, gave me my requisite three outs in the field, I asked him if I could take those three outs at third base. Mr. Tibideau glanced reflexively at the scoreboard, noted how badly we were losing, and said sure. And so I replaced our third baseman for a change, instead of our right fielder.

The very first batter that inning was left-handed. He was a long-haired little boy named Lonnie Lamberti, and like me he was a scrub. When my father saw that I was at third base and there was a left-handed scrub at the plate, he climbed down from the bleachers and stood beside the little boy in the coaching box and said to me, "He won't be able to pull the ball, he's going to hit it your way. Be ready."

I nodded politely, but I didn't believe him.

I should have. Lonnie Lamberti slammed an eyeball-high line drive right at me that I dove away from with less than a millisecond to spare. The ball rolled for a double, Lonnie later scored, and we lost that day by eight runs instead of seven.

This all happened when I was nine.

My own son, Nathaniel, was a much better baseball player than I was. He was a much better Little League player at any rate. Little League and baseball are actually very different games, and it's important to make this distinction. Little League is throwing the ball, hitting the ball, and catching the ball. The basic mechanics, pure and simple.

Baseball is all of these things too, but it's also a great deal more cerebral, a great deal more strategic: in baseball, batters bunt runners to second, pitchers throw sinkers while infields are set at double-play depth. Batters hit behind runners, and infields have rotation plays for bunt situations. These sorts of things don't happen in Little League. The kids aren't ready.

In any case, Nathaniel was much more talented than I was. He was, perhaps, much more talented than any other ball player in the Havington Little League (his coach's appraisal, not mine), including the older kids in the league above him. He was tall and lanky, and like most tall and lanky Little Leaguers, he "gravitated" instinctively toward first base. (Or, more likely, his first coach gravitated him in that direction. Tall kids make better targets than short ones.) Nathaniel had no fear of the baseball, in the field or up at the plate, and he had a good, graceful swing with the twenty-eight- and thirty-ounce bats Little Leaguers use. He also hit long, hard line drives with those little bats that carried regularly well past the three (and sometimes four) outfielders positioned deep against him.

It is also worth noting that I saw a lot of Nathaniel's games. My son told me of no superstitions, and he let me come to as many games as I wanted. Consequently, I saw each of the six games his team played when he was an eight-year-old in the Sprout League and almost all of the fifteen games his team played when he was a nine-year-old superstar in the Pee-Wee League.

He never had the chance to play in the Triple-A League in our town: although he reached the mandatory ten years of age one September, he died in the following March.

Harper is a Southern girl, as comfortable with that description now at thirty-five as she was when I met her at twenty-two. She never saw her son play baseball on Saturdays, but she went to many of the night games—Tuesday or Thursday evenings at six o'clock, when the air here in Vermont is just beginning to feel moist. When she went with me to a game, we would stand to-. gether on the ridge just past the third base bleachers by the edge of the outfield. She liked this angle because she could see Nathaniel clearly at first base, but unless he turned away from the batter (which he was much too good to do), he couldn't see her.

She was afraid he might become self-conscious if he saw us.

Harper wasn't (and isn't) wild about baseball, having come from a family of girls. She's the oldest of three sisters, with a father who had a fair amount of interest in ol' Miss football, but who had never in his life driven east to an Atlanta Braves baseball game or north for the St. Louis Cardinals. But she picked up almost immediately on the importance of repetition and ritual to the game, especially "all that stuff they do between innings."

That was always her favorite part of the Little League games: the stuff the kids do between innings. The first baseman throws grounders to the other infielders, slamming the baseball into the dirt so hard that it kicks up little dust clouds before the second baseman. The outfielders throw a baseball back and forth among the three of them, lofting it to one another in what must appear to nine-year-olds as great, soaring arcs. And the pitcher throws a baseball to the catcher, warming up, testing his control, his velocity, the feel of the pitching mound.

The irony of all this activity is that most of the kids still drop or miss or shy away from the baseball the majority of the time. As Harper said once, "The whole scene looks like a game of Asteroids." It does indeed. The balls fly and swirl everywhere: the third baseman scoops up his warm-up grounder and heaves it eleven feet over the first baseman's head. The center fielder throws his warm-up pop-up well past the left fielder, and the two of them wind up retrieving the ball from the marshy weeds in foul territory. And it's a sure thing the pitcher will bounce at least one pitch past his catcher, "experimenting" with a change-up, or knuckleball, or split-fingered fastball.

Have you ever seen a boy try and split his little fingers around a baseball? It's not a pretty sight.

Nathaniel died at 9:58 on a Thursday morning. When I'm wearing my watch, without fail I glance down at my wrist as ten o'clock approaches, and I watch as the second hand announces 9:58. I have this tendency whether I'm daydreaming at my desk or repairing the clapboards on the barn. It's a nervous tic of sorts.

Once, when I was on an airplane, I saw the entire passenger cabin do the same thing—stare at their watches at a set time, wondering if a select moment in time was damned or hexed or just plain unlucky. The day was January 28, 1986, the day the space shuttle blew up. (Fortunately, we don't have to say the day the space shuttle *Challenger* blew up; so far, only one of these blunt-nosed rockets has gone the way of a Fourth of July buzz bomb.) I was sitting in a passenger jet on the runway at Los Angeles Airport, number nine on a long conga line of planes waiting to take off. It was early morning in California, late morning back east. The airline was piping into the cabin some cable news network's coverage of the space shuttle lift-off as entertainment while we waited to take off and fly east to New York City.

At exactly one minute and fourteen seconds into its flight, the shuttle blew apart. I know it was exactly one minute and fourteen seconds not as a matter of historical record that I checked, but because the network broadcast the explosion over and over and over, a small digital computer noting the seconds from take-off in the lower right-hand corner of the screen.

For reasons that I will never understand, the airline failed to cut the broadcast. Instead, they let two hundred and fifty soon-to-be-airborne passengers watch seven of their fellow flyers go up in the air for exactly one minute and fourteen seconds, and then explode. And they let us all watch it at least a dozen times.

Consequently, when we did take off, all two hundred and fifty of us stared at our watches from the moment the jet's wheels left the runway, following the second hands as they strolled slowly around the faces of our watches, past sixty seconds, and—eventually—past seventy-four seconds.

At exactly one minute and fifteen seconds into our flight, that seventy-fifth second, we all heaved a collective sigh of relief. The seventy-fourth second in time on the twenty-eighth of January was jinxed for seven people only, not for us all.

Of course, this isn't exactly the same thing as looking at my watch at 9:58 every day of my life. But it is nonetheless related: I try to avoid meetings that may be in session at 9:58 in the morning, as well as visiting doctors, lawyers, accountants, or any other professional contractor who may in any way be responsible for bad news. I just won't do it.

The day Nathaniel died, Harper and I left the hospital and went home and went to bed. We fed the cats—two calicos from a nearby barn and the closest thing Nathaniel had to siblings—and then we went upstairs to sleep. We didn't know what else to do. We were incapable of seeing anyone, and—perhaps fortunately—Nathaniel's condition had deteriorated so rapidly that no grandparents or aunts or uncles or cousins had arrived from Mississippi or Connecticut. I doubt they had even been called.

But we went to bed also, because—pure and simple—we were exhausted. The hospital in Burlington had called the night before, just after midnight, and told us that Nathaniel was in trouble and we should be by his side. And so we had been up all night.

Of course, we were also emotionally exhausted, tired in a way I hope never to be tired again, tired from trying for six months to give a terminally ill boy—and each other—hope.

Someone at Nathaniel's funeral told my brother that Nathaniel and Harper and I were fortunate that Nathaniel died after only nine months: some kids are forced to battle it out for one, two, or even three years. And, my brother said, this person added, "It only gets worse."

* * *

There was a small irony in Nathaniel's dying of acute lymphocytic leukemia. It wasn't simply that both Harper and I have distant relatives who died of leukemia—a great aunt on her side, a second cousin on mine. The irony was that it was Little League that led to the diagnosis. It upset Harper when I pointed this out to her, and I had to explain to her quickly that the irony did not diminish for me in any way the sense of loss and sadness and frustration. The sense of bewilderment.

It didn't make any of it any easier.

But Harper said there was nothing ironic about her little boy's death, nothing at all.

Nathaniel sank into his final coma fifteen minutes before we made it back to the hospital. We had said good night to him about nine o'clock that Wednesday evening, and then driven home in silence to Havington. (Neither Harper nor I said much to each other—or, quite probably, to anyone else—during that last month.) We had been home for two hours and were just falling asleep when Todd O'Connor, one of the specialists who had supervised the last, desperate bone marrow transplant, called and said we should return to Burlington as fast as we could.

And so we did, returning just in time to see one nurse insert an intravenous tube into a spot on Nathaniel's neck (a painful spot, I thought, a spot just above his collarbone), and a second one switch on the heart monitor that read my son's chest through a series of little white suction cups.

"Is he still with us?" Harper asked, the first traces of the numbness that would hold her steady for a time in her voice.

The older of the two nurses, a woman named Lorraine who Nathaniel said gave shots and took blood best ("She holds my right hand, see, and acts like that's what she's interested in, and then, zap, the needle's in."), answered with a nod that yes, he was still with us.

It was about one-thirty in the morning.

O'Connor evenly explained to us what was happening: Nathaniel, essentially, had just about run out of good blood cells. Healthy blood cells. Red corpuscles and white corpuscles and platelets that worked. There were just none left. His arteries and veins were now filled with abnormal blood cells that were incapable of carrying oxygen, or fighting infection, or clotting when exposed to open air. His circulatory system was a road map of back roads and highways jam-packed with bad cars, bad drivers, and bad directions. It was no longer a matter of weeks, it was now a matter of days. Perhaps hours.

When O'Connor was done recapping for us what he and a dozen other specialists, radiologists, and well-meaning hospice workers had explained to us in great detail many times before, Harper looked over Nathaniel's shoulder at the heart monitor behind him, watched it jump once, and asked again, "Is he still with us?"

"He's still with us," O'Connor said.

And he was still with us for another eight hours and twenty-eight minutes. It is possible that we could have kept select organs in Nathaniel's body functioning well past eight hours and twenty-eight minutes, but Harper and I had agreed long before that there would be no heroic measures for our bald and gray little boy (and he did look very little at the end). When it was time, it was time. No senseless extra innings here.

It was somewhere around six or six-thirty in the morning that I explained to Harper the irony of Nathaniel's dying of leukemia. It was a stupid thing to say to Harper, and a stupid time to say it; and although Harper has forgiven me, I still regret bringing it up. But I was tired and scared and perhaps just a little bit delirious. And unlike Harper, I wasn't tranquilized: convinced that I was expected to remain stoic until the bitter end, I had turned down the Valium that O'Connor had offered us in the middle of the night.

Nathaniel had not evidenced any of the more common signs of leukemia nine months earlier: bleeding gums or a bloody nose, a sudden tendency to tire easily, an unusually pale complexion. Were it not for Little League, it might have been many more weeks before Harper and I would have realized that Nathaniel was even sick.

The first symptom occurred in the championship game against Sedgebury. Or, more accurately, the first symptom occurred in the weeks immediately following the championship game. It was a sliding strawberry on Nathaniel's left thigh, a tremendous bruise that remained black and blue for two and then three weeks after the game. A bruise that lasted three weeks, and even then showed no signs of healing.

That was the first symptom, the first indication of trouble.

"For whatever it's worth," I said to Harper sometime around six or six-thirty that morning, knowing it was worth to her less than nothing, "He got that strawberry when he slid home with the winning run."

Harper's favorite moment at all of the Little League games she saw had nothing to do with Nathaniel. She loved to see him get hits and run as fast as he could with his head weighted down by one of those monster batting helmets, and she loved to see him smile when he stopped a baseball at first base with his glove or his chest or whatever part of his body got in the way of the thing; but the Little League moment that she says she thinks about most actually occurred while Nathaniel was sitting on the bench, waiting for his turn to bat.

One of the stronger little boys in the town, Jesse Parker, was up at the plate. Along with Nathaniel, Jesse was largely responsible for the winning season that the Havington Pee-Wee Tigers enjoyed. On the first pitch, Jesse hit a ball about as high as a nine-year-old probably can, sending it almost straight into the air.

The catcher reflexively threw his mask away, mimicking the urgency of the professionals he had seen on television, and stood up to find and follow the foul ball. The ball drifted a bit, beginning its long descent perhaps a half dozen feet up the first baseline and a dozen feet into foul territory. Everyone playing or watching the game must have had a vague sense that the ball was drifting toward Obie Northrup's silver pickup, parked—as usual—too close to the ball field. Someone, probably the boy's mother, screamed loudly, "Watch the truck! Stop and watch the truck!"

We were convinced the catcher was going to crash into the parked truck, a collision from which neither his shin guards nor his chest pad would protect him. The little boy would be pulverized, the first time in recorded history that a speeding child had smashed into a truck, instead of the reverse.

We were wrong. The catcher may have heard the one woman who thought to warn him about the pickup, he may have known all along that the pickup was there. With the grace and agility of an Olympic gymnast, the boy approached Obie's truck as if it were a vault and this were a practiced part of his Olympic routine

—the floor exercises he had rehearsed for years in preparation for this one moment. Placing his gloved hand on the truck's rear door, he swung his legs over the side, and then standing in the middle of the back of the truck itself, he caught the pop-up.

Harper said she had never seen anything like it, especially by a nine-year-old boy. I told her I hadn't either, and that I had seen a pretty fair number of Little League games in my life.

Of course, Harper has not seen a Little League game since Nathaniel died. It's not that seeing a group of little boys (and these days, girls) together is especially painful for her: she is, after all, a third-grade schoolteacher. But the game only held interest for her while her son played. Consequently, the games I saw last year, in those months just after Nathaniel died, I saw alone.

It was an odd feeling to stand by myself at a Little League game, a spectator without a son. When there was a game in the late afternoon last spring, I would drive to the field straight from the college where I'm director of development—essentially, a fund-raiser. I would park my jeep beside the station wagons and pickup trucks in the firehouse parking lot, and wander down the left field foul line. I would stand often in the exact same spot where Harper and I stood together the year before, when Nathaniel was still alive.

But it was an odd feeling indeed to watch a game without a son.

This is another difference between baseball and Little League: baseball is a wonderful spectator sport. Little League isn't. The first time I stood alone on Harper's and my spot, I looked back at the third base bleachers and across the diamond at the first base bleachers, and I noticed that every single person watching the game was a relative of one of the kids on the field. A father or mother, a grandfather, an aunt, or—and this is very common in the little town in Vermont in which we live—a cousin.

In the little town in which we live, everyone seems to be a cousin of everyone else.

This is not a catty comment about inbreeding. Havington is simply a town of extended families, with new blood from other counties added as needed.

In any event, last spring I was always the only spectator without a vested interest in the game. Perhaps that's why I vowed that this year I would coach. I would forget the fact that I myself had been a horrid Little Leaguer, relegated most innings of most games to keeping score and lending moral support, and I would coach.

And I vowed I would coach at the town's Triple-A level, the level that Nathaniel would have reached had he lived to play one more year.

II.

Chapter 2

I am on top of Harper, moving in the dark, her legs wrapped around the small of my back as she too moves against me, churning her hips in little circles. The heels of her feet bounce gently against my sides, and she purrs, small soft moans.

I lean forward to kiss her on her forehead, her nose, her mouth, and then abruptly I pull out from inside her, and she opens her eyes, surprised. Her eyes reflect the moonlight in our room and glow like a cat's.

She starts to open her mouth, but I place one finger there and say, "Shhh." Her legs relax, descending soundlessly back onto the bed, and she stretches her arms over her head, trusting, reaching for the cherry wood headboard and giving to me her breasts to suckle.

I kiss her neck, a long strand of her blond hair a surprise against my teeth, and I run my tongue in small circles around the small nipples of her small breasts, and then I crawl downward on the bed, and lick at the small furry patch that only a moment before I had been deep inside.

I know that tonight we will make a baby, tonight it will happen, and I want the night to last and last and last.

Showered and shaved and dressed, I pull on the navy blue blazer I wear whenever I am spending the day with alumni from Boston or Chicago or New York. It has the school seal stamped on the gold-look buttons and sewn onto the worthless chest pocket, touches that I and the alumni know are extremely hokey, but therein lies their charm. It makes my love of the college look more sincere, and my requests for money sound less tawdry. It makes me look like a good-hearted rube.

The elementary school where Harper teaches is out for spring break, and so she is still upstairs in bed, taking advantage of the week off to catch up on her sleep.

I pad softly up to our bedroom, taking the steps as I envision our cats do, moving silently but fast.

Harper rolls over when I open the door, and smiles, her eyes still shut.

"Do you feel maternal?" I ask, sitting beside her on the bed.

She shrugs, the smile fading.

"No, huh?"

"Maybe," she says, opening her eyes and looking up at me.

"Good. You have to think positive. It's all attitude."

Harper ignores this. She runs one finger along the lapel of my jacket. "Who are you seeing today?"

"Toby Nesmith and John Wrightman. They're from Boston. They're in charge of their class's fortieth reunion this June."

"Ah, the sixty-plus crowd," Harper says knowingly. Like me, she now calculates automatically a person's age and likely net worth from his reunion class. "Loyal, successful, rich. Willing to revise their wills."

"We hope."

"What time are you seeing them?"

"Late morning. And then we'll go to the Maple Tree for lunch."

"Will you be home early?"

"I have to be. There's an organizational meeting for the Little League coaches tonight at five-thirty. It's at the firehouse." I kiss Harper on the forehead and remind her, "Attitude," repeating the word as much for myself. "Attitude."

When I say the words "Little League" to Harper, I am reminded always of Nathaniel. I have never told Harper this equation, but I know she is aware of it.

Nathaniel has been gone now for almost fourteen months. Twelve months plus forty-six days, I count to myself, as I walk to the barn where we keep the jeep.

Because it is early May, the jeep turns over easily, the ignition starting the moment I turn the key. Were it even one week earlier, in April, it would have been sluggish and slower to start. The jeep is very much like me: it hates winter and mud season and any kind of weather that makes the driving unpleasant.

The college is a twenty-five-minute drive from Havington on a blue-sky day like today, on roads that are photographed often for travel magazines and features on Vermont. Although I drive under no covered bridges, I pass seven working dairy farms, the cows ("the ladies," as my neighbor Norman refers to his own herd) grazing or sunning themselves within feet of the almost invisible electric fence that keeps them away from the road. I pass through two towns only slightly larger than Havington, towns with small churches with immaculate white steeples, towns with general stores that advertise in their windows, "Vermont Maple Syrup." And I pass through the village of Sedgebury itself, with the college of the same name spreading out onto the rolling hills just past the village.

My eyes tear this morning, as they do many mornings on the drive to work. They tear because of a story I hear on the public radio station: a group of cartoon illustrators have opened a small animation museum in Los Angeles, dedicated to the memory of Mel Blanc.

That's all it takes these days to reduce me to tears: a museum dedicated to the voice, now dead, of Bugs Bunny. And Foghorn Leghorn. And Elmer Fudd. I have no special fondness for any of these characters, and I don't recall watching Bugs or Daffy or Yosemite Sam with inordinate pleasure on Saturday mornings as a child. Nor do Mel Blanc and his voices conjure up for me memories of Nathaniel. At least not directly. Nathaniel never watched Bugs Bunny. Like other children his age, he watched cereal boxes turned into cartoons. He watched Smurfs, and Turtles, and Masters of the Universe.

But the animation museum makes my eyes tear nonetheless. As did the story last week about the slaughter of elephants in Kenya's Amboseli National Park, (I didn't use to care about elephants, and I don't even know where Amboseli is located). Or the one two weeks ago about overcrowding at a big city animal shelter.

For over a year now, alone in the confines of my automobile, I have become a softie.

I silently cry.

As usual, I am the first person in the development office, and the person therefore responsible for brewing the coffee. Two pots these days—one regular, one decaffeinated. I bring the coffee to my desk, nodding at the two photographs that sit on the corner as they have now for years, a photograph of Harper holding the calicos when they were kittens, and a photograph of Nathaniel in a swimsuit in Florida, visiting his grandparents.

I will never remove that photograph.

I push to the far side of my desk Doug Bascomb's charts, his weekly progress report as thick as a big city phone book. Projections for the alumni fund. The growth of the endowment. Contributions to the capital campaign, broken out by class, by region, and by the size of each gift. Some of Doug's charts are in color, some of his graphs appear three-dimensional. I stare at these charts at least once a week—each one a special effect of sorts, computer-generated art at its best—and try to discover how they've changed.

But I won't stare at them right now. Instead I pull from my briefcase the list that matters to me far more: the list I received over the weekend of my Little League team's personnel, the kids who signed up for Havington's Triple-A Tigers.

There are fifteen kids on the team, all ten or eleven years old. I count the names twice, relieved that whenever my team is in the field, there will still be six kids on the bench—enough of a crowd that our bench warmers won't stand out.

I had hoped to have an all-male team since I know almost nothing about little girls, and I know absolutely nothing about teaching them baseball. There are, unfortunately, at least two girls on the team this year, each ten. They are very sweet and enthusiastic, and as I look at their names I am fairly confident that—unless they've improved dramatically since last year, when both played for the Pee-Wee Tigers—neither will be capable of swinging a bat at the first practice next week. Only one, Jack and Carrie Edington's little girl, Melissa, will be able to throw a baseball on a fly from third to first base.

Melissa isn't any bigger than the other girl, Cindy Fletcher, but she has at least the advantage of an older brother. I've seen them play one-on-one Whiffle ball.

I recognize all but one of the names on the roster. Many of the boys were friends with Nathaniel, some closer to my son than others. But there are on the list the names of at least a half dozen boys who played with my son at our house. Boys who built six-inch-wide roads in the dirt by our garden, then tracked mud onto the celery-colored carpet in the den; boys who played war games set in the future as well as the past, finding always a role for the loft in our barn; boys who would drag their sleds and saucers to the top of the small hill beside our house in the winter, and race down it again and again until their wrists and ankles burned from the wet snow lodged underneath their wet snow-suits.

I was to them, I imagine, a vague adult presence. Mr. Parrish. The guy who drove the jeep. Nathaniel's dad.

Now I may be to them something more: I am afraid I may become to these little boys a ghost of sorts, an uncomfortable reminder that even ten-year-olds die.

Little League in Vermont lagged years behind Little League in a lot of the country. This fact didn't surprise me when I learned it. Vermont didn't get a Little League organized until 1950, and of course that was up in Burlington. The city. Havington didn't field a team until 1968, and there wasn't really a "league" in our area with multiple teams from multiple towns until 1971, when Lincoln, Starksboro, Sedgebury, and Havington agreed to organize the nine-year-olds in their villages and find sponsors for uniforms.

The local sportswriter for the *Sedgebury Independent* told me all this, an old man named Hilton Burberry. Hilton must be in his mid seventies. After escaping to a second home in Havington his entire life, he came here to live eleven years ago, retiring from an apparently successful career as a sports attorney in Boston. He represented the Red Sox: its owners and general managers, not its players, and so by his own admission got out just in time. "A gentleman by the name of Mr. Flood changed the rules in some very positive and decent ways," he said to me once in his careful, clipped manner. "But he made my life a living hell."

When we first moved to Vermont, I heard stories that Hilton had been "asked" to retire by the Red Sox. Fired, actually, in his mid sixties, after working forty-plus years for the team. But it wasn't age that led to his dismissal, people said. It was Ben Slaughter. Slaughter was a twenty-two- or twenty-three-year-old prospect for the Red Sox, who must have hit nine or ten home runs in the half dozen games that he played in the majors.

It was an astonishing streak, and for one week in April, a kid named Ben Slaughter was the toast of the majors, and the biggest sports story in New England. And then, abruptly, he died. He smashed his sports car into the underpass of a bridge near Dedham in the middle of the night, early that April. He had been drunk, so drunk supposedly, that it was a wonder he could drive at all. And, I've been told since moving to Havington, he had been drinking at a small party the Burberrys had held for some of the younger players.

Perhaps because Hilton retired from the Red Sox that May, only weeks after the Slaughter car crash began filling the tabloids, people in Havington assumed that the Red Sox were blaming the old man for the accident. After all, why else would a man like Hilton Burberry have not waited until the off-season to retire?

In any case, now Hilton writes about local sports. The affairs of the Sedgebury Colonials, the college football team. The wins and losses of the teams from the local high schools. The summer slow-pitch softball league ("Dorset Dairy Hammers Simmonds Precision 27-1"), skiing at the Snow Bowl, and even the triathlon held here last year with national athletes. Hilton and his wife, Eunice, agree that Hilton's job as a sportswriter preserves their sanity.

Hilton is also the commissioner of the Sedgebury County Little League, and has been for a decade. He meets me tonight at the firehouse in Havington just before five-thirty, holding a clipboard. We both are a few minutes early.

"Evening, Bill," he says, extending his hand to me, his grip bony but firm. "Glad you could make it." Hilton smells tonight of Ben-Gay.

"I wouldn't have missed it."

He nods, and we stroll together across the gravel parking lot into the tremendous two-story garage that houses the Havington Volunteer Fire Company. Two swallows dive underneath one of the eaves, a few of the dozens of families of birds that nest at the firehouse each year, and fly like the jets at Shea Stadium over the Havington diamond.

As we walk, Hilton reaches into the chest pocket of his red plaid lumber jacket for a pen. "I'll need some things from you, some information. I might as well get it now."

"Ask away."

"I need to fill in your home telephone number, and I need to know your work number. I also need to know when you can meet and when you can't. And I guess I should know whether you get along with Pete Cooder."

He holds his clipboard ahead of him like a waiter as we walk. I tell him my phone numbers, including my extension at the college, and that I like Pete Cooder just fine (it's impossible not to like Pete Cooder). I tell him I'm available any weeknight or evening, and whenever necessary on the weekends. Except 9:58 in the morning—weekday or weekend. I will coach games already in progress at 9:58, but I would prefer not to attend any special meetings or get-togethers which may happen to occur between nine-thirty and ten-thirty in the morning.

"Sure you want me to write that down?" he asks, rubbing the thin mat of white hair that coats his head like a bathing cap.

"I'm sure."

Inside the garage we pass beside Havington's two fire trucks, each polished to a sparkling red luster, and by the silver pumper, a monstrous metal sausage filled with river water. Two of the firemen are at the station right now, unpacking the new hip boots that arrived last Friday and initialing the top left cuff of each. I read about the new boots in the *Sedgebury Independent*.

Our meeting is in the fire company's "training room," the second floor of the firehouse. Someone, probably Hilton earlier in the day, arranged seven chairs around the fold-up card table by the window: one for Hilton and two for each set of coaches on each of Havington's three teams. We have a team for seven- and eight-year-olds in the Sedgebury Sprout League, we have a team for nine-year-olds in the Sedgebury Pee-Wee League, and we have a team for ten- and eleven-year-olds in the Sedgebury Triple-A League. Our team in each league is called the Tigers. We are always the Havington Tigers.

I take one of the chairs with a better view of the ball field, noticing in the late afternoon May sun that someone—again, probably Hilton—has ordered a small mound of soil, now piled neatly off the first base line.

Hilton sits beside me. "We're burning the field tomorrow afternoon," he says. "Infield and outfield. Kevin Trellis wants to burn some of the grass in foul territory too, at least on the first base side, but I don't know if we'll have the time. We've only got a couple fellows from the fire company from three to five o'clock. Then they have to go up the hill a bit, and burn the first of Rosemary Nicholson's grazing pastures."

In the suburbs of southern Connecticut where I grew up, people used chemicals and fertilizers and specially treated sods to get rich, green lawns. Here in Vermont, we simply scorch the earth. We set select patches of the ground on fire, let them burn to the dirt, and then watch as nature heals herself with an almost supersonic infusion of nutrients. The grass grows back faster, richer, greener than anything I ever witnessed in southern Connecticut.

"I think the infield is most important, anyway," I tell Hilton agreeably. "What's the extra soil for?" I then ask.

"You been out to the field?"

"Not this year."

"Well, it needs work. The pitching mound is low, even for these kids, and there's a hole big enough to build a basement between second and third base. If we don't fill it in, we're liable to lose someone." Hilton is smiling, but I know that as an attorney Hilton doesn't use the word *liable* lightly.

"I'll have to get out there," I say, and I realize suddenly that I am nervous. It crosses my mind that bad Little Leaguers may make bad coaches. Or at least incompetent ones: ones incapable of hitting grounders for infield practice or pop flies to the outfielders. Coaches unable to teach kids to bend their knees and their backs when reaching down to scoop up a ball at shortstop, or to extend their arms when batting.

How do you begin to teach a little girl without an older brother —Cindy Fletcher, for example—to pivot at second base during a double play?

"That sounds like Pete's truck," Hilton is saying, rising and going slowly to the window. "Yup, that's Pete. Mike Boley's with him." He turns back to me and continues, "Pete says he'll be happy to be your assistant coach. He won't be able to make Wednesday night practices and one or two of the Thursday night games, because he's playing softball again this year. But he says he'll be happy to help you out."

Pete Cooder is twenty-three or twenty-four years old. I am both relieved and frightened to have him as my assistant: on the one hand, he is an amiable, nice enough sort. On the other hand, I have no doubts that he will be able to hit grounders and pop-ups and fungos with embarrassing—embarrassing to me—ease. I have not seen him play softball, but I have read about his exploits in dozens of Hilton's articles about the slow-pitch softball league. "Cooder Pitches Goddette Construction Past Price Chopper with Five-Hitter." "Cooder Slams Two Home Runs in Goddette Victory."

Pete Cooder is a jock. A happy jock. He runs up the firehouse stairs two, perhaps three at a time, and before I know it he and Mike Boley have joined Hilton and me, two energetic young men in windbreakers and blue jeans and mustaches.

"I love May," Pete says to Hilton as he takes off his jacket, smiling. "It takes more than one bluebird to make a summer, but I saw one this afternoon. I love it. I love May."

Harper and I sit next to each other at the dining room table, not on the same side but on adjacent sides. With the exception of a few select restaurants that gave us no choice (and so we never went back), we have never sat at opposite sides of a table. It's just how we are. We like to be close, even when we eat.

I tell her about Toby Nesmith and John Wrightman, the Boston alumni who guaranteed 80 percent participation in the alumni fund from the fortieth reunion class.

"How many people does that mean?" Harper asks, meaning, How many people are still alive?

"About one hundred and twenty separate gifts. The class has around one hundred and fifty people left."

"And it's a wealthy one hundred and twenty." It's a statement from Harper, not a question.

"Right."

"How old do you think Hilton Burberry is?"

"Older than Toby Nesmith and John Wrightman. Hilton probably has ten or fifteen years on that pair."

"God, I hope we're as well-preserved as Hilton when we're his age."

"Me too." I perform some quick math in my head: if Harper becomes pregnant this year, I will become a parent again at thirty-six. I will see my child graduate from college when I am fifty-seven. When I am seventy-five, my estimate of Hilton's age, my child will be thirty-nine. Four years older than I am now.

This all sounds reasonable, acceptable, good.

"So, do you feel maternal?" I ask, trying to make the remark sound casual, by cutting into my chicken as I speak.

Harper knows there is nothing light about my question; it weighs heavily on her too, and she answers simply by shaking her head that she doesn't. I don't even have to look up to know that her head is moving slightly, almost imperceptibly, from side to side.

After dinner, I pull on a heavy sweatshirt and walk to the town baseball diamond. It's a short and pretty walk from my house, pretty even at night. I walk past the church, lit by a spotlight across the street, parts of it so bright and the paint so white that it looks almost like daylight. I walk past the Havington town marker, a carved rock boasting that the town was chartered in 1782. I walk over the bridge (new, not covered) that spans our small part of the New Haven River, past our white clapboard firehouse, and then along the New Haven, gurgling loudly with spring runoff from the mountains.

At the ball field I wander first to the backstop behind home plate, our wooden and wire wall to help keep the ball in play. Unlike more modern backstops—chain-link fencing cut from rust-proof metal—our backstop could pass for a length of prison fence, especially in the dark. There's no overhang or ceiling to our backstop, it just goes straight up into the air, climbing perhaps thirty feet toward the sky.

The dirt around home plate is damp under my feet, damp with dew, and I can almost feel the moist ground through my sneakers.

I walk up the first base line, past Hilton's pile of fresh soil, and stand where Nathaniel stood for two years' worth of Little League, and look at what he looked at. It's a new view for me, since my vantage point—Harper's and my vantage point—had always been from the third base line, out toward left field. We saw Nathaniel and we saw first base; we saw some of the parked trucks, trucks like Obie Northrup's, and we saw where the field began sloping into the river. We saw some trees.

Nathaniel had a different view when he stood by first base.

Standing there now I see that he saw the white firehouse, fifty, perhaps seventy-five yards past the backstop—a white building that must have camouflaged line drives and pop-ups, making his job in the field that much more difficult. He saw the bridge beside the firehouse, and if he turned slightly to his left for any reason, he saw our general store. Perhaps once or twice he might even have seen the streetlights come on toward the end of some of the early spring games.

There are not many stars out tonight, and the moon darts constantly behind drifting clouds, offering them each the barest, briefest of halos. A plane rumbles somewhere overhead, a lumbering passenger jet.

I don't know why I do it, but suddenly I take off as fast as I can from first base and run toward second. It feels good to run, wonderful to be winded. I take my lead off second: I look to my left and imagine Nathaniel leaning forward on his toes, his hands on his knees, one swallowed up in a massive lobster claw that poses as a first baseman's mitt, and then abruptly I sprint to third. I hadn't planned on it, but suddenly I'm sprinting, trying to accelerate as quickly as possible.

I practice running the bases, veering slightly into foul territory just before first base to lessen the arc I'll have to make between first and second, angling my approach to third so that I can run straight through the bag and toward home plate. Oh, how I love to run the bases. I wasn't on base a whole lot in Little League, but when I was—oh, how I loved to run the bases.

My eyes become used to the darkness. I can see, it seems for a second, like the sun hasn't quite set.

My second time around the bases I slide into home, a beautiful hook slide, my left toe just catching a corner edge of the plate. I'm thirty-five years old, and I'm sliding. I'm sliding into home plate for the first time in over twenty years.

After my slide I stand up, I brush off my jeans. I walk to the pitching mound, so close to home plate in Little League that pitchers are practically on top of the batters.

It occurs to me that most Little League stars are pitchers. Nathaniel was the exception. Only in practice did he ever have the feeling of standing on the mound, staring down at the batter.

I start to run the bases one last time, slowly, but as I reach first base I stop. What I had thought initially was a tree, and then just a shadow, is something else. A deer, perhaps, except that it looks to me like it has three legs, not four. It is standing three hundred feet away, out past right field, at the edge of the woods. I watch it, anchoring my left foot on the first base bag, trying to focus. It seems to be watching me too, and it probably has been for the whole time that I have been wandering and running around the infield.

I open my eyes wide, as wide as I can. It's definitely not a deer.

But it isn't a tree either.

I begin to move toward it, padding softly and slowly through the wet outfield grass. It remains unmoving as I approach, and for the first time since I have noticed it I am more than curious. I am frightened.

Two clouds race past the moon, and in the brief moment between them there is enough light on the image that I can see clearly the brim of a baseball cap and that what I had thought was a deer's third or fourth leg is actually a baseball bat, leaned casually against a boy's thigh.

Behind me a car passes on the bridge by the firehouse. Reflexively I look over my shoulder, watching it pass for perhaps as long as a second.

When I turn back to the woods, the boy before me has gone.

Chapter 3

The development office at Sedgebury College is at the edge of the campus, along a residential street bordering the village of Sedgebury itself. It is a wealthy street, a factor that I doubt was lost on the trustees when they approved moving the development office here two years ago, and placing it (placing us) in Jensen House, a Georgian brick home built in 1841. Our offices consist of the top floor of Jensen House, with the first floor staffed by admissions. We share as a conference room something that I imagine was an extremely dark, unpleasant living room in a different era, a room that the college decorators managed to make even darker last fall when they paneled the walls.

Ironically—and perhaps unfortunately—no sooner had we in development arrived at Jensen House, than the tremendous, eight-bedroom colonial across the street was sold to a pair of Burlington doctors who were starting a small rest home for the aged. They call it the Trillium Extended Care Facility, although only the word Trillium is carved into the elegant wooden sign that hangs on a post on the lawn. The residents of Trillium tend not to need round-the-clock medical attention or emergency medical care, but they do need help remembering such details as turning off the gas range, or—in the case of Russell Godwin—putting on pants and shoes and socks before going outside. Especially in January.

In any event, I have been told by many elderly alumni that it can be extremely disheartening to discuss a will or legacy gift after passing "that blind guy with the chimes across the street," or "a pair of seventy-five-year-old women playing Chutes and Ladders in the grass."

When I arrive at the college the morning after racing around the Havington Little League diamond, I see Mr. Godfrey sitting in a rocking chair on the Trillium front porch. The porch really does have rocking chairs, and they really are made of wicker. I call Mr. Godfrey "Mr. Godfrey" because I have no idea what his first name is, but also because he's about ninety years old, and he seems to have earned the respect that comes with the word "mister."

I drop my attaché case beside the jeep and cross the street to say hello to Mr. Godfrey. I have no idea if he ever had any family, but I assume if he did they've been dead longer than I've been alive. I do know that he receives few, if any, visitors.

While he is telling me something about his days with the old Vermont railroad, Lorna Strickland scoots by in her electric wheelchair, waving as she passes, and hugging the left side of the street. Although Lorna is one of Trillium's younger residents, a mere sixty or sixty-five years old, she is the home's only resident who is bound to a wheelchair.

"Lorna," I say to her good-naturedly, "where do you think you are, Liverpool? You should be on the right side of the road in that contraption!"

"Oh no," she says, "I don't go that fast. I'll stay over here, thank you very much. Those cars just move too fast. Too fast!"

Mr. Godfrey nods, and then says to me, "I had a question 'bout that on my drivin' test. It said, 'If you're walkin' along a back road, and it's dusk, what side of the road should you be on?'

"I thought about it, and I decided left. Common sense said to me left, left-hand side of the road. The instructor told me I got it right. Yup, he did. I got myself a lot of questions right—enough to get my license.

"'Course, I probably knew the answer as much 'cause a my nephew as common sense. He was walkin' along a road up near St. Johnsbury one night, along near dusk—just like the question. He was on the right-hand side of the road, and a car went by, and got him from behind. Killed him. Just like that. Killed him dead.

"Car was probably goin' too fast. Cars 'round St. Johnsbury do that, you know. They go too fast."

Stunned and saddened, I ask Mr. Godfrey when this happened.

"'Round near twilight, I think."

"No, I mean how long ago?"

Mr. Godfrey thinks for a moment. "Well, let me see. I had seen him at a family gathering, just a couple weeks before it happened. And he was twenty-one at the time.

"So it was thirty years ago, I guess. I guess it happened thirty years ago."

Diamond.

It is the one name on the roster that I don't recognize. L. Diamond.

"Are you free for lunch with President Ketchum?" Doug Bascomb asks, leaning over the edge of my desk. I never even heard him enter my office.

I nod. "Sure. Anything special on his mind?"

"No, he just wants an update on the capital campaign. A couple trustees will be in town this weekend, and he wants to have a vague idea what's going on."

"What time?"

"Doesn't matter, his calendar's pretty clear. Noon?"

"Noon is fine."

He stares at me as if I'm ill. Then: "Are you okay?"

"I'm fine. Why, do I look sickly?"

He waves his hands. "No, you look . . . you just seemed to be in a daze." He looks down at the piece of paper before me. "What have you got there?"

I hold up for him the roster of Havington's Triple-A Tigers. "These are my Little Leaguers."

He rolls his eyes. "I'll come back about ten of twelve."

"I'll be here," I mumble, as lineups begin to form in my mind. Before Doug has even left my office, I am envisioning for the first time the black spiral-bound score book in which I will actually pencil in the names of these children.

I study the list, alphabetized by Hilton Burberry on his ancient Smith-Corona: R. Bissonette, D. Casey, M. Edington, L. Diamond, J. Fenton, C. Fletcher, M. Harris, P. Hayden, M. Lamphere, L. Northrup, J. Parker, D. Pratt, C. Thorpman, R. Wheelock, R. Wohlford. The *e* on the commissioner's typewriter looks very much these days like a *c*, and the Xerox machine on which he copied the list left a long smudge along the bottom of the paper.

I recognize that the *R* before Wohlford is an error, (the Wohlford boy prefers Bobby to Robby), and that L. Northrup goes by Carl (his middle name), not Leon.

I lean back in my chair, and try to guess what the *L* before Diamond stands for. Lawrence, Luke, Lewis. Maybe—just maybe —it stands for Lisa.

Beside most of the names I can put a child's face, or—in some of the cases—a parent's face. I can envision J. Parker, Jesse, pitching with his exaggerated windmill windup, his arms flung back as much like a diver as a pitcher. In my mind I can see Donnie Casey, with his small pug nose and spare tire: a belly that in Havington rivals only his father's, and necessitates that his mother take him to shop in the "husky boy" section of Ames' or Ben Franklin. And although M. Lamphere's face escapes me at the moment, I can remember his father's, and the man's nervous smile when he picked up his son at our home not long before Nathaniel died.

The only face that eludes me completely, the only name with which I am completely unfamiliar, is L. Diamond. I cannot recall ever seeing or hearing the name Diamond in Havington, and I don't believe Nathaniel ever knew any boy or girl with that name.

I wander outside my office to the credenza by Kim Swanson's desk, and reach inside it for the Sedgebury County phone book. The local phone book feels thin in my hands, no more substantial than a coloring book. It is less than one half as fat as Doug's weekly pile of progress reports. I flip to the section of *D*s, past the Darbys and DeGrays, past the Demars and Desordas, and on the page bounded by the Devans and the Dibbles, I stop and look for a Diamond.

As I had suspected, as I think I had known, there is no Diamond listed. Diana follows the Diabetes hotline.

I glance again quickly at the roster Hilton gave me, and like an old family photograph in which someone has died, the name L. Diamond stands out from the crowd on the page.

I can see the smoke from Havington before I can smell it, a column of powdery black ash winding up into the sky above the village, and then smothering the town in a grimy soot canopy. It reminds me of the films I've seen from the Second World War of German or British towns after air raids.

I've seen farmers burn their fields before, a fairly common sight in Vermont in May, but I've never witnessed a fire department (or at least select members, including its chief) burn a baseball diamond. This will be my first time.

It's just past four-thirty as I approach Havington, and the smoke from the fire begins to tickle my nose. It smells, I decide, a bit like a monster barbecue, like one of those summer Saturdays I remember as a child when virtually every house on our block was grilling something.

I pull into the firehouse parking lot and coast to a stop beside Hilton Burberry's battered red station wagon. I had hoped he would be here, and therefore folded into my wallet the roster for the Triple-A Tigers—twelve boys, two girls, and a fifteenth child of indeterminate gender (and origin) named Diamond.

Another copy of the roster, a copy I made myself, is back in my office in one of my two Little League files. (Harper can't believe that I actually have Little League "files"—one specifically about my team, one with coaching tips I have copied from books and magazines. She has always teased me about my unnatural, perhaps unsavory, obsession with order, and believes this is one more manifestation.)

As I approach the ball field, the lines and the patches of fire become clear. The half of the infield between the pitching mound and second base is burning now, as is a shallow portion of center and right field. The flames rise no more than a foot or two into the air, but they dance and undulate like throw rugs beaten in the breeze, and send thick black plumes into the sky. The rest of the infield, the half closer to home plate, is charred, as if a group of giants has used the area for a massive campfire pit.

No, it looks more ominous than that. The place looks like it has been napalmed.

Hilton is not immediately visible in the haze, but Ken Morton and Obie Northrup are. Together they are corralling the fire behind the pitching mound, spraying its edges with their water packs whenever the flames rise too high or stretch beyond their limits.

I wander over to Jamie Sturman, the Havington volunteer fire chief. In addition to serving as our town's fire chief, Jamie is also a state trooper and—along with his radar gun—a first-rate source of revenue for the state of Vermont. He has told me that from the second week in September through Columbus Day, the month when the down-country leaf peepers descend upon Sedgebury, he catches anywhere from fifteen to twenty-five speeding flatlanders a day.

"Evenin'," he says to me as I approach, removing his sunglasses in a gesture of friendliness. Although Harper and I moved to Havington from Manhattan, and represent in many ways the sort of leaf peepers he finds most irritating, Jamie likes us: we sought his advice when we bought our wood stove, and we had him inspect our installation every step of the way.

"Evening, Jamie."

"Hear you're coachin' this year."

"I am indeed."

He runs a hand through his thinning black hair, wiping some of the sweat off his forehead. It's probably no more than sixty degrees right now, but Jamie has been watching this fire for perhaps an hour and a half.

"'At's nice of you," he says. "Coachin' can take a lot of time."

"That's what they tell me."

"I didn't know you liked the game so much."

"I'm a pretty big fan." I turn my head to cough, my throat already becoming sore from the smoke.

"You play in school?"

I shake my head that I didn't, trying to catch my breath. It amazes me, but except for the sweat on his forehead, Jamie seems completely unaffected by the fire.

"I played a bit in high school," he volunteers. "'Course 'at was years ago. But I had a nice swing, 'a sweet swing,' the coach said. I don't 'member his name, but he knew what he was talkin' 'bout. And he said I had a nice, sweet swing."

"Was that at Sedgebury Union?"

"Yup. But it wasn't called Sedgebury Union then. Then it was just Sedgebury High." He pauses, and when he continues he is smiling, needling me. "I think it was some of your buddies at the college who probably insisted on givin' the place a 'union.' Sounds more to 'em like Vermont."

Obie Northrup picks up a shovel from the ground beside him and begins tossing dirt from the base path onto a thin tentacle of fire trying to burn its way toward the third base line. He finally steps on it with his new fire boots, blackening them for the first time.

"This is a big job," I comment, watching as Cal Burack joins Brad Fenton behind second base. Their faces are dirty, and the soot has settled on their white tee shirts like a second color.

"Nah, it's not so big. Drop a couple fire lines from the drip tanks—circles make most sense—and jus' let the fires inside the lines burn 'emselves out. The most important thing is to watch the wind. If it's a calm day, like today, it's not a big job at all."

"And if it isn't a calm day?"

"You lose a couple acres of forest. Maybe a house or two," he says, trying to look serious.

Together we watch Cal rake some of the dirt from around second base onto a small flame, smothering it. "Yup, your kids will have a good spot when we're done," the fire chief continues, "a real good spot."

I consider suggesting to Jamie that he encourage Helen, his ten-year-old daughter, to come out and join the team. But I stop myself: two little girls will be tough enough.

"Well, we appreciate your doing all this," I say, waving my hand across the field of fire.

"It's nothing. Really, it's nothing."

I scan the field for Hilton, but he doesn't appear to be anywhere in sight. "I saw Hilton's car back in the lot," I tell Jamie. "Is he around?"

"Yup." Jamie turns his head just the slightest bit, motioning toward the firehouse.

I look back, and through the smoke I can see the silhouette of a person in the window of the second floor training room. He is standing with his hands behind his back, unmoving, a black shadow of a man.

"I gather the smoke bothers him?"

"Nope. Ol' Hilton jus' likes a bird's-eye view of things."

I nod. "There's someone on my team named Diamond. L. Diamond. I want to ask Hilton if he knows the child."

Jamie shakes his head. "I don't think I've ever come across anyone 'round here named Diamond. New boy in town?"

"Or girl, I guess. Maybe a new girl."

"Maybe. But I'd have expected Helen to have told me if a new girl just showed up one day in the fifth or sixth grade."

We stand together for perhaps a minute, saying nothing, a moment of awkward stillness that signals in small towns that a conversation is over and it's time to move on. Finally I break the silence. "Well, I thank you once again for all that you're doing," I tell Jamie. "It's going to make a big difference."

I then turn and start back toward the firehouse, stopping once to make sure that my roster is still with me. As I reach the building, however, and start toward the side with the door, I hear the sound of an automobile accelerating. I look up in time to see Hilton's red wagon leave the firehouse parking lot and cross the bridge over the New Haven River.

My father got into a fight over Little League when I was nine years old.

It was a fistfight, a knock-down, drag-out, roll-in-the-dry-dirt-by-home-plate affair, the sort of unexpectedly violent explosion that the seventeen-year-old umpire calling balls and strikes that day was powerless to break up.

Grayson Brodie was pitching that day, and I was batting. Grayson was a Little League star, a dominating sort of talent like Nathaniel, (except, of course, that Grayson also pitched). It was the last inning, and Grayson's team was winning by something like sixty runs.

We weren't going to win that day.

I came to the plate with one out and nobody on base.

"A walk's as good as a hit!" Mr. Tibideau shouted as I took my spot on the right-hand side of the plate, "Walk's as good as a hit!"

Mr. Tibideau shouted this at me whenever I came to bat, my coach's gentle way of reminding me that I was probably going to strike out if I did anything other than keep my bat on my shoulder and hope to God that the pitcher threw four balls before he could throw three strikes.

I didn't swing at Grayson's first pitch, a called strike, but I did at his second—a swinging strike. I took a ferocious cut at what amounted to his Little League change-up, his "slow pitch," twisting my body up into knots and falling on the ground in an embarrassing (though predictable) display of incompetence.

I stood up, trying to ignore the comments from the benches of both Grayson's and my team, ("Feel that breeze," "Rusty gate, rusty gate," "Fan, fan, fan!"), and took my spot back in the batter's box. I dug in, trying to plant my back foot firmly, anchoring my rubber cleats into the dirt.

And that's when all hell broke loose.

"Did you see that?" Mr. Brodie screamed at the high school kid calling balls and strikes that morning. "Did you see that?"

The umpire called time, pulled off his mask, and walked to the chain-link backstop to ask Grayson's father what it was he was supposed to have seen.

"You mean you missed it? Oh, for crying out loud, you missed it!" Mr. Brodie said, disgusted. He turned to Mr. Tibideau, our coach, who was standing perhaps a dozen feet away at the end of our bench, and continued, "You saw it, right, Clark? You saw what Billy just did!"

Mr. Tibideau smiled. "Calm down, Dan. He didn't mean anything."

Billy. Didn't mean anything. I realized that Mr. Brodie was talking about me, and that whatever it was I had done, Mr. Tibideau had seen as well.

I started to wander to the backstop to listen more carefully, but Mr. Brodie saved me the trouble. He ran onto the field, standing across from me on the opposite side of home plate.

"Look what you did!" he said, chastising me. "Look what you did!"

His son yelled from the pitching mound, "Dad, I can see the plate just fine! I can see the plate okay!" and Mr. Tibideau followed Mr. Brodie to the batter's box, saying softly—but sternly— "Dan, would you lay off him? You're making an ass of yourself."

I followed Mr. Brodie's eyes, trying to learn from them what horrible sin I had committed, what rule I had broken. He was looking down, so I looked down.

And that's when I saw what Mr. Brodie was talking about.

When I had dug back into the batter's box after falling down, I had kicked some dirt onto home plate. Not a lot, certainly not enough to obscure Grayson Brodie's view of the plate as he pitched, but some. A small corner of the plate was covered, covered accidentally by an embarrassed little boy trying to look tough.

"Don't you know that's against the rules?" Mr. Brodie asked

me. "Don't you know that kicking dirt on home plate is cheating?"

Cheating. I wanted to cry. I wanted to run off the field and hide somewhere far in the woods. Not only was I a lousy baseball player, I was a cheater. I didn't answer Mr. Brodie's questions, because I was afraid that if I opened my mouth, all that would come out would be sniffles.

"I can see, I can see," Grayson kept saying.

"Take it easy, damn it, you're scaring the boy!" Mr. Tibideau hissed.

Mr. Brodie squatted in front of me, so we stared into each other's eyes. "Why did you do that?" he asked, pointing at home plate and softening just the slightest bit. "It was because you missed that last pitch, right?"

I shook my head no, trying to communicate without words that he was mistaken, that I hadn't done it because his son had humiliated me, that I hadn't even done it on purpose.

"Would you goddamn take it easy?" Mr. Tibideau said again, louder now.

And that's when my father appeared. He walked up to Mr. Brodie with one hand in the pocket of his plaid Bermuda shorts, the other holding a paper cup full of soda. He never gave Mr. Brodie a chance.

"Dan, you've always been a real dick, you know that?" he said, and then, standing over him, he poured onto Mr. Brodie's head his cup of soda. Sticky caramel Coca-Cola. And then he slugged him, hitting him hard enough that Mr. Brodie toppled over onto his side like a bicycle with a broken kickstand.

For a moment he lay there, astounded that my father, George Parrish, had just slugged him in front of thirty-plus children, their sponsors, friends, and families. And then, with a whispered, "You bastard," he dove at my father's knees, bringing him down onto the ground with an open field tackle that would have impressed any Big Ten coach.

They rolled back and forth in the dirt, and taught all of us boys who gathered around them at least a half dozen new words: cocksucker, shithead, wanker, shanker, son of a bitch, and stupidest motherfucker on the face of the earth.

Mr. Tibideau, Mr. Friedman, and Mr. McKenna finally pulled them apart. I noted that unlike when two of us boys would get into a fight, the umpire didn't make my father and Mr. Brodie make up and shake hands.

Amazingly, until my father appeared beside me at home plate, I hadn't even realized he was at that game.

Chapter 4

When I come home from the baseball field, Harper is sitting on the living room floor, surrounded by perhaps a dozen of Nathaniel's books. I am, as I often am, surprised by how lovely she is. Not because there are times when she seems less attractive to me, or because I have ever taken Harper for granted.

Far from it. I am struck by Harper's beauty because I hadn't expected to have a beautiful wife when I was growing up. I don't believe it ever crossed my mind that the woman I would someday marry would be small and blond with soft Southern eyes, that she would have skin so smooth that not even my tongue can find imperfections.

"You're home early," she says, standing to greet me, and brushing some cat hair from the carpet off her jeans.

We kiss once, gently, on the lips, and then I kiss her again on her forehead. "What's all this?"

"A summer reading list for the kids," she answers. "I want them to read more than Garfield comics this year, so I thought I'd give everyone a list of twenty books to think about."

"And perhaps even read."

"Right. And perhaps even read. Looking over Nathaniel's books seemed as good a first step as any."

We kneel on the floor, and I reach for his biography of General Custer. It is one of three biographies he read from a long series of "Signature Books," stories of famous men and women written for eight- or nine-year-olds. The books had belonged originally to his uncle, my brother, but they had become Nathaniel's favorites as soon as he found them in my brother's attic one Thanksgiving. In addition to General Custer, he had read about Robert E. Lee and Lafayette in this series.

The books are almost antiques now.

"Can kids even find these books today?"

Harper nods her head that they can. "The Sedgebury library has almost the entire series, and even Lincoln and Havington have a couple each."

I flip through the life of George Armstrong Custer, pausing to glance at some of the line drawings: young "Autie" Custer telling his father that he's going to be a great general someday; George Custer as a defiant plebe at West Point; Captain Custer as an aide to General McClellan in the Civil War; and, of course, General Custer facing death bravely (as he always had in the past) at the Little Big Horn.

"Nathaniel really liked these."

"Especially that one," Harper says, referring to Custer. "He never figured out that the man was an idiot." She shakes her head, remembering something suddenly, something about Nathaniel: something he may have said to her once about the book, or about the general, or perhaps about one of the drawings. It's a beautiful memory, I can tell, because of the way she takes a deep breath and turns away from me.

My first reaction is to reach for her and touch her shoulder, to bring her close to me. But I know that I can't, that I shouldn't: I know if I do she will cry.

"He never figured out that the man was an idiot," Harper says again, staring off at a memory I'll never quite know. "He just never knew."

Harper and I fuck like bunnies. We make love these days in beds, on couches, on the floor before the wood stove. We are on vacation from condoms and jellies and foams, and the diaphragm has been hidden away for God knows how long in its space-age plastic case, buried deep behind sweaters Harper never will wear again.

I know, because I put it there.

Making love this way is a wonderful feeling. It's like being naked again for the first time, it's like being uncivilized. It's like being animals—bunnies, and that's just how we go at it.

After dinner we take a bath, and after our bath we quickly—very quickly—towel each other dry, and then we return to the living room, pushing aside the books of a ten-year-old boy, and there we make love on the floor.

Lying on the living room floor with Harper, I am confident that there is a heaven, and I am confident that Nathaniel is there. We are wrapped together in a garish yellow and blue quilt that Harper's mother made us when we moved to Vermont, the room an almost pitch-black decanter of smells: Harper's shampoo, our bubble bath, the appealingly sour aroma of our own spent bodies.

What I cannot imagine, however, is what heaven is like. Specifically, I cannot imagine what people—angels—really look like, or how old everyone is. Is my son now ten years old in heaven, and will he be ten forever? Will he spend eternity playing with Transformers and Lego and a plastic mutant turtle named Donatello? If I, on the other hand, live to be ninety, will I be ninety forever, with whatever aches and pains and infirmities accompany my old age?

When Nathaniel died, our age difference was twenty-four years. I was thirty-four, and he was ten. I liked that age spread, twenty-four years seemed just about right. I'm not sure I'd be crazy about heaven if the age difference between me and my son were eighty years.

"What are you thinking about?" Harper asks, resting one of her warm, soft hands on my chest.

"Heaven," I answer, kissing her lightly on her ear. "I'm thinking about heaven."

Harper has told me that she is not at all sure I should be coaching Little League. She believes it is too soon for me to surround myself with the likes of Jesse Parker and Cliff Thorpman and Donnie Casey, little boys in whom I will see my own sweet son.

But that is, of course, exactly the point. I may be an unfortunate reminder for them that even nine- and ten-year-olds die, but they will be for me a reminder that they don't.

"Wait till you see Jesse Parker's new haircut," Harper says as we turn out our bedroom light and crawl underneath the sheets of our bed. "It's a mini-Mohawk—like that crazy skier who was pictured in all the magazines last winter."

Jesse's parents, a couple older than Harper and me, came to

Vermont over twenty-five years ago, to join a commune up in Lincoln. Jesse's oldest sister, now twenty-one, was born on that commune and named Free Love.

"A mini-Mohawk? What's a mini-Mohawk?"

"Well, it's not a full-blown Mohawk. The sides of his head aren't completely shaved. But pretty close."

"Has he spiked the hair that he has?"

"Yup."

"That will look great under a baseball cap."

"I was surprised, but none of the kids teased Jesse when he first came to school with the haircut."

"Jesse's a jock. An athlete. At his age, that gives him a certain amount of license."

Harper is silent for a moment, weighing the liberties that may be taken by little boys who are graceful, or fast, or strong. She then rolls over so that she is facing me, her mouth barely an inch from mine. She whispers with an urgency that surprises me, "If you change your mind, you know, everyone would understand."

"I know."

"I'm sure Pete Cooder could take over the team."

"I'm sure he could too."

"I just don't want it to make you . . . unhappy."

I kiss her mouth, soundlessly. "It won't. You shouldn't worry about me."

"I do, you know."

"I know."

"You've seemed awfully tense lately."

"Have I? I haven't felt tense."

She nods. "You seem to be taking it all so seriously. All those meetings, all that time at the field last night and today, all those folders—"

I kiss her again, this time to silence her. "I have two folders," I remind her. "Two."

"You bought a clipboard," she says, trying to be light.

"I'm fine," I insist. "You have nothing to worry about."

I am awakened by noises from another bedroom, sounds that might be small footsteps in a room down the hall. Someone is pacing in Nathaniel's old room, wandering back and forth between the toy chest and his bureau, perhaps between the toy chest and his bed.

At least that's what it sounds like, at least that's what I envision. Somebody pacing. Somebody pacing in my little boy's bedroom.

I can feel the movement as well as I hear it; I can sense the way the rhythms of my sleeping house have been disturbed.

I open my eyes and stare at the doorway to Harper's and my bedroom, and out at the hallway beyond it. The moon, waning, is hidden almost completely by clouds, making the hallway look like a long thin tunnel without windows or doors. Without my glasses I am unable to read the clock on the bureau, and my glasses are still downstairs on the coffee table, where I had placed them when Harper and I began to make love.

I have no idea what time it is, only that the sun has not yet begun to rise.

Harper moves slightly beside me, curling up one leg underneath her and nuzzling deeper into her pillow. These footsteps will never wake her.

Lying in bed I continue to listen to the sounds of someone methodically exploring my dead son's bedroom. The bookcase is jostled as books are removed, perused, returned; the bed creaks as someone sits, kneels, lies down on the mattress; the three drawers of his bureau squeal as each one is opened.

Were this Manhattan, were these noises coming from a room in our old apartment, I might now be whispering into our telephone a desperate cry for help. In Vermont, however, in a little town such as Havington, the police are a distant option: in the middle of the night, my only alternative are the state troopers in Sedgebury, sixteen miles away.

But I know also that the state police would be no help with the . . . intruder . . . in my boy's bedroom, they would be useless. Despite the noises that continue to spill from that room, sounds that become louder and more distinct with each passing second, Harper continues to sleep, unmoving and undisturbed.

The intruder is there for me, and me only.

I have heard these exact noises in my boy's room in the middle of the night at least a half dozen times since Nathaniel died, noises that exist in my mind somewhere between dreams and despair. It was, I assume, the sight of Nathaniel's books earlier that evening, scattered like leaves on the living room floor, that has conjured for me the intruder tonight.

And yet I try to reassure myself that the sounds that I hear are actually the sounds of our cats, Alexis and Elsa, at play. Somehow one or both of them has gotten into Nathaniel's old room, a room in which they once spent hours at a time on a sick little boy's bed, keeping him company . . . although how they got in there tonight is beyond me. Harper always keeps that door shut tight. But as my eyes grow accustomed to the dark, the blobs on Harper's easy chair in the corner become Alexis and Elsa, curled up together, each as soundly asleep as my wife.

Unable to tolerate the noise any longer, I sit up and reach for my bathrobe, hanging on the wrought iron arch of the reading lamp on my side of the bed. I push my arms through its sleeves, slide out of bed, and walk soundlessly across the floor of the bedroom, shivering. The hardwood floor is cold against my feet, and I say to myself that my shaking is caused solely by the chill in the house.

I pause in our doorway, wondering if I want truly to continue. Venturing into the hallway represents a commitment to go on, to turn toward Nathaniel's room and open the door that is most times kept closed. And yet I know from experience that the only way to make the intruder go away is to confront my son's silent, unused bedroom.

The toy chest slams shut, the lid of what is actually an old blanket chest plastered now with stickers and decals of futuristic robots and weapons and spacecraft. The crunch of wood on wood echoes through the house, and I look back at Harper and watch the blankets upon her quiver rhythmically with her breathing. I will continue.

The floor of the hallway is colder than the floor of our bedroom, and there is a draft in the tunnel that is new to me. It may be coming from the guest bedroom; it may be coming from underneath the door to the attic. But it is a new draft, and a musty one at that.

I pause when I turn the corner toward Nathaniel's old room, and then I jump back slightly against the hallway wall. Nathaniel's door is open tonight, our buffer zone against sadness is inches ajar. While it is possible that Harper inadvertently left the door open this afternoon when she was looking for books for her reading list—it is in fact likely, it has to be—I can't imagine why she would have left it only six or seven inches ajar. After all, if her hands were full of books, she would have been unable to close the door at all, and the door would now be wide open.

I run my fingers along the wall as I approach the room, the ancient wallpaper a dry and flaky reminder of the age of the house. On the other side of Nathaniel's door there is rustling, a sound I know well: Nathaniel sliding his toys under his bed as I approach his room to "inspect" it after he cleans it, Nathaniel on his knees, desperately trying to wedge a pile of dirty clothes under his dresser before Harper and I open the door.

And then the rustling stops, and the room becomes quiet. For the first time since I was awakened by the noises from Nathaniel's room, the entire house becomes still, asleep. When I hold my breath, there is nothing. Even the draft is gone, the breeze that cut across the hallway like a river of cold.

I hesitate for a brief moment outside my son's room, considering one last time whether I want to open the door all the way. Suddenly, my wife seems very far away, my image of her sleeping shape something I must have seen a very long time ago. It seems odd to me, almost impossible, that I could be back with her under the covers in seconds.

Standing squarely in the frame of the door, I graze the knob with two fingers and push the door open. Of course I will go inside; it's why I've been awakened, pulled from my bed, and led here.

And it does indeed feel as if I've been led. Teased along with the noises and sounds I know well.

The door glides on its hinges away from me, like a curtain from a stage play, and unveils a room too dark even for shadows. The room is blacker than Harper's and my bedroom, blacker than the hallway in which I stand holding my breath. Automatically I reach for the light switch by the door, and even in the split second between when the lights go on and when I must shield my eyes from the light, I see what has happened, what is different about Nathaniel's room—what has made the small bedroom as black as a coffin.

The shades on all three windows have been pulled down, blocking out the streetlight across the road that shines on the church and the small slivers of moonlight that escape even tonight's heavy cloud cover. In all the years that Nathaniel slept in this room those shades were never drawn, because as tall and as brave as my son was, he still died at ten, an age when it is perfectly all right to be afraid of the dark.

Chapter 5

The next morning when I kiss Harper before leaving for work, she smiles and stretches, asking me how I slept.

"I slept fine," I tell her, lying. "I slept just fine."

"Did I hear you get up in the middle of the night?"

"I was getting a glass of water," I explain, smiling back. "I was thirsty."

"You've been thirsty a lot lately."

"Think so?"

"I do. Why don't you start leaving a glass of water on the nightstand?"

I nod in agreement. "That's a good idea. I'll try and remember tonight."

I call Hilton Burberry at his home, the fifteen-man roster of my Little League team unfolded before me on my desk.

It is now well past 9:58 in the morning, a perfectly reasonable time to phone anyone in Vermont on a Thursday. His wife, Eunice, answers the phone.

"Morning, William," she says after I identify myself. Her Boston accent has not diminished with age or with years of living in Vermont. "Hilton tells me you're a baseball manager this year."

"It's a tough job, but someone's got to do it," I tell her lightly.

"It's only tough if you let it get to you. Just don't let Bobby Wohlford's parents make you crazy, and you'll find it all as easy to take as sugar on snow."

"I'll remember that."

"I doubt you will. The Wohlfords get to everyone. You calling for me or Hilton?"

"Well, I have to admit, I am calling for Hilton."

"I figured. Hold on, William, I'll go find him. Good speaking to you."

A moment later, I hear Hilton's heavy footsteps as he pounds across what I assume is their kitchen floor. (For some reason, whenever I call people at their homes during the day, I envision them in their kitchens.)

"Hello, Bill," he says to me.

"Good morning, Hilton. How are you today?"

"Never ask an old man that, son. Unless you got a free morning."

"Are you feeling a little under the weather?"

He grunts slightly, making a noise somewhere between a growl and a sigh. "Seventy-four-year-old men always feel a little under the weather. I think I spent too much time on my feet yesterday, watching Jamie Sturman burn the ball field."

"I stopped by to watch it myself. I guess I just missed you."

"What did you think? You ever see that sort of thing down country?"

"Nope. People don't even burn leaves anymore in New York or Connecticut."

"It impress you?"

"It impressed me."

"Good. It should have. So, what do you need?"

"Oh, I don't really need much of anything. I just have a quick question for you."

"Shoot."

"I was looking over my roster yesterday, and think I recognized every name on my team. Every name but one."

"Uh-huh."

"Diamond. There's a child on the team named L. Diamond. I was just curious, do you know him? Or her?"

"It's a him."

"Well, that's a start."

"His family's only been in town a couple weeks."

"Was he at tryouts?"

"Bill, you sound just like that imbecile, Russ Wohlford. What are you worried about—afraid you got a loser on your team? Some kid who can't scoop up ground balls like a vacuum cleaner?" Hilton is chuckling as he asks me the question, but I nevertheless feel chastised.

"No, not at all," I insist, trying to laugh with him. "Just academic curiosity. But I must admit, I find the fact the child's a boy very reassuring."

"Now why is that?"

"Because I don't have the slightest idea how to teach little girls baseball."

I can almost see Hilton shaking his head in disgust, appalled at the stupidity of the New Yorker today. What next? he's thinking, what next? But Hilton is nothing if not unpredictable. "Oh, that scares most first-year coaches. But you know something? It's no more difficult to teach a little girl to catch a fly ball with two hands than it is a little boy. Fact is, it may even be easier."

"You think so?"

"I do. You see, almost every little boy plays Little League, regardless of whether he has any athletic ability whatsoever. It's . . . expected. It's part of growing up male. But that's not true with little girls. In my experience, the kinds of girls who want to play baseball are usually pretty good athletes."

I nod, wondering if I have somehow misjudged Cindy Fletcher or Melissa Edington, if my memory of their play in the Pee-Wee League has grown faulty.

"Of course," Hilton continues, "that's not true with the two girls on your team. The two girls on your team are . . . well . . . awful. Just awful."

"Thanks, Hilton."

"No problem. Anything else?"

"No, I think that about does it."

"Well, I'm glad I could fit you into Eunice's and my busy schedule."

I put my eyeglasses down on my desk beside the telephone, and rub my eyes. I should have asked Hilton the Diamond boy's name, I should have asked him what that L stands for.

Because I'm sure Hilton knows. Hilton is, after all, commissioner of the Sedgebury County Little League. Our Mountain Landis, our Happy Chandler, our Bart Giamatti. What some people might mistake for mere overzealousness, I know is actual—in the context of one small Little League in one small county in Vermont—omniscience. Hilton knows everything there is to know about our Little League, and he pulls all the strings that he can.

I am a case in point: I am firmly convinced that were it not for Hilton Burberry, I would not now be coaching the Triple-A Tigers. Wes Pratt would be the manager, as he was last year.

Last December, however, about two weeks before Christmas, I approached Hilton about coaching. I ran into him at the post office, and told him that I'd be available to coach a Little League team this spring, and that, in fact, I wanted to. He said he didn't think there were any openings, but—if I didn't mind—I could drop by his house Saturday morning and he would see what was available.

Saturday was one of those hideous gray winter days in Vermont, when there's no snow on the ground and the mud on the dirt roads is frozen into rock-hard ripples. I drove up to Hilton's and Eunice's farm, convinced I would come home with a team: the Triple-A team, in fact, the team on which Nathaniel would have played. After all, why else would Hilton have suggested I drop by his place?

I was wrong. Sitting across a round oak table from Hilton in the man's library, he told me that there wasn't a single coaching job available in Havington. Not one. If I really wanted to try my hand at this sort of thing, he said, there was no reason why I couldn't be an "extra" assistant coach for the Sprout League: he was always looking for parents to help out with the Sprouts, and that was the best way to get one's feet wet anyway.

I agreed, but I was disappointed. I had invested so much emotional energy and anticipation into the idea of managing the Triple-A team that past summer and fall, that I hadn't even considered whether the ten- and eleven-year-olds already had a coach. But of course they did: Wes Pratt, Dickie Pratt's dad. He had coached them the year before, his son's first year on the team, and there was no reason to believe he wouldn't coach them again this year, his son's second.

I was honest with Hilton, and I told him that I was disappointed. I told him that I had hoped to be around the older kids, the boys who had been my son's friends. I told him that it was an odd and empty feeling to watch a Little League game without a vested interest: a son, a grandson, and these days, a daughter.

And I told him to let me know if anything changed and he needed a coach or assistant coach at the Triple-A level.

He said that he would, but it was highly unlikely. Highly unlikely. Wes Pratt and Pete Cooder were all lined up as coach and assistant coach, and they seemed to have everything under control.

And then, less than four months later, Hilton called. He called at the beginning of April, on the night of the first of that peculiar month's two full moons, to tell me that Wes had just received some sort of promotion at work, and was going to have to spend a lot more time on the road—too much time to allow him to be the head coach. If I were still interested in the job of Triple-A manager, he said, the job was mine.

I decide to drive past the Little League field on my way home from work and stop by to examine it closely. I've never seen a field, baseball or corn, after it's been burned, or wandered around among the blackened dirt and weeds and grass.

It's windy this evening, windier than yesterday. Jamie probably wouldn't have burned the field on a day like today.

I drive into the firehouse lot, the only car there, and coast to a stop facing the river. I recall that I have a pair of sneakers in the trunk, remnants from a tennis game last week with Doug Bascomb, and decide to get them so I don't have to walk in my good shoes across the giant ashtray on which we will soon play baseball.

And that is truly what the ball field is like: a tremendously wide, flat ashtray, with a fine black dust all around. I look behind me at our antiquated backstop, imagining that its sloping creosote-covered posts were designed actually to support a giant cigarette, and for a brief second I can almost see that cigarette (it's two to three times as large as a person, and if I'm not careful a burning ember may fall upon me—such are the dreams and delusions of ex-smokers). Certain landmarks on the ball field are unchanged, despite the black sootiness of it all: the pitcher's mound still rises in the middle of the infield, and the shapes of the wide dirt fans between first and third base are still clearly visible. Hilton's pile of new soil has also remained untouched.

Nevertheless, the field doesn't look like a particularly appetizing place to play baseball.

I wander aimlessly around the infield, the ground feeling like another planet beneath my feet. The portions of the field that will soon be grass feel too hard, while the portions that should be dirt feel too soft. Nothing gives properly.

I end up at first base, Nathaniel's position, and stand there for a moment, surveying the field from what had been his perspective. I look toward the first base bench, only a half dozen yards to my left, and imagine myself there with my new clipboard, scanning the score book and roster. Perhaps I'm counting names to make sure that everyone has gotten a chance to play, perhaps I'm wondering if the Hayden boy is ready to try his first bunt in a game situation.

I would have liked to have coached Nathaniel. I really would have. I almost feel badly for Wes Pratt, because this year he will miss the chance to coach his son, Dickie.

After a moment I start back across the blackened infield to my car, the ashes occasionally crunching as my sneakers press them into the ground. And then abruptly I stop, and a small gasp escapes from my lips. There is a child not forty feet away from me, sitting on a spot that hasn't been burned in foul territory by the third base bleachers, a patch of grass still winter brown. I can't imagine how I could have missed him when I drove in or when I strolled out to the field, but clearly I did. He looks like he's been sitting there for a long time, perhaps hours, leaning against one of the bleacher's support columns, his legs comfortably stretched out before him.

I walk toward him, annoyed with him for surprising me, annoyed at myself for being surprised. I don't believe the child is from Havington, because I've never seen him before, but at the same time I have no idea what a child from Sedgebury or Starksboro would be doing hanging around the Havington diamond at dusk.

He stands up as I approach, a ten- or eleven-year-old boy with hair as black as the ash around us. He might be five feet tall, but he might also have gained a couple of inches in my eyes from the assertive way that he stood up to face me. He's a thin boy, and—as I do with all children his age—I compare him with my own son: he's thinner than Nathaniel, with a longer face and a more pronounced chin. His eyes, however, are what stand out to me, even at twenty-five feet. He has blue eyes, eyes as blue and round as my son's.

I don't think I've ever met anyone before with jet black hair and blue eyes. I didn't even know it was possible.

"Howdy," I say to the boy, trying to compensate for the shock that must have registered on my face when I first looked over and saw him. "You from around here? From Havington?"

He nods that he is, smiling. He jams his hands into the pockets of his gray windbreaker.

"I'm Bill Parrish," I continue, extending my hand to the child. "You play baseball?"

He nods that he does, and removes a wallet-size notepad from the back pocket of his blue jeans. He flips open the cover to reveal the first page, and gestures for me to read the sentence hand-printed there in bold block letters:

I don't speak. But I can hear.

I start to tell the boy that I'm sorry for him, but I catch myself. When Nathaniel was dying, Harper and I were taught not to show pity overtly: a handicapped child, we were instructed, needs hope and love and respect. Not pity. So although I am genuinely saddened for the boy, I simply nod back at him in understanding, and continue, "Where in Havington do you live?" I point toward the town, asking, "That way?"

He shakes his head that he doesn't, and writes something with a blue felt-tip pen. He then holds the note up to me, and points over my shoulder:

Past the bleachers.

"You live past the bleachers?" I ask, looking off at the hills in that direction.

He smiles.

"Where about? Is it too complicated to write down?"

I watch him scribble, his hands appearing to me deceptively small because of the way he has gnawed his fingernails. He holds up the pad once again:

Off the Logging Highway.

Now it's my turn to nod. I nod because I'm not sure I believe him. Harper and Nathaniel and I have hiked up there, there was a time when we cross-country skied up there. And we never saw any houses. We never even saw any signs of houses: no power lines, no telephone poles, no mailboxes.

"What's your name?" I continue, hoping no hostility has crept into my voice because I believe he has lied.

Lucky.

"Lucky what?"

And then, as he's writing, I feel a wave of dizziness sweep over me, the sort of dizziness I felt when I waited for the doctors to tell me Nathaniel's white blood cell count, or the survival statistics by month. I recognize it well. But while that dizziness was triggered always by reasonable, explicable dread—every parent's worst nightmare—this particular vertigo is brought about by an altogether unreasonable fear. I know exactly what the boy is going to write. I know now exactly who the boy is, and for reasons that I don't understand this knowledge disturbs me. It frightens me.

And yet it is almost anticlimactic when the boy turns toward me his little spiral-bound tablet and reveals to me his name. I should have known it all along, I should have known the moment I saw the boy appear out of nowhere that his name would be

Lucky Diamond.

Chapter 6

I am a dinosaur when it comes to baseball bats, a relic from a different era. I am part of the last generation of little boys to grow up with wooden bats, the last group of kids who thought about issues like hitting with the label away, who learned from experience that a bloop single to right was going to sting your hands an awful lot more than a home run slammed over the left fielder's head. I can remember breaking baseball bats (yes, even lousy hitters like me had the thrill of breaking a bat now and then), feeling them crack or sever or chip when I made contact with the ball, occasionally even splintering one in half.

Today, all Little Leagues use aluminum bats. Even small ones in Vermont, like our league. Aluminum bats cost three times as much as wooden bats, but they're virtually indestructible. They last for years, the only indications of wear and tear the small scratches along the sweet spot where the paint eventually begins to peel away.

Moreover, a ten-year-old can hit a ball harder and farther with an aluminum bat than he can with a wooden one. (Undoubtedly a forty-year-old can too, but I've never spent a morning watching forty-year-olds hit baseballs.) I know the companies that make baseball bats dispute this, and I understand that there are actually university studies that prove and disprove this theory. But I've watched the Havington kids use their longer, thinner, and lighter aluminum bats for three consecutive years now, and I know they're better hitters than my peers were when I was their age. It may be a simple result of the fact that they like the aluminum bats more than wood—perhaps they believe they look more contemporary, perhaps they swing them with less fear of being stung along the palms of their hands—but I believe strongly they're better hitters.

I don't miss wooden bats, however, because they gave me a feeling of strength as a child when I broke one, or because I identify them now in some ritualistic way with traditional baseball.

I miss wooden bats because of the noise they made when they made contact with the ball. Wooden bats made a sound like a gunshot, a deeply resonant clap of thunder. Wooden bats created lightning that could electrify a crowd.

Aluminum bats don't. Aluminum bats make a plinking sound when they hit the ball, one high, metallic clink. It sounds as if someone threw a quarter against a piece of glass; it sounds insubstantial. It sounds weak.

I watch Lucky Diamond swing the bat at our first practice, a Tuesday night in the middle of May. Pete Cooder is grooving slow pitches that are belt high to everyone, giving them a chance to hit the ball hard, while I toss a baseball with the two boys who I expect will be our star pitchers: Jesse Parker and Bobby Wohlford. The infield grass has begun to grow back, and it looks now like a lush, rich crew cut.

No one, I have noticed, hits the ball anywhere near as hard as Lucky Diamond. One shot flies over pudgy Donnie Casey's head in left field, another zooms past Paul Hayden in center. One of Lucky's line drives comes straight back at Pete Cooder with such velocity that the star of the Goddette Construction softball team barely has time to duck. It is almost difficult for me to believe that anything that originates with such an ineffectual plink can move so fast.

A lot of the children are scared of Lucky. None of them know him, none of them have ever seen him before. He has told me on his little tablet that he just arrived in Havington, and he won't be attending the public school: beginning in September, he has explained to me, he will be going to a special school in Granville.

The two little girls on my team, Melissa Edington and Cindy Fletcher, seem especially wary of Lucky. While some of the boys grunted in his general direction when I introduced Lucky to the team, Melissa and Cindy shied away from the boy, and even now seem to be refusing to look in his general direction.

I imagine that part of the children's reticence stems from Lucky's handicap. They have never met a mute before, and are unsure of how to deal with him. He's different, he's abnormal, he carries around a notepad. But there is also something about Lucky's eyes that is disquieting, something unnatural about their blue—especially since they radiate from a dark-skinned boy with hair as black as a chimney pipe.

"Attaway," Pete tells Lucky, grinning, when the boy sends another fly ball over Donnie's head. Donnie is somewhat less pleased, since this is at least the third ball he has had to chase into the woods that border the Little League field, his spare tire jiggling visibly in a sweatshirt a size too small. "Keep swingin' through the pitch, through the pitch," Pete continues.

Lucky does have a marvelous swing: he strides into the pitch the way a professional does, waiting on his back leg until the last possible second, and then stepping toward the pitcher, keeping his hips closed. He swings the bat extremely fast, ("good bat speed," as the hitting coaches say), a quick but graceful stroke.

I am relieved that Pete is pitching the first batting practice. As I throw a ball with Jesse and Bobby, I realize that I lack Pete's control and accuracy. My batting practice could degenerate into a series of wild pitches that result in eleven-year-olds swinging at stuff over their heads, and balls that bounce in the dirt.

"Can I try some curves, Mr. Parrish?" Jesse hollers at me.

It is hard to tell that the boy has a Mohawk underneath his baseball cap. He has combed his hair so that it hangs down the sides of his head like small waterfalls.

"Nope." I throw the ball back to him.

"How 'bout next practice?"

"Nope."

"Then when?"

"Oh, maybe in three or four years."

He looks over at Bobby Wohlford, sharing with his friend a conspiratorial grimace: this Parrish guy is a real idiot. He then looks back at me, nods agreeably, and proceeds to throw me a huge lollipop curve.

"Bend your knees *and* your back, Melissa, knees and back," I say good-naturedly to Melissa Edington, after another ground ball I have hit to her at second base has rolled through her legs and into the outfield. I try to make eye contact with her, so that she focuses on me and not on Dickie Pratt, rolling his eyes in disgust at third base.

I find I enjoy hitting grounders to the infielders. They say that those who can do, and those who can't teach. Clearly I exemplify this expression. I had been afraid of my ability to manage infield practice, to literally throw the ball into the air and hit grounders consistently around the diamond. My fears were unfounded: I am good at this.

In the outfield behind first and second base, Pete Cooder is working with the five kids who say that they're outfielders, hitting them fly balls and pop-ups to chase. It was interesting to note that the moment we broke up into two groups after batting practice—outfielders and infielders—and Lucky Diamond wandered behind the four other boys joining Pete, both Melissa Edington and Cindy Fletcher beelined for my group.

Having since seen their throwing arms, I think this was a wise decision on their part, and I begin immediately to envision the two of them platooning at second base. They have not been apart for more than half a minute throughout the entire practice.

After hitting ground balls for fifteen minutes, with each infielder expected merely to scoop the ball up and throw it to Carl Northrup at first base, I decide to liven things up a bit. I ask Roger Wheelock, the little boy beside me who has been catching the baseballs as they're thrown in from the infield, if he feels like being a runner for a few minutes on first base.

"You got the wind for it?" I ask.

"Yup," he says. "I got plenty of wind," and he removes the shin guards and chest protector he has been wearing, and jogs to the first base bag.

"Okay," I yell to the infielders, "this is the drill. Roger is a runner on first base. If there's a grounder to one of you, what would you do with the ball?"

"Bean him on the head!" Dickie Pratt yells back from third base, and everyone giggles.

"After you bean him? What would you do after you bean him?"

"Bean him on the butt!" Cliff Thorpman volunteers from shortstop, and he and Dickie Pratt begin to convulse with laughter, Dickie trying to hide his face in his glove. I had forgotten that to an eleven-year-old, "butt" is an extremely funny word.

"Good answer," I tell them. "Of course, if you do that, the ball will probably roll into the outfield, Roger will wind up on third base, and whoever hit it will be on first base. So instead of one man out and a runner on first base, you'll have nobody out and runners on first and third. And then whoever's pitching—let's say it's Jesse—will have every right to kill you on the spot."

"Darn right!" Jesse agrees from the pitching mound.

"Okay, Dickie, a grounder's coming your way: where are you going to throw it?"

"To second base," he answers, just a hint of exasperation in his voice. Clearly, this is very basic stuff to a knowledgeable kid like Dickie Pratt.

"Right. You want to get the lead runner. Here goes." I send him a fairly sharp grounder, sharper than I'd planned, but he scoops it up cleanly, and makes a solid throw to second. Unfortunately, I had neglected to explain to either Melissa or Cindy that one of them needed to cover second base to catch the ball, and Dickie's solid throw to second rolls about fifty feet into the outfield.

In the outfield there is a collision. I see it from the corner of my eye while hitting ground balls around the infield. Donnie Casey has slammed into Lucky Diamond, crushing the boy into the ground while racing for a pop-up between them.

I put the bat down and jog out to the spot where Lucky lies on the ground, trying not to look alarmed in front of the kids. When I arrive, Pete Cooder is already kneeling over the boy, and it's clear that Lucky will be fine. He has merely had the wind knocked out of him. He is shaking it off, rubbing the back of his neck, while Pete tells him it was a heck of an effort.

"It wasn't my fault," I overhear the Casey boy telling Mark Lamphere. "I can't help it if the kid can't call the ball for himself."

I can't tell for sure if Lucky heard the remark, but judging by the way he stopped rubbing his neck for the slightest second, I believe that he did.

*　*　*

Once Lucky is up and around, I call an end to practice. It's almost seven-thirty, and it's getting dark. I schedule the next practice for Thursday, two days later.

As Pete and I are tossing the burlap bags of baseballs and bats into the back of my jeep, he tells me that he has a practice of his own tomorrow night, Wednesday. Goddette Construction practices every Wednesday night down at the Sedgebury Union High School field.

"Hilton tells me you'll win the softball league again this year," I say.

"Yup, we better. We got ourselves a real good team," he agrees, smiling. "You interested in comin' down, joinin' us?" he asks. I can't tell for sure, but I believe this is a serious offer.

"I don't work for Goddette," I answer. "How can I?"

"Goddette just sponsors the team. Most of us work for Goddette, but a lot of us don't."

"In that case, maybe sometime I will," I tell him vaguely, both flattered and panicked. I doubt I have either the ability or the time or even the temperament to play in the adult softball league.

"Well, you think about it," he says, taking my hand and shaking it hard. "I'll see you right here Thursday night!"

As he turns his truck around in the firehouse lot and begins to speed away over the bridge, I walk back to the diamond, and stand on the first base bag. I stare at the field and the bleachers and the backstop, all becoming fuzzy in the darkness, and I wonder about a myriad of might have beens.

Chapter 7

"My friend was named Costas," Mr. Godfrey says, rocking gently in his wicker chair on the Trillium porch. "He came to this country from Greece, just after the Second World War. Lost his whole family there, and came here to start again. He was about my age then, maybe a little older. Maybe fifty. But, oh, he looked like an old man.

"Well, one day I told Costas that he had to see himself a baseball game. It was nineteen fifty-eight. If he was going to live in New England, he had to see Fenway Park. You ever been there?"

I sip the coffee I have carried across the street from my office, although it has become so cold by now that I could finish it in one long swallow.

"Many times," I answer, enjoying the mid-afternoon sun. It's warm for Vermont this time of year, almost seventy-five degrees, and it's nice to wander away from my office for a few moments and sit on Trillium's front steps.

"I loved Fenway Park," Mr. Godfrey continues. "I loved goin' to games on Patriots' Day. Sometimes they'd begin at eleven in the morning, those games."

"Did Costas like baseball?"

Mr. Godfrey shrugs. "The Greeks, they don't play much baseball. That was part of the problem."

"I gather he didn't. . . ."

Mr. Godfrey stares across the street. "First inning, we see three men come up, three men go down. Second inning, same thing: one, two, three, the Red Sox are gone.

"I can tell Costas isn't havin' a real good time, and so every time someone comes up—Red Sox, Detroit Tigers, I don't care—I start rooting for some action. A couple singles, a double, a home run.

"You see, I loved the game, and I wanted Costas to love it too.

"But I guess it just wasn't meant to be. Seemed like every inning, we'd see three Sox up, three Sox down. Three Sox up, three Sox down."

"Costas was bored?"

"Costas was more than bored, he was confused. By the eighth inning, me and the thirty, thirty-five thousand people there were on our feet screamin' our lungs out. We were screamin' for the Sox to keep goin' down one-two-three, even though this was Fenway Park and the Tigers had a couple runs!

"And when the ninth inning came around, and—sure enough —the Red Sox went down one-two-three, we all stood around clappin' and yellin' like there was no tomorrow. And poor Costas, he just sat in his seat scratching his head, bored to tears. He must have thought we all were nuts."

I turn to Mr. Godfrey, looking up at him in his rocker. "I can't say that I blame him. I can't imagine I'd do much clapping either if I saw the Red Sox get shut out in Fenway Park."

"Costas didn't just see a shutout!" Mr. Godfrey says, raising his voice, evidently astonished by my colossal naïveté. "He saw a goddamn no-hitter! He saw Jim Bunning pitch a goddamn no-hitter, and didn't even know enough to appreciate the thing of beauty he was given a chance to see!"

As I walk back inside Jensen House, Kim Swanson races downstairs from the development office to greet me.

"Good, you're back," she says breathlessly. "Harper is on the line upstairs. I was just about to run across the street to get you. She says it's important."

"Did she say what it was about?"

Kim shakes her head no, so I race up the steps two at a time, forgetting about Mr. Godfrey, Costas, and no-hitters.

I wonder why Harper is calling me at three-fifteen in the afternoon, when it is clear that she must still be at school. It isn't likely that she wants me to pick something up at the supermarket in Sedgebury, or that she will be unable to get our dry cleaning. Those sorts of calls come at four-thirty or five, when she is home in Havington and doesn't need to use the phone in the teachers' lounge.

"Hi, sweetheart," I begin, when I get to the phone at my desk. "Is everything all right?"

I can tell instantly by her voice that it isn't, that something is decidedly wrong. "It's Donnie Casey," she says, whispering. "Something terrible has happened to Donnie Casey."

I sit down on the edge of my desk, incapable of imagining what could have happened to Havington's fattest child that could be so terrible as to merit a mid-afternoon phone call. "Go ahead, I'm listening," I tell Harper, while she catches her breath.

"When he didn't show up for school this morning, Judy called his mother," Harper says, referring to Judy Markham, the sixth-grade teacher. "But there was no answer. So in the cafeteria during lunchtime, she asked me if I had any idea whether Donnie had been at Little League practice last night. I said yes, I thought he had been there. Didn't you tell me that Donnie had some sort of collision with the new boy?"

"Yes, with Lucky."

"The school nurse finally got through to Donnie's mother after lunch, and she said that Donnie had left for the school bus right on time, a little after seven o'clock. So we asked the bus driver if he remembered seeing Donnie on the bus, and he didn't. He said he didn't think Donnie had gotten on at all this morning."

Behind Harper I hear the voices of Patty Glover, the elementary school principal, and Joe Deveroux, the fourth grade teacher. They are alternately shouting at each other, and then apologizing.

"Has anyone found the boy?" I ask.

"Yes, they've found him. Jamie Sturman and Obie Northrup found him. He was by the baseball field, on the slope that goes into the river."

"By the first base line?" I ask the question to stall, because I can't bring myself to ask the real question, the question hovering inside me and making me sweat.

"Right by the first base line," Harper answers, before pausing. She is capable right now of telling me that something terrible has happened to the boy, but she is evidently unable to blurt out the specifics without prompting. She needs my help here.

"Is he—is Donnie—alive?" I ask finally, holding my breath. I can think of nothing worse right now than John and Susan

Casey going through the wordless hell that Harper and I experienced just over a year ago.

"He's alive," Harper says, "but barely. He's in a coma. No one knows what happened."

"An eleven-year-old boy?"

"I know, it sounds crazy. But that's what they're telling us."

"Why was he at the baseball field? That's not on the way to the bus stop, is it?" I recall where the Caseys live, and wonder whether it's even remotely possible that the boy could have taken a shortcut by the diamond. It doesn't seem likely: the bus stop is between the Caseys' house and the ball field.

"No, the field is nowhere near the Caseys', you know that," Harper says, confirming my fears. "No one has any idea what the boy was doing there."

"Which hospital is Donnie at, Burlington or Essex Junction?"

Harper takes a deep breath before answering, gathering the strength to utter words that resonate for her in ways that have nothing to do with Donnie Casey. "He's in Burlington," she says, thinking no doubt about her own lost little boy, "at the Medical Center. He's in the intensive care ward."

Harper leaves me after dinner to take a bath. Sometimes I join her, bathing with her; other times I sit beside her at the edge of our old antique tub and simply wash her hair. But I can tell that tonight she would like to bathe alone, and so I let her be.

When she has shut the bathroom door and become insulated by the sound of the running water, I wander quietly upstairs to Nathaniel's bedroom. I know it would upset her to know I have gone there.

I turn on a light, the bedside lamp that is connected to the wall switch by the door, and I sit at the foot of the small single bed. The sheets were changed last over a year ago, about two months after Nathaniel died, and the bedspread has sat undisturbed ever since. Harper and I changed those sheets together, when we attempted to clean up his room one Sunday. Unsure of what to do with his belongings, we did nothing.

The room no longer smells like Nathaniel, and it hasn't for months. It smells clammy and musty and stale. It smells more like a basement than a bedroom.

I lean back on my hands on the bed, sinking momentarily into

the mattress, when I feel a lump in the bed, a lump in the mattress—rather, a lump underneath the mattress. I bolt upright and
turn, running my hands over the small, unexpected anthill in the
middle of the bed. I know instantly what it is, how long it has
been there, and I am both moved and horrified by my son's
optimism.

Standing up, I pull aside the bedspread and reach deep underneath the mattress, scraping my knuckles slightly on the box
spring, and grab Nathaniel's baseball glove. It has sat there for
fifteen months now, oiled and packed with a baseball, held
closed with two wide rubber bands. It is a ten-year-old's exercise
in hope. As late as February or March last year, as late as the
week or two before we left for the final bone marrow transplant,
Nathaniel was still preparing for what he hoped would be another baseball season.

"I told you," Harper softly reminds me, "no one named Lucky
Diamond ever went to our school. No one named *Diamond* ever
went to our school."

Harper and I lie together in the dark, both of us tired, but
neither of us able to sleep. I'm not sure how long we have lain in
bed. It might be fifteen minutes, it might be an hour. It is sometime after midnight, meaning John and Susan Casey have probably left their boy for the night up at the Medical Center and
returned to Havington.

"I understand that," I say, as much for myself as for Harper.
"But no one had even heard of the family?"

"No one I asked. No one in administration or registration. But
why would anyone know of them? Didn't the boy tell you his
family had just moved to Havington?"

"That's what he told me."

"And you don't believe him?"

"No, I believe him."

"Then what?"

"It's only May. There are still five weeks of school left. I would
have thought that someone—his parents maybe, perhaps the
state—would want him in school for those five weeks. I would
have expected someone to have contacted the principal or something."

"Not if he's enrolled in a special program someplace else in September."

"In Granville. He said—he wrote—the school is in Granville."

Harper's breathing changes slightly, and she rolls toward me. "Granville?"

"Uh-huh. Granville."

"I didn't know there was a school for handicapped children in Granville."

"That's what he told me."

She stretches her legs, her toes grazing my feet. "I thought I knew of most of the special schools in the state."

"Maybe I misunderstood him."

"Maybe. Maybe I just don't know as much as I think I do," Harper says lightly, but I am not reassured. I find it hard to believe that I misunderstood the boy, or that my wife is unaware of a special school in Vermont.

Nathaniel's baseball glove had something called the Grip-Tite Pocket and Hold-Tite Straps, trademarked but essentially meaningless terms that did nothing but teach my son to spell the word "tight" incorrectly, (as he did in his Cub Scout notebook in the little section on square knots). It was a more sophisticated tool than the glove I had used growing up, just as my glove had more bells and whistles than my father's. Nathaniel's mitt had a specially designed hole for his index finger, and webbing that seemed to grow from the glove's fingers, rather than being simply stitched to them.

The glove was a first baseman's mitt, meaning it looked as long and round as a small animal. A barn cat, perhaps, or a raccoon. It was red, relatively common among boys today, but unheard of when I was a child. When I was a child, baseball gloves were the color of rawhide, either tan or brown.

Like my glove, however, Nathaniel had used a small wood burner to brand the mitt with his name and phone number. That was exactly how I had personalized my glove, and how my father had personalized his. No conventional Magic Markers or ballpoint pens for this family, no smeared or faded ink here. Nathaniel had in fact used the same wood burning kit my parents had given me one Christmas decades earlier, a small electric branding iron that seared wood (or leather) with small triangular points.

As far as I know, I was the only child in my Little League to use a wood burner, and Nathaniel was the only child in his.

Chapter 8

When I first started working at Sedgebury College, late May was one of the busiest times of the year for me. Graduation occurs here the Sunday before Memorial Day, and is followed then by two consecutive alumni weekends —weekends when the members of every fifth graduating class are invited back to the campus for reunions. Reunions are extremely important to anyone involved in development or fundraising: at them alumni become especially dewy-eyed and nostalgic, and their generosity especially great.

Last year, however, my first May at Sedgebury without Nathaniel, I began taking our alumni weekends less seriously. Part of it was an inability to cope, but part of it was a simple unwillingness. It suddenly seemed ludicrous to spend hours double-checking the dormitory accommodations the alumni office was providing the class of '51, inspecting the small single beds being made up for sixty- and sixty-five-year-old men and women. It seemed almost grotesquely mercenary to make sure that our estimated wealthiest returning alumni, our illustrious "Top 40," were attending a series of carefully orchestrated dinner parties and teas with the president.

And so despite the fact that the first alumni weekend begins three weeks from tomorrow, on Thursday afternoon I pull the top back on the jeep and go for a drive during lunch. I begin aimlessly, driving with no specific destination, but as I'm passing through the town of Sedgebury I veer east. The sun, almost directly overhead, warms my hands on the steering wheel, and I understand where I want to go exploring. Within minutes the few streets and neighborhoods that comprise the Sedgebury suburbs are behind me, and I'm passing through the farmlands that surround the town. Most farmers have planted their cow corn by now, making the fields almost uniformly rich, brown, and flat.

I pass quickly through Pelham and Clinton and Bristol without seeing another car on the road, until I'm soon on the far side of the mountain from Havington. I come to a stop at the base of a dirt road known unofficially as the French Highway, and reach underneath the passenger seat beside me for the *Vermont Road Atlas,* a book with pages as large as a coloring book that lists almost every road in every county in Vermont.

Even the French Highway is in the road atlas, noted with a tiny red line and referred to as the Bristol-Havington Road, (although even on the map it is clear that the road does not go all the way over the mountain to Havington). There is a second capillary cutting across the French Highway at the top of the small mountain that does wind its way into Havington. It is unnamed, but I believe this is the old logging highway, a thin dirt road that was used decades ago for dragging timber from the forest. The road is used now for cross-country skiing, snowmobiles, and hiking. It may in fact be Harper's favorite cross-country ski trail. As far as I know, no one lives up there, except, perhaps, Lucky Diamond.

I put the jeep into four-wheel drive and start up the hill, unsure how far I will be able to go. I have no delusions that I'll be able to turn onto the logging highway and follow the road all the way through to Havington—I'm sure that at some point now the road thins to a small deer path—but I am nevertheless curious about what's up there. I've never seen this side of the French Highway.

At first the jeep groans as I switch gears, irritated with the steep climb I'm asking it to make. Once we have gained some momentum, however, the engine chugs ahead more happily, and I stop glancing down at the gauge with the engine temperature.

I start glancing instead at the woods around me, woods that become thicker as I drive up the mountain. Spring has come to the base of the mountain and valley towns like Sedgebury, but many of the trees up here have only the tiniest buds on their branches.

Nevertheless, the road becomes darker as I climb: although the trees have fewer leaves at the higher elevations, there are many more of them, and they branch over the road like a tunnel. The sky becomes a thin blue window at the top of the trees much of the time, and for whole seconds will disappear completely.

Perhaps a yard or two in from the road I note the remains of a century-old stone wall, drowned almost completely now by trees and ferns and moss. At some point, even the steep hills this side of the mountain were needed for fields, if only as grazing pastures for plow horses or cows. Some of the larger boulders have their own little moonscapes, seas of craters and pockmarks.

Nathaniel loved stone walls. He equated them with the black and white photographs he had seen from Civil War battles, the sketchbook horrors chronicled by the likes of Alexander Gardner and Mathew Brady. Harper was truly appalled by my brother when he gave our seven-year-old son one Christmas an illustrated history of the Civil War, a history that included some of the more grisly pictures taken immediately after Antietam and Gettysburg, (although she did admit later that the stuff was nothing compared to the polychromatic gore served up by television while we were growing up with Vietnam).

Across the road from the stone wall, in a patch perhaps the size of an acre, someone has recently been logging. The forest is at least a third less dense there, and I can see in the ground the tracks of the equipment and the fallen trees.

And beside the stone wall, often running parallel to it, is a thin white tube connecting maple to maple. Someone has tapped the trees in this area, and spent March sugaring. These tubes are undoubtedly part of a complex feeder network that uses gravity to funnel the sap down into holding tanks someplace at the bottom of the hill, where it is eventually boiled down into maple syrup.

I can see from the jeep that one of the tubes hangs flat and limp against an especially old, wide maple, its connection with the rest of the system severed. I stop where I am and put on the parking brake, and stare at the tree more closely. I know—I know without looking, I know with complete confidence—that between the tree and the stone wall beside it is a gray work shirt covered with blood. Blood that is still damp to the touch.

I know this because I have seen this tree before, I have seen it in this exact proximity to this stone wall, and I have seen it in a moment when—like today—the sun was high but crowded out by the forest.

I know too this is neither déjà vu, nor a premonition, nor something I saw once in a dream.

I know because I have seen this tree with Nathaniel, on a day hike we took together two summers ago. A day hike we took over one hundred miles east of here, up a little hill in Landaff, New Hampshire.

I leave the engine running in the jeep as I climb out, and I approach the stone wall. Despite the engine's steady gurgle, there is a ringing in my ears, the sound of a faint and distant metal wind chime. (I can't recall: was there ringing in my ears in Landaff, the chimes from some distant farmer's porch?) I recognize immediately the smell from the hike two years ago, the aroma of pine and dirt, and I can feel on my cheeks the same moistness in the air.

I step carefully over a small gully at the side of the road, unsure of the footing underneath the piles of slushy leaves, and lean on one of the rocks at the top of the stone wall. If I am willing, I need only look down now to see again that shirt, with its frayed collar and brown cat's eye buttons. I know my eyes would gravitate immediately to a red splotch that begins along the right sleeve and travels across the right breast pocket. I know I would reach instinctively for the cloth, exactly as I did two years before, and my knuckles would graze the wetness that I assumed was merely dew, until I saw that only the redness was wet.

I think I may be ill. The ringing in my ears becomes louder, and my forehead begins to burn. My collar feels tight.

I breathe deeply, and let my eyes drop to the ground.

There is no shirt there, no bloody cloth.

But there is no relief either, because instead of a shirt there's a little wallet-size notepad, a small, spiral-bound tablet exactly like the kind carried by a mute child who claims to live someplace up on the mountain. It is covered partly by pebbles and partly by leaves, its pages water stained and its tin binding rusted.

I reach carefully for the pad, as if it's a small but violent animal, as if its metal spirals will snap at my fingers. Bending over makes me dizzy now, almost nauseous.

I flip through the pad like a paperback, searching for a word or words on any of the pages, a clue into the mind of the little pad's owner, but they all appear blank. At least they do at first. On a second pass, it looks as if there may be some writing on two or three of the pages toward the front of the tablet. The cardboard is cool in my hands, damp, and I have to pinch the tips of the soggier pages apart to separate them, to read the few words scribbled there by Lucky Diamond:

Mr. Burberry
~~**Mr. Pratt**~~ **(Tigers) Mr. Parrish**
Mr. Cooder (Tigers)

At some point the boy crossed out the name of the man originally slated to coach the Triple-A Tigers, Wes Pratt, and replaced his name with mine.

I turn to the next page, and discover there a partial list of the children on the team. I am not positive, but I believe the list only includes those children who played on the Triple-A team last year—in other words, the team's eleven-year-olds.

Mark Lamphere
Leon Northrup
Jesse Parker
Dickie Pratt
Cliff Thorpman
Bobby Wohlford

I assume the boy got the list from the commissioner himself, since only Hilton Burberry insists on calling poor Carl Northrup "Leon."

Taking the pad with me, I return to the jeep. My imagination—overactive, disturbed, perhaps on some level out of control—has tired me. I've gone far enough, at least for today, so I decide to turn around and head back to the college.

As I coast in low gear down the dirt road, I recall how Nathaniel and I had turned in that bloody work shirt to the New Hampshire state police, and then never heard another word about it. We read the *Manchester Union Leader* and the *Littleton Courier* for perhaps a month afterwards, every single page of every single edition, but we never saw a single word about a murder or a missing person up on that mountain.

Chapter 9

Doug Bascomb and I are interviewed Thursday afternoon by a twenty-year-old news editor from the *Sedgebury Student*, the Sedgebury College newspaper. The student is writing an article for the paper's commencement issue about capital campaigns, and how a small liberal arts college like Sedgebury raises the hundreds of millions of dollars it needs. I know this editor's name from her other stories, predictably well-meaning but strident baubles condemning CIA recruitment on campus or demanding an expansion of the vegetarian dining commons.

Nevertheless, I am unprepared for the student's questions.

"Why do the portfolios at Amherst and Williams outperform Sedgebury?

"Why are women's colleges like Smith capable of raising more money per alumna than we are?

"Why is our current goal only ninety-five million dollars?"

I had expected a left-wing reflection from my own college days, and have received instead a future money manager. I had anticipated a woman in blue jeans and Birkenstocks, and sit facing instead an aggressive child in Lycra running tights and Nike cross-trainers.

"How important is the eighty/twenty rule to Sedgebury?

"Do you view Theodore Ketchum as an academic president or a fund-raising president?

"How tight are your battle plans?"

When she has left, I collapse back into one of the conference room chairs, and rub my eyes. Someday that student will be responsible for a very large gift to Sedgebury College.

* * *

I stand at home plate and hit a slow roller to Melissa Edington at second base, so slow that it barely reaches the edge of the infield turf. No matter. She still flails at it with her glove as if swatting a fly, knocking the ball twenty or twenty-five feet to her right.

Amazingly, no one laughs, not even Dickie Pratt.

That is how subdued the boys are at practice Thursday night. I don't believe Donnie Casey is a particularly popular little boy, but the fact that someone they know—someone their own age—is now in a coma has frightened them.

It has probably reminded them as well of Nathaniel's death.

And so they are very quiet this evening, very well behaved.

"Two hands, Melissa, two hands," I tell the half of my second base platoon currently taking infield practice. She nods, covering her mouth and her nose with her glove.

Behind her I see Pete Cooder leading the outfielders over to the right field foul line, and then walking them in toward home plate. As always, Lucky Diamond lags about three feet behind the other boys, bouncing his glove against his hip as he walks.

"Carl, this last one's for you—a short hop," I shout at Carl Northrup, our first baseman, and then slam a line drive into the dirt directly before him. Reflexively he turns away from the ball, but he keeps his glove before him and manages to scoop it up.

"Attaboy," I can hear Pete tell the child as he walks past him in foul territory. "Very nice snag."

I call the entire team together around home plate, and inform them that Pete Cooder is going to lead them in their first sliding drill. As I had expected, the boys love to slide, and I can see more excitement in their faces now than I've seen all evening. They throw their gloves into a pile by the on-deck circle along the third base line, and begin rubbing their hands together and slapping each other on the back as they prepare for their turns.

Pete has the situation well in hand, so I wander over to the small wooden bench behind third base for my windbreaker, and then sit down to watch and to listen: I too expect to learn from the Pete Cooder Sliding Clinic.

"You all know what a strawberry is," he begins, and I nod with the other boys, thinking actually of Harper. I wonder: does Harper remember my explaining to her the irony of Nathaniel's final sliding strawberry the morning our little boy died? We never talk about it, although it is only one of perhaps hundreds of memories we each have relegated to some cerebral attic where they can be ignored, forgotten, left to gather dust. Memory can be selective, especially when it wants to heal, and I hope—I believe—that she has been granted amnesia on at least this one particular incident.

"There are three reasons to slide, at least three I can think of," Pete begins, most of the children immediately enraptured. Even Bobby Wohlford, who until now has made it quite clear that he knows everything about everything, stands at attention. The only player who seems uninterested is Lucky, who stands just beyond the semicircle gathered around the assistant coach. He bites his nails, he fidgets, he bobs on his toes. He glances again and again at the pile of baseball gloves over his shoulder, as if he's afraid his will disappear.

Abruptly he turns away from the circle, and for a split second I believe he is walking toward me. He stops instead at the heap of gloves, finds the one that I assume is his, and places something inside its webbing. He then pulls a rubber band from his sweat-shirt pocket, and winds it around the mitt to prevent whatever's now inside it from slipping out.

"Goin' in headfirst looks real good on the instant replays, but it ain't always the smart way to take a base," Pete says, answering someone's question.

Lucky notices that I have been watching him, and smiles in my direction, nodding just the slightest bit. He then returns to the other children, although he continues to stand a few feet behind them. When I follow him with my eyes back to the group, I catch Jesse Parker and Cindy Fletcher staring at him, curious.

The children are still not sure what to make of Lucky. On the one hand, he is handicapped, crippled, an object of pity and disgust. He is an oddity, a freak, a kid who can't speak. But he is also the team's single best hitter, by far, the child who hits the longest fly balls and the hardest line drives, the child who will be —without question—our cleanup hitter.

"Okay, Roger, you stand by home plate," Pete tells our catcher. "Stand like you're waiting for a throw from an out-fielder. Pretend it's Mark or someone. You can't block the plate 'cause you don't have the ball, but you want to stand as much in my way as you can. I'm goin' to be a base runner comin' in from third."

When Roger is set, Pete jogs about thirty feet up the third base line. "Don't do anything, Roger, most of all worry. I got about eighty pounds on you, and I'll end up breaking your skull if you try and tag me. Got that?"

Roger nods, and Pete immediately races for home, hitting the dirt nine or ten feet from the plate, and sliding just within the baseline. He barely grazes the outside corner of the plate with his left toe, as he slips past Roger in a small eddy of dirt and dust.

"Safe!" Dickie Pratt screams, waving his arms palms down before him, while some of the other boys clap and whistle.

Pete stands up and brushes himself off, and suggests the team line up midway between third and home to practice. "I want everyone to get two slides in this way. I'll be the catcher."

A small shoving match occurs between Bobby Wohlford and Joey Fenton, but Joey defers to one of the evolving team leaders after a second, and lets Bobby go before him.

While the children race toward Pete Cooder, no doubt bruising their hips and sides unmercifully, I stroll over to the pile of baseball gloves. Telling myself that it is only academic curiosity (though knowing full well it is more than that), I scan the pile for the glove with the rubber band, the one that I know belongs to Lucky Diamond. I want to know what the boy has hidden inside it.

I discover it on the far side of the small mound.

"Start your slide a little later, Cindy, just a step or two later," Pete says to the girl, lying flat on her back now about four feet in front of home plate.

Without lifting Lucky's glove off the ground, I wander around it until I am at an angle that allows me to see down inside it, through the conical opening at the top. When I see what Lucky has hidden there I smile, I smile at my own curiosity. I smile at my own stupidity.

"Perfect, Lucky, that was just perfect!" Pete yells, pounding the air with a fist.

It was obvious what Lucky had placed in his glove, at least it should have been. The boy was practicing sliding. He was about to throw himself onto the ground and land hard on his hips and his bottom. The boy had simply thought ahead, and emptied his back pocket of his wire-bound notepad.

"Nicely done, Lucky," I shout encouragingly at the boy, when I see him looking in my direction.

I start toward the team to watch their second tries, when something about Lucky's glove itself strikes me. Something I hadn't noticed immediately because I had been so obsessed with what was inside it. I turn back to the pile and focus on the Rawlings mitt with the rubber band, and find myself inadvertently biting my lip when I see what Lucky Diamond has done to it.

Up the slot for his pinky, and along the slot beside it, Lucky Diamond has used a wood burner to brand his name into his glove.

Harper taught Nathaniel to say his prayers each night, and for years he said them with Harper present. He would regurgitate his "Now I lay me"'s while Harper sat at the side of his bed, and ask God to bless whoever he knew who was sick or unhappy, and then roll over and fall instantly asleep.

About three months before he became ill (rather, about three months before he was diagnosed as being ill), he looked up at Harper and told her that he couldn't remember everyone who needed to be blessed, there were just too many of them. It was too hard. There was his grandmother, Harper's mother, who was just beginning to battle glaucoma. There was Mrs. Walters, a schoolteacher for one of the older grades, who Nathaniel saw once a week when she was the cafeteria monitor; Mrs. Walters had recently begun to depend upon her crutches to get around, the result of multiple sclerosis. There was his godfather, fighting melanoma so severe that he had grown a huge mountain man–style beard to protect his face and his neck from the sun, and never wore short sleeved shirts. And there were the assorted missing (or run over) village dogs, the aunts and uncles with arthritis, and the local friends and neighbors hurt each year in car accidents, hunting accidents, or at the Kreiser-Dale plant where many of them worked.

"Can't I just ask God to help everyone who's sick?" Nathaniel asked Harper, and Harper said sure. Otherwise his list really would have become way too long.

Chapter 10

"It was an arrhythmia," Judy Markham, the sixth grade teacher at the school, explains to Harper Friday night, referring to Donnie Casey. "It was some sort of heart attack."

Harper nods. She is not even pretending to eat, despite the fact she is sitting between our hostess, Patty Glover, and Patty's husband. Her fork rests on the edge of her plate, the small mound of spinach and salmon fettuccine undisturbed.

"Is he still in a coma?" Stan Markham asks his wife.

"Yup."

Patty offers the pepper mill to her husband, passing it to him before he requests it. She turns toward Judy, asking, "Are they sure? He's just a boy, how can he have a heart attack?"

"Well, they're sure he had a heart attack. An arrhythmia, Susan called it," Judy continues, referring to Donnie Casey's mother. "But they're not sure why. They're still waiting for all of the blood tests to come back."

"Is there anything they can do?" Harper asks, her voice soft and small.

Judy shrugs. "It doesn't look like it. He's on a respirator, and they're giving him drugs to prevent a relapse—"

"A relapse?" George Glover asks, incredulous.

"I guess a second heart attack. But I'm not a doctor, George, so I'm just guessing."

"This is delicious," I hear myself telling Patty, speaking too loudly while motioning with my own fork at the pasta on my own plate. "Really wonderful stuff." I'm not sure whether the words have gushed from my mouth because of the untouched serving on Harper's plate, or whether it was a pathetic attempt to steer the conversation away from sick little boys.

"I just don't see how an eleven-year-old boy could have a heart attack," George says, shaking his head. "Did he have a history of heart problems?"

"Not that anyone knew about."

"Maybe it was a virus," Stan suggests. "Can't a virus cause heart or muscle problems?"

Judy nods, remembering something from her conversation with Susan Casey. "You know, that is one of the things they're considering. Viral myo . . . myo-something. But it's a virus. Susan said that Donnie had had some sort of chest cold last week. Nothing major, nothing that kept him out of school—"

Patty snickers. "Oh, great. Whatever he has, he's now given it to an entire elementary school."

"No, I don't think it's that kind of virus. I don't think it's contagious like that."

George turns toward her. "Then how did he get it?"

"I have no idea," she says.

"Maybe it was a bug bite or something," Stan offers. "Maybe it was a deer tick."

"You're coaching a Little League team this year, aren't you, Bill?" George asks me.

I nod that I am.

"Think this deer tick thing will end the season before it begins?"

"George, there's no 'deer tick thing.' No one ever said that Donnie Casey was bitten by a deer tick."

"Stan just did."

I shake my head. "Well, I doubt we would cancel Little League on the kids. Even if Donnie was bitten by a deer tick."

"Bill!" On the surface, Judy Markham's voice is merely good-natured disbelief. On some deeper level, however, I know there is genuine concern. She is a mother of twins, three-year-old boys, and I can tell that were they six or seven years older, their Little League season would now be over. Someone has suggested that a deer tick may have bitten a small boy in the woods or fields around our town, and as far as Judy is concerned, she would sooner allow her children to become bullfighters than play baseball in Havington.

"I don't know, Bill," Stan says, "I wouldn't want to risk the kids out there. I wouldn't want to be out there myself."

I survey the table before answering. We are a dinner party of six people, two Glovers, two Markhams, two Parrishes, none of whom are originally from Vermont. With the exception of Harper, who is from Mississippi, we are all from suburbs of New York City, we all grew up in the sort of pristine neighborhoods where children were taught to fear raccoons and skunks and squirrels, where disease lurked in every insect and wild animal that dared venture onto our acres of split-levels and shingle oak colonials.

Vermonters, however, do not fear the woods the way we flatlanders do, nor do they cower from the animals that live there. After all, they sugar in those woods in the early spring, they hunt in them in the late fall; they chop the wood they will need to heat their homes throughout the winter in June and July, and—real Vermonters—roar through them on snowmobiles in January, February, and March.

"If we were in Connecticut," I finally answer, "or Westchester County, the season might be scrubbed because of a deer tick. But not here. I'd go along with whatever the parents wanted, but I really don't think we would cancel the season on the kids."

Patty Glover, who as the school principal has been working with Vermont parents and children for three years now, nods in agreement. "I think the town would be pretty sensible about this. A couple years ago there was some sort of encephalitis scare in Miami. Mosquitoes, I think. Five or six kids came down with the disease, but nobody panicked. The city took some precautions—I think they scheduled all Little League games and outdoor functions during daylight—but I certainly don't believe the city took all organized activities away from the kids."

Stan smiles. "I can see it now: Bill Parrish leading the kids in tick-check drills."

"Touch your toes, toss a tick—"

"No, no, it's *pick* a tick, it's pick a tick—"

"And of course no one would be allowed to chase the foul balls that went near the river or high grass—"

"And the good news would be that the kids wear white socks, right, Bill?"

I start to say yes, yes the kids do wear white socks, but before I can answer Harper says to the table, "This isn't funny. Donnie Casey is up in the hospital. If . . ."

I watch as everyone turns toward her and then away, staring down at the food on their plates. If . . .

I know that the four of them are finishing in their minds Harper's sentence for her, each of them finishing it in his or her own way.

"I would have let Nathaniel play baseball this year," Harper says, staring out the window of the jeep as we drive home from the Glovers. "I wouldn't have let my fears about a deer tick ruin his spring."

"I know."

"I would have worried about him. But I wouldn't have kept him home."

"I know."

"Do you?"

"Yes."

As we round the Havington church and come to a stop in our driveway, I pause before climbing out to open the barn door. "Something's been bothering me," I begin quietly.

From the streetlight behind us I can see Harper's eyes. She raises an eyebrow, waiting, and I can tell she was crying at least part of the way home.

"What do you think Donnie was doing at the Little League field Wednesday morning?" I ask.

"I don't know. I don't think any of us will know the answer to that question unless . . . until Donnie wakes up."

"Well, I've been thinking a lot about it, and I have a theory. It's probably not a very good one, but here it is. Donnie collided with Lucky Tuesday night, and really knocked the wind out of him. He said something mean about Lucky, something mean about the boy's handicap. And then, the very next day, for reasons nobody knows, Donnie wanders down to the river by the Little League field before school."

She pats my knee softly. "I don't see any connection, sweetheart."

"Don't you think it's possible the two boys went there to fight or something? The Little League field was the only place they both knew where they could . . . where they could have it out."

"Donnie's not the fighting type. He's a big, fluffy Twinkie. And from what you've told me about Lucky Diamond," Harper says, "he has enough problems without you blaming him for Donnie Casey's illness."

Saturday afternoon, Harper and I start to hike up our side of the mountain, beginning with the road that passes the baseball diamond. Harper has packed us a small picnic, and tossed the lunch into our red and blue Jansport knapsack: pints of blueberry yogurt and small plastic containers of chopped apples in peanut butter. It's the perfect lunch for a warm and sunny spring afternoon in Vermont.

As we approach the spot where the pavement ends, about a quarter of a mile up the hill, Harper reaches into the back pocket of her blue jeans and pulls out her trail guide.

"What do you think?" she asks. "Should we head straight into the national forest? We've never taken the Courtney-Battell trail."

I pause. I should have told her earlier this morning where I wanted to go. "How high does it go?"

"Thirty-two hundred feet," she says, staring at the map in the guide. "Not quite to the top of the mountain, but almost. I think it will have some pretty nice views of Camel's Hump and the Adirondacks when we get there."

I nod, but suggest, "I thought we might head up to the old logging highway." I try to sound casual, but I know immediately that Harper has seen right through me. I can see by the sudden annoyance in her eyes that she knows exactly what I'm thinking.

"The logging highway." It is a statement, not a question.

"Uh-huh."

"Why do you want to spy on a ten-year-old boy?"

"Eleven. And I wouldn't call it spying. I'd call it curiosity."

"Is it any of your business where Lucky Diamond lives?"

"Nope."

"Then why go?"

"I want to see if he really lives up there. I want to see how he lives up there. I worry about him."

"You worry about him? You've never told me that."

I nod. I've never told myself this.

"You know what you're going to find, don't you?" Harper continues.

"No."

"You're going to find that he's lying. You know as well as I do, there's no electricity or phone lines up along the logging highway."

Where the pavement ends and the dirt road begins there is a huge pothole, filled in partly by chunks of asphalt and small stones. I press one of the rocks into the dirt with the toe of my hiking boot, testing the ground.

"We haven't been up there since January, when we went skiing. A lot can change in four months."

She smiles at me, knowing that I know what I have said is idiotic. We both know that nothing has changed. "You think so?"

"No, not really," I confess. "At least not up there."

"Then we'll take Courtney-Battell?"

"I'd rather not. I really want to take the logging highway," I insist, motioning over my shoulder.

Harper sighs. "Okay," she says finally. "It's your hike. I think this is foolish, but we'll go your way."

It is not a rectangular mobile home, not one of those conventional shoe boxes that I have seen on so many of the roads between Havington and Sedgebury, or Sedgebury and Burlington. It is cylindrical, a tube rounded off at both ends. I have seen pictures from the 1950s of diners shaped just like it.

The trailer sits a foot off the ground, on cement blocks, perhaps three or four yards in from the thin dirt road. Its siding is spackled with great splotches of rust, but I can tell that in its better days it had been blue and white. Something—a toaster, maybe—reflects the sun in a side window, and sparkles.

I have never seen the trailer before, not hiking here in the summer, nor cross-country skiing here in the winter.

Trying not to stare, Harper and I move cautiously past the trailer in a wide arc. No one seems to be home, although we watch our steps carefully in any case, walking whenever possible on rocks, each of us always keeping one eye on the trailer.

When we are just past it, I stop, and Harper stops with me. I try to convince myself that there is no reason to feel guilty, that we've really done nothing wrong: my wife and I have gone for a hike, and out of the blue there has appeared a trailer on the old logging highway. We have stopped to look at it now, that's all.

"I think we should turn back," Harper whispers.

Perhaps because she has spoken so softly, I cannot tell exactly what she is thinking. I reach for her hand, surprised by the way her palms are sweating.

"In a minute," I whisper back.

For a long, quiet moment I stare at the trailer, trying to determine for sure whether anyone is there. The yard is about twenty feet wide and the rough length of the mobile home. The grass isn't cut, it's beaten down, a small patch of ground cut from the forest. At the far corner of the plot, hidden partially by a pile of rusted car parts, is a red kick ball. It is identical to the ones I saw Nathaniel use in elementary school, except that this one has less air.

I try to recall in which direction Lucky walks after practice. I believe, but I'm not positive, that he walks alone up this very part of the mountain.

"How far do you think we've walked?" I ask Harper.

"A mile and a quarter. Maybe a mile and a half."

I look up at the trees, wondering if a telephone or power line could possibly be hidden anywhere up there, hidden anywhere at all. I can't see how. If the trailer has electricity, it's in the limited quantities provided by a small generator. And there are clearly no telephone lines—although I have to assume it is at least remotely possible that whoever lives there has some sort of cordless or cellular telephone.

I turn back to Harper. "This definitely wasn't here in January, right?" I ask, referring to the trailer.

She nods. "It's new. New to this spot, I mean."

I look back at the dirt road along which we have walked, wondering if it truly is wide enough to allow a mobile home to pass. It doesn't seem to be, but I can't imagine how else the trailer got there.

"Do you think anyone's home?" I ask.

"Why? Do you plan on breaking in?"

"I'd like to know if Lucky really does live here."

Harper adjusts the strap on the knapsack across my back. "It's none of your business," she says softly into my ear. "It's none of our business. We shouldn't even be here. I think we should turn around right this second, and head back down the mountain."

She's right: how the boy lives truly is none of my business. But I do wonder about him. I wonder why he has been dropped out of the blue into my life. Because that's what it feels like. And while I know my curiosity about the child is unreasonable, I know my concern—the concern of a father, the concern of a parent who has seen his own little boy swallowed up by disease —isn't.

I worry about the boy, I feel bad for him. He has no friends, at least none on the team, and his home sits isolated in a dark patch of woods. The kid can't speak, and when—*if*, I realize uncomfortably, if—he starts school in September, it will be at a school over an hour away.

Even the child's name is a misnomer, an ugly and mean-spirited joke of sorts.

"Is this road plowed in the winter?" I ask, trying to envision Lucky's mother or father driving him to Granville.

Harper doesn't answer, and starts past me toward the trailer. She walks slowly, on her toes, and when I say her name she doesn't respond.

"Harper?" I repeat, this time a little louder, but she continues to ignore me, gliding in a trance to the trailer. She wanders up to a window at the far end, a window coated with a thick film of plastic, and she stands on her toes to peer in. I walk behind her, trying to see over her shoulder, wondering what could interest her so.

I place one hand gently on her side, trying to turn her toward me. "What do you see?" I whisper, glancing both at her and into the window before us.

Never taking her eyes off the room through the window, she raises her hand and with her finger points at something inside it, something that has almost hypnotized her.

I follow her finger, peering with her into the room. I see a pair of twin beds, unmade, and between them a metal card table. A small model airplane hangs from the ceiling above the far bed, a fighter jet from the Vietnam War. In a crumpled ball on the card table rests a pair of striped pajamas, and beside them a pile of books.

I grip Harper more tightly, pulling her to me. I've never seen her like this. "What's so interesting?" I ask, trying desperately to sound light. "What's there?"

"Look," she says, her voice peculiarly hoarse. "Look at the books."

I do as she says, surprised momentarily by the idea that from the dirt road she had noticed the books, but only momentarily. When I see the books—and I know what they are by the designs on their spines, I know what they are before I even read their titles—I understand why they have drawn Harper to the window. *The Story of Lafayette.* And *Robert E. Lee.* And *George Armstrong Custer.*

There on the table are some other child's copies of Nathaniel's three favorite stories from the antique series of "Signature Books." Their size and design is unmistakable to the woman who is Nathaniel's mother, unmistakable at perhaps any distance.

By the light from the fire in the wood stove, Harper and I undress each other on the living room couch, kneeling and necking like teenagers. This will be our last fire until late September, and we are both excited by the warmth from the stove and by the knowledge that winter is behind us once and for all. I pull Harper's gray sweatshirt over her head, thrilled to find she is wearing the blue silk bra I gave her for Valentine's Day, and then extend my own arms above me so she can remove my turtleneck.

I smell talcum powder on her tummy, as I run my tongue along the base of her ribs.

She lies back on the couch and I crouch on the floor beside her, and together we kick off her sweatpants, and throw them onto the carpet behind us. The panties that match the bra, loose-cut tap pants, come partly off with her sweats, so I pull them back up over Harper's hips, and then rub her crotch through the silk.

She is already as damp as I am hard, and the wetness comes through the material and moistens my fingers, and she presses herself up against my hand.

I rest my head on her belly and watch my fingers move in circles on the light blue silk, dreaming of the moment when the taut stomach muscles of my wife will again house our baby.

Chapter 11

I am reminded late Sunday morning of a baseball card convention Nathaniel and I once attended. There is an ad in the *Burlington Free Press* for another convention, one of those shows in which a local high school gymnasium is packed with boys of seven to men of seventy who want to sell or swap their baseball cards.

I remember that I had been appalled by the convention Nathaniel and I attended. Unknowingly, I had brought my little boy into a trading pit that made the commodities market look refined. We were surrounded by eight-year-olds who knew the monetary and book values for baseball cards the way a used car salesman can tell you the blue book appraisal of every Trans Am and T-Bird on his lot. Little boys would dicker toe-to-toe with grown men, rifling off the dollar values of a 1974 Henry Aaron or a 1986 Roger Clemens, and debating the worth of Ben Slaughter (you don't have to attach a year to a Slaughter, because the Red Sox's six-day superstar only appears in one year's worth of cards).

Nathaniel, like any boy who suddenly discovers a treasure chest in his own backyard—although in this case it was a lunch box in his closet—would have sold his entire collection on the spot if I hadn't talked him out of it. He would have sold his rookie Don Mattingly; he would have sold his rookie Will Clark. His collection of New York Mets, the entire 1986 world championship team, would have become a snowboard or a Ninja Turtle if I hadn't convinced him that the cards would be worth even more next year, and to reconsider selling them for at least one more day.

Ironically, the convention almost convinced me to sell my baseball cards (yes, I still have them). The collection, which has survived intact in the attics of five separate homes now, came precariously close to becoming my tax payment two Aprils ago. For one brief and depraved afternoon, I flipped through the three shoeboxes that house the cards, trying to estimate the dollar value of my 1968 Tom Seaver or my 1967 Johnny Bench.

Fortunately, that moment passed. The dark brown smudge from an ancient chocolate bar that covered Bob Gibson's birth date probably took ten or fifteen dollars off the card's value, but it made the card priceless to me. That stain, after all, came from a chocolate bar eaten by Kevin McNichol, my best friend when I was nine. A dog-eared Gary Gentry could not in all likelihood be sold for much more than a cup of coffee, but the card would always have tremendous value for me, because it would always remind me of my buddy Todd Farris. Todd not only had a Gary Gentry autograph, he had an older sister named Margaret, a girl of thirteen or fourteen when I was ten, who was for me my first older woman crush.

No, I couldn't sell the cards. I had kept them all those years for the same reason that people keep old slides or photographs, videotapes of Halloween costumes and Christmas toasts. I had kept them because I knew they would become for me someday a Proustian scrapbook of sorts, an opportunity to bring back for one moment my memories of Ping-Pong in Glen Morrisey's basement or building a tree house with Tim Minot.

As a result of retaining my own collection, I now have the very strange sensation of knowing there is in my house the baseball cards of not one but two generations of collectors. And, while it pains me to admit this, I will never know the real value—the value that cannot be measured by any of the baseball card guidebooks advertised in the *Sporting News* and sold at the shows—of that second, more recent set.

"I had no quarrel with Abigail about staying an extra day on Monhegan Island," Mr. Godfrey continues, rocking gently in his wicker chair on the Trillium porch. "I had no quarrel at all. It meant calling my supervisor, of course, and feeling more indebted to the man than I would have liked, but no, I had no quarrel with Abigail."

"I've never been to Monhegan Island," I tell Mr. Godfrey, smiling.

"Well, I'm glad we stayed that extra day. If we hadn't, I would never have met Adlai Stevenson—he ran for president, you know."

I turn to the old man, astonished, and look up at him in his rocker. "You met Adlai Stevenson on Monhegan Island?"

He nods, chuckling slightly. "I did, I did. He was a mighty interesting politician in his day, I must say."

"He certainly was," I agree, trying to envision Mr. Godfrey and Adlai Stevenson together on a small island off the coast of Maine.

"I met the man walking along one of the deer paths. I was with Abigail, and I remember saying to her, 'Look, there's Adlai Stevenson,' and she said to me, 'Where?' And I had to point, just a tiny bit, so Mr. Stevenson wouldn't see."

"What did you talk about?"

Mr. Godfrey stops rocking, and sits forward in his chair. "Power," he says thoughtfully. "We talked about power."

"Do you remember what Adlai Stevenson said about power?"

"I do, because like everything the man said, it made a good deal of sense to me."

I lean closer to Mr. Godfrey, wishing I had a faculty member from the history department here beside me. "And?"

"And Adlai Stevenson said to me, 'Mr. Godfrey, we need a stronger generator on this island.' And he was dead right, you know. We used to lose all power on that island every night about nine o'clock. That meant you could barely even read in bed after dinner. Imagine!"

Doug Bascomb and I sit on the top of Mount Intrepid Monday afternoon, a foothill on the Sedgebury campus with a view of Lake Champlain in the distance, and Sedgebury's twenty-two tennis courts at its base. I have just spent my lunch hour down there losing two sets to Doug, serving as little more than the man's backboard until he tires of the rally and puts me away.

This is not because I am an especially bad tennis player, but because Doug is an especially good one. He was seeded number one at Sedgebury for four years while he was here as a student, and then spent three years as a teaching pro at a Florida resort before deciding to return to Vermont, and the reassuring sine-cure of a job in development at the college.

"Harper do anything special over spring break?" Doug asks,

referring to the fact that the public schools were closed for a week earlier in the month. He stretches his legs before him, his navy blue sweatpants bubbling over his knees.

"Nope, not really. She caught up on some sleep, some reading. That was what she really needed." I open the can of tennis balls beside me and check one more time that all three are there, the sort of compulsive behavior that will someday give me a stroke. "But I do have some news for you," I continue, snapping the rubber lid back on the can.

He looks once up at the sun, squinting, and then turns to me, expectant.

"We've decided to try and have another baby," I tell him, verbalizing the idea for the first time outside of my house, savoring the very notion. I am grinning, and I'm unable to stop. Harper isn't even pregnant yet, at least as far as either of us can know, and yet I'm smiling, smiling as if I've just told my friend that Harper and I are indeed again parents.

Doug nods, and smiles with me, but I can see in his eyes some concern. "That's wonderful news," he says softly, as if I've just told him I've had a wisdom tooth successfully extracted. "I couldn't be happier for you. For you both."

"It feels good."

"It was a long time."

"No, not that long. It took us a year to figure it all out. That's not a long time. In some ways, it doesn't seem very long at all."

Doug fans the air lightly with his tennis racket. "Can I ask you something?"

I shrug. Of course he can. If what he asks is none of his business, I can explain that to Doug.

"Any special reason Nathaniel was an only child?"

I—we, both Harper and me—have been asked that question a thousand different ways in our lives. We were asked it constantly by Nathaniel's grandparents before he become ill (and then not at all after), and by Harper's teacher friends both in New York and Vermont. One well-intentioned neighbor in Havington, an elderly woman in the local senior citizens volunteer program, actually stopped by to tell Harper that the best time for offspring is when the moon is full and the raccoons first get in the corn.

And yet despite the number of times I have been asked why Nathaniel was an only child, I have yet to craft an adequate response. I'm not sure there is one. The fact is, when Harper and I decided to have children, there never was a conscious decision to have just one. We hadn't planned on stopping with Nathaniel. It just happened that way. On those rare occasions when we talked about how many children we would have, we usually assumed we would have two. Having come from a family of three sisters, Harper was almost envious of the closeness my brother and I shared because there were only the two of us.

Unfortunately, we allowed the simple logistics of life and living to stand between us and a second child. We convinced ourselves that we couldn't afford another baby in Manhattan, because a second child would have necessitated a larger apartment. So we decided we would wait until we had moved to Vermont. And then we chose to wait until we had established ourselves in our new careers, and settled into our new town. And then, before we knew it, Nathaniel was sick, sicker than we had ever imagined a child of ours would be, and we channeled whatever dreams and visions we had of a family into him, and into our desperate prayers that he would, somehow, get better.

I look over at my friend Doug Bascomb, a father of three children, and I answer his question as best I can. "There was no real reason Nathaniel was an only child," I tell him. "I guess the three of us just always got along as we were."

I couldn't have wished for more perfect weather opening night. I stand along the first base line with Pete Cooder and the Triple-A Tigers Tuesday evening, my head bowed and my cap over my heart, while Commissioner Hilton Burberry thanks everyone for coming, and then says a short prayer from the pitching mound.

"Don't forget," Hilton concludes gravely, "although this is a boys' game, it has men's rules. Play hard, but play fair."

It is exactly half past five, the sun still high in the west, and the temperature a balmy seventy degrees. Both sets of bleachers are filled with parents and sisters and friends, with the first base side belonging to Havington, and the third base side to the team from Starksboro. As Hilton passes home plate, he pats the teenager who is one of tonight's two umpires on the shoulder, and the skinny fellow from Sedgebury Union yells at the top of his lungs, "Play ball!"

I gather the Havington Tigers around me in a small circle before they can race onto the field, and I kneel in the middle of them.

"Okay, guys," I begin, "what are the three most important things we learned at practice Saturday morning?"

Melissa Edington and Cindy Fletcher roll their eyes in distaste: they know this is about bugs, and it's more than they bargained for when they signed up for Little League. Although the doctors have now ruled out the possibility that the virus that attacked Donnie Casey's heart—viral myocarditis is the formal diagnosis—was carried by a deer tick, I have decided that I can't be too careful. I have implemented a series of precautions.

"Cindy, why don't you start?" I suggest.

She sneers at me, and then mumbles, "No chasing balls into the river."

"Right. No chasing baseballs into the river. Mr. Burberry has generously agreed to buy us all the baseballs we need." I turn to Joey Fenton. "Joey, what's rule number two?"

"Always wear white tube socks, even at practice."

"Bingo." I glance once again at the ankles of the Havington Tigers, making sure they're all covered. "And rule number three?"

Cliff Thorpman volunteers the answer: "Tick check, every half inning."

"Yup. When you come in from the field, and when you go back out to the field: check your legs and arms to make sure they're clean."

"And if you do find you got yourself one of the little buggers," Pete Cooder adds, "it's no big deal. But you have to let me or Mr. Parrish know. Okay?"

The team is silent for a moment: they came out here to play baseball, not check their arms and legs for ticks. "Now, before you hit the diamond," I tell them, "Jesse has something he wants to say."

Jesse Parker, our captain and our opening day pitcher, perhaps one of Nathaniel's closest friends when he was alive, joins me in the center of the group.

"We all know Donnie Casey isn't here tonight," Jesse says, his voice intense, determined. He is trying very hard to sound like a grown-up. "We all know he's still real sick. So I think we should play this game for him. I think we should go out and beat the crap out of Starksboro for Donnie Casey!"

I put my hand on Jesse's shoulder, calming the boy just the slightest bit.

"Okay guys, you all set?" I ask the group, and they nod silently together, thinking perhaps of their friend at the Medical Center.

"Then what are we?" I ask.

"We're a team!" they shout, but they shout it without much energy.

"What are we?" I ask once again.

"We're a team!" they repeat, this time a little louder, a little more in unison, a little more like the battle cry that Pete Cooder and I taught them each practice.

"I can't hear you: what are we?"

"We're a team!" they scream, everybody but Lucky, "We're a team!" and they finally approach the sort of deafening exuberance I expect from children ten and eleven years old.

"And what does it take to win?"

"Teamwork!"

"What?"

"Teamwork!" they yell, as Lucky's eyes dart excitedly from teammate to teammate. If the fact he can't speak disturbs him right now, it doesn't show on his face.

"Right on, right on, right on," I tell them, imitating a disc jockey from my own youth they will never in their lives understand, and then sit back on my heels and watch as the home team Havington Tigers explodes onto the field, some screaming, some jumping, some pounding their fists into the palms of their mitts as hard as they can. Jesse races up onto the pitching mound, and immediately starts bouncing his warm-up pitches into the dirt before home plate, and the infielders begin whipping a baseball back and forth among them, slinging the ball between first and third and—inadvertently but inevitably—our bench.

From the corner of my eye I can see Hilton standing beside the Homer Harvey Pittmann Memorial Water Fountain, smiling with his hands on his hips. In a square cardboard box in the water fountain's basin (a basin that has held nothing but rainwater since the well went dry over five years ago) sits the opening day baseball, the ball Hilton will throw to our catcher to inaugurate the new season.

I scan the outfield, and for a moment watch Lucky Diamond throw pop-ups to the right and left fielders flanking him, balls that seem to spin straight up into the air like rockets, and then fall to the earth near the foul lines.

"You gotta love that kid's arm," Pete says to me, as together we watch Lucky launch baseballs into the sky.

Around us mill the members of the team who are not tonight's starters, some pacing, some chatting, some—like Paul Hayden—standing beside me to remind me they're there. They needn't worry, I won't forget. Having been no more than a backup throughout my years in Little League, I know well the indignity and frustration of warming the bench. I know well what it feels like to fail.

I turn quickly to Joey Fenton and Mike Harris, two of my little boys on the bench, hoping I can find the words to cheer them up. As I approach them I hear Mike explaining to his small friend, "The stirrups are the most important part! You gotta get your mom to make 'em longer for you, see, by sewing a four- or five-inch piece of elastic into 'em."

"But I don't want to show any more of my white socks! I don't like 'em!"

"Doesn't matter! Making your stirrups longer makes your legs look longer!" the Harris boy insists, swiping at the air with his hand for emphasis.

I look down at their shins, and the part of their uniform in question. Mike has taken the blue nylon stirrups that the boys wear over their white sanitary socks, and had his mother insert a piece of stretch nylon into the thin part that wraps around his foot. The result is that his white socks appear to extend to his knees, with only a thin blue band separating them from his uniform trousers. Joey Fenton's stirrups, on the other hand, cover his socks almost completely, exposing only a small half moon just above his cleats.

Mike Harris is absolutely right: his legs look remarkably long. I pat him on the back lightly with my clipboard, and then do the same to Joey Fenton.

"Keep your head in the game, guys," I tell them. "I'm going to need you both around the third or the fourth inning."

* * *

I watch the coach of the Starksboro team try—and fail—to get a drink of water from the Homer Harvey Pittmann Memorial Water Fountain. Homer Harvey Pittmann grew up in Havington, the third or fourth or perhaps even fifth generation to live in the farmhouse at the end of the Chelsea Road.

He had been, I am told, an extremely popular member of the community, and when he was killed in Vietnam in 1972, the town was devastated. There had been some talk about building a statue in the center of town, perhaps placing a memorial plaque on the porch of the general store.

But statues and plaques weren't Homer's style. He, like many an uncorrupted Vermonter, prided himself on his practicality, on his ability to "make do." Markers and memorials did no real good, at least not the sort of good that can be seen and touched and used, and so the town selectmen put their heads together one meeting, and proposed to the community a variety of "usable memorials to Homer Harvey Pittmann." Among them were a new guardrail on the bridge over the New Haven River, storm doors for the town clerk's office, even a small shelter for one of the school bus stops.

After a fairly lengthy debate one meeting over "what Homer would have wanted," his cousin, Jordon Mathews, stood up and said to the town, "You know what Homer liked? Homer liked to play softball and Homer liked to drink beer. That's what Homer liked. You want to build somethin' to remember him by? Then build a goddamn keg cooler down at the ball field. That's what Homer woulda wanted." And then he sat down.

The water fountain was as close as the town would come to combining Homer's love of softball with his love of drink.

Lucky Diamond stands at the plate and lets two pitches sail past him for balls, both a good foot and a half outside. He strides into the third pitch, a waist-high slow ball thrown by a little boy behind in the count, and hits a screaming line drive straight down the third base line, fair by inches, that rolls and rolls and rolls well past the diving left fielder.

It is a home run, the first—I am sure—of many.

He rounds the bases, head up, and smiles at me just the tiniest bit as he rounds third base.

Our substitute second baseman, Cindy Fletcher, has rare perspective for a ten- or eleven-year-old Little Leaguer, and like all prophets causes a bit of a stir when she takes the field for the first time in the top of the fifth inning.

"Time out!" the field umpire screams when he sees her, and he walks briskly over to where she is standing beside second base.

"It's kind of neat looking, I think," Pete whispers to me, while behind us some of the boys on the team begin to snicker.

I nod in agreement. "But as fashion statements go, it's probably a little too bold for baseball. If I'd noticed what she was doing, I would have stopped her before she ran onto the field."

Cindy smiles at the umpire when he arrives, and while we cannot hear a word he says to the child, it is clear that he is handling the situation with appropriate delicacy. The child removes her baseball cap from her head, and then begins methodically to remove each of the two dozen bright yellow dandelions she has slipped through the wire mesh at the back of the cap.

I am astounded. It is the top of the seventh inning, Starksboro's last turn at bat, and unless they can put together some sort of miraculous rally, my team will win. I look down at the score book on my clipboard, and count again the number of runs we have scored. Fifteen. We have scored fifteen runs, and are about to win our first game by a rout of 15 to 4.

I have let Cliff Thorpman, our shortstop, pitch the final two innings. This has, in all likelihood, prolonged the game another ten or fifteen minutes and made it a little closer: Cliff throws hard, but he has walked almost every other batter.

But I know we will win, and Donnie Casey will have, if nothing else, a victory in his honor.

As the children begin to depart, piling into their mothers' station wagons or their fathers' pickup trucks, I wander over to Lucky Diamond, tying his sneakers alone by the first base bleachers.

"You played a great game tonight," I tell him. "You hit the ball well, but I also thought you had two nice grabs in the outfield."

He looks up and nods, smiling. There is that light in his eyes, a joy that is apparent even at quarter to eight in the evening.

I zip up my windbreaker against the early evening chill, and ask the boy, "Your mom or dad here?" I regret the question the moment the words escape my lips, especially when Lucky looks down at the ground and kicks at the dirt with his toe. The boy shakes his head that they're not here, and starts to walk away.

"Hey," I say impulsively, reaching for the boy's arm, "if you don't have to be home right away, would you like to have dinner with me and my wife?" I ask the question without thinking, the words triggered on one level by the sadness I saw when he kicked at the ground. On another level, however, I asked the question with images in my mind of baseball gloves with wood-burning scars on their fingers, and bedside tables with biographies that are perfect for little boys. Harper and I have not had a child in our house since Nathaniel died.

"I could drive you home afterwards," I add quickly, trying to ground my invitation in something that resembles responsibility.

Lucky looks up at me as the light returns to his eyes. He grins, a wide, broad smile, and I can tell by his expression that yes, yes indeed, he would.

Chapter 12

"Well, I still wish we could phone your family," I say to Lucky, while Harper tosses an extra handful of spaghetti into the pot of boiling water on the stove. "I know this was my idea, but I still feel like I'm kidnapping you."

The boy shrugs, smiles good-naturedly, and scribbles quickly,

No one is there.

handing me the piece of paper to hold.

No one is there, I think to myself, surprised at the words the boy has chosen. Not, *No one is home. No one is there.* This feels to me like no small distinction. It is as if until I return the boy with the dark, dark hair and the sky blue eyes to his home in the woods, no one will be there.

Beside me, Harper slices in half a stick of sweet butter, and drops one piece into the pan on the front burner.

I shield her from the four words Lucky has written, and find myself raising an eyebrow dubiously as I reread them. "I suppose they said they were going out tonight?"

The boy smiles, nods his head vigorously, and then writes,

Besides we dont have a phone.

Have you ever had dinner with a mute?

I can almost imagine myself asking Doug Bascomb this question tomorrow, a straight line just waiting for a joke.

But I have no idea what the joke is, because there is nothing funny about Lucky Diamond, just as there is nothing funny about any little boy with a handicap.

But there is especially nothing funny about Lucky Diamond, a mute who, evidently, was never even taught how to sign. I watch him at dinner respond to my questions and Harper's, occasionally eating with one hand so he can write with the other, nodding whenever a question demands simply a yes or a no answer. He is as determined to hold up his end of the conversation as he is to hit line drives, as capable of communicating in his own way with Harper and me as any little boy his age.

His penmanship is far from perfect, but he writes legibly, using a blue felt-tip pen to allow his words to glide almost effortlessly across his small pocket tablet.

Some moments, when he is responding to a question with a full sentence or two, or while he is scribbling an observation he wants to share, I find myself babbling idiotically.

"Lucky really took some Starksboro kid downtown tonight," I hear myself telling Harper. Or, "You should have seen some of the shots he caught in the outfield."

It's as if silence has begun to frighten me. It's perhaps because something in the boy himself frightens me.

But at the same time, I'm proud of Lucky, as if he's my own discovery, my own personal find.

I am proud of his prowess on the Little League field.

I am proud of the way he has charmed my own wife.

Do you like your job?

he asks her on his tablet.

This is delishus!

he tells her after he tastes the spaghetti, and the fact he has butchered the word "delicious" becomes irrelevant, even to a hardworking schoolteacher like Harper.

I watch, mesmerized, as she applauds the child, as she finds reasons to praise him. It is astonishing the way a few compliments can make him smile, astounding the way they make his eyes glimmer.

"What do your parents do, Lucky?" I ask, determined to break whatever spell I have fallen under, although my voice still has more of an edge to it than I want. "Do they work around here?"

Lucky chops in half a remaining noodle with his fork, and pushes the two pieces apart. He seems almost to be stalling, before nodding yes, they do work around Havington—or wherever he perceives here is.

"What do they do?" I continue. Although I am smiling, Harper can tell by my voice that I have not asked this question lightly. She directs at me a small frown, and I wish there were a way for me to take the question back. The question is, after all, only one of a dozen questions that I've thought of, all of which I have chosen consciously to ignore. What is the name of the school you'll be attending in Granville, Lucky? How will you get there? Did you, by any chance, any chance at all, see Donnie Casey the day he became ill?

I watch almost nervously as Lucky flips his pad to a clean page, and begins to write his answer to my inquiry. He writes more slowly now, concentrating on every letter. Eventually the words begin to take shape, the sentences to form:

My Mom died. My Dad is a Logger.

Harper looks down at her plate, brushing a loose strand of hair away from her eyes. If I know Harper, and I believe that I do, she is as moved by the way Lucky has written his father's occupation, capitalizing the *L* with respect and admiration, as she is saddened by the fact that his mother is dead.

Against the black and white bars of bare birch trees, caught in my headlights like deer, the trailer appears abruptly before me. It sits in the clearing like a giant lunch box, exactly where Lucky had written it would be. It is, as I had come to expect from the boy's directions, the trailer Harper and I discovered the other day.

I can see through a window that somewhere inside it a dim light is on, or perhaps a small television. Either way, I am pleased: it means that the boy and his father do indeed have an electrical generator.

Parked beside the trailer is a huge blue and silver chrome pickup truck, with a white cab hooked over the back.

"It looks like your dad is home," I murmur. "I'll walk you inside."

Lucky turns to me and shakes his head no, that isn't necessary.

"Well then, why don't you make sure he's in there?" I suggest, trying to read his face in the light from the dashboard.

The boy nods his head in agreement, and opens the door on his side of the jeep. He jumps to the ground, and then, just as he slams the door shut behind him, he smiles at me and drops onto the passenger seat a short note:

Thanks alot!

I let the paper lie where it has landed, and watch as he runs to the trailer's front steps. He pushes the front door open, and as he gives me a very small, very quick wave, I see moving behind him a shadow. For a brief second I see the man himself, the man I assume is a Logger with a capital *L*. Before I can focus on the man's features, however, before I can take in more than the fact that the man looks . . . young . . . the door is shut and the shadow is gone.

I drive in the dark down the hill, my jeep bouncing in low gear on the dirt. I try to think only about the road, navigating each turn carefully, always aware that this time of the year and this time of the night the roads can be filled with small animals.

I find it difficult to concentrate, however, because I know that I should have walked Lucky to the door. I should have explained why the boy was late. If I had, I would have met the boy's father.

Instead, all I saw was a shadow, a feature—his hair, his face, I'm not really sure—that gave me the impression the man was young. No more than thirty, perhaps younger. And I know I had wanted to see more. I had wanted to see a strong, burly fellow with a beard—my idea of a logger—lift Lucky Diamond to his chest and hug him.

I had wanted to see something that would make the boy less disturbing, less frightening, less mysterious.

I reach a point in the road where I can see below me the lights of downtown Havington, with the street lamp that shines on the church the brightest among them. Using that light as a guide, I can see the lights of my own house, and I imagine Harper at that moment in the kitchen, placing the last of the dishes in the dish-washer, or drying the pots she has scoured.

Harper likes the boy, she likes him a good deal. He won her over tonight.

If I were to tell her that the child unnerves me as much as he impresses me, she would tell me that I am being ridiculous. And I would know in my head she was right. But I would know in my heart, I would know with a knowledge that is visceral, instinctive, reflexive, that something about Lucky Diamond is wrong. It is as if there is a lie hovering around the child, circling him—circling me—like a hawk.

These are unfair thoughts. What is more likely is that the lie is within me. Alone in the dark, it almost seems plausible that I have conjured Lucky Diamond from the depths of my own despair, a demon boy born of a grief-stricken father. I have taken some anonymous child and invested him with all of the sadness I have lived this past year, the tears shed in silence on the roads to and from Sedgebury, the longing that comes when I see Harper's students, the depression that seduces me into my boy's empty bedroom in the dead of the night.

The jeep bumps slightly when the road turns to pavement, less than a quarter of a mile up the hill from the ball field.

I tell myself that Lucky Diamond is a little boy with a handicap. With many handicaps. I say these words out loud.

"Lucky Diamond is a little boy with a handicap. Lucky Diamond is a little boy with many handicaps."

This is what I must remember; this is all I need know.

Chapter 13

I park the jeep in the barn and swing the door shut behind me, and wander up the front porch steps to our house. I watch Harper briefly through the kitchen window, noting the way the overhead light casts her shadow first on one wall and then, as she moves, on another.

Inside I kiss the back of her neck, while she replaces the coffee pot she has rinsed by the coffee machine, and I can feel immediately that she is tense. She neither turns to me to return my kiss, nor purrs just the slightest bit in response.

"You made it," she says simply, running a sponge along the side of the coffee machine.

"I did indeed."

"Does he live in that trailer?"

"The one we found on Saturday? Yes, yes he does."

She dries her hands on the dish towel with the small blue rabbits. "Did you meet his father?"

"No. I probably should have. I never got out of the jeep."

"Did you see him?"

"Yup."

"What was he like?"

On the counter beside the dishwasher sits one of the boy's white terry cloth wristbands, forgotten on his way out the door. "I only saw him for a split second. I really can't say."

"But there was someone home."

"Yup. There was." I hang my jacket on the hook inside the closet door, and then continue, "You'll be relieved to know they have a generator. His father was watching television when I got there."

"Good," she says, shrugging as she surveys the kitchen. "Well, I'm finished in here. I'm going to go run the bath."

"You don't seem very happy right now."

"I'm not."

"You want to talk about it?"

"Not really. But since you ask, I'll tell you: I didn't like your tone with that child." She leans against the door to the front hall, inhaling deeply. "It was like you were interrogating him. He doesn't need that."

"I asked him what his parents did. Hardly the stuff of the Spanish Inquisition."

"You asked him what his parents did. You asked him who his friends were. You asked him—"

"I also told him over and over how well he played tonight."

"Yes, you did. And that was good of you. But when you weren't babbling about hits, and runs, and whatever else it is you all do over at the ball field, you were . . . you were grilling the poor child! You should have heard your tone some of the time!"

I go to her, taking her hands in mine, but she remains cold to my touch. "I want to take a bath," she says angrily.

"You're really upset with me, aren't you?"

"Yes!"

"Well, I'm sorry," I tell her, trying to look into her eyes. "I'm sorry. I am. The last thing I meant to do was grill the kid or upset you."

Slowly she allows herself to fall against me, sighing as her body relaxes. "He's just one of the best behaved little boys I've ever seen," she murmurs. "I see children almost every day of my life. I see little boys who are seven and eight years old, I see little boys his own age. And I don't think I've ever seen one quite like him. It's just that simple."

I nod silently. If I want, this argument is now finished. I need only remain quiet, or nod my head in agreement, or move on to another subject, another part of our life. Harper's bath. Our bath. That's all I need do. I know that's what I should do. Didn't I just promise myself in the jeep that I would view Lucky as a little boy with a handicap, nothing more?

I am compelled, however, to ask the question that gnawed at me through dinner, that has gnawed at me since we finished.

"Did you see the cats during dinner?" I ask, my tone almost accusatory.

Harper pulls away from me, and I watch as she tries to recall where Alexis and Elsa, our two calicos, were during the meal, and whether they had done something strange.

"No, I didn't," she answers. "Did something happen?"

"No, nothing happened," I tell her. "That's my point. The cats have been hiding since the moment the boy entered the house. They didn't even come out when you opened the cream for the Alfredo sauce, and that's just not normal."

Harper knows I am right, that this is indeed unusual behavior for our cats. Usually they are very friendly animals, and they have always greeted and examined our guests. They sniff them, they rub up against them, they knead at the cuffs of their pants. Moreover, their particular Pavlovian bell is the sound of the refrigerator door opening, and the small pop that occurs whenever either of us opens a container of cream.

"Where are they now?" she asks me.

"I have no idea. They're hiding somewhere."

More perplexed than frightened, Harper opens the kitchen cabinet in which we keep cat food, and starts shaking loudly a box of cat treats.

"Elsa? Alexis?" she calls. "Elsa? Alexis?"

From the floor above us we hear rustling, what may be the sound of claws scooting along the hardwood floor.

"Elsa? Alexis?" Harper calls once again, rattling the box of treats.

We wait for the sound to resume, the reassuring rush of our cats down the stairs. But it doesn't come. We stand there in silence for perhaps thirty seconds, before running through the kitchen together, and then up those stairs to the second floor.

"It came from our bedroom?" Harper asks, referring to the sound.

I nod, flipping on the lamp on her side of the bed. Perhaps because the noise that we heard had sounded to me like cat claws on wood, I am not surprised that the cats are not on the bed or in the easy chair in the corner.

Beside me, Harper kneels and pulls the bedspread up off the floor.

"Elsa, Alexis, what's the matter?" she says softly. "What are you two doing under there?"

I look under the bed with Harper, fascinated by the way our two unusually outgoing cats have become misanthropic and filled with mistrust. Their eyes are wide open and their tails are fluffed like feather dusters; they are in their defensive crouches, their haunches raised, their claws protracted and prepared at any moment to lash out.

"Hey, guys, it's me, mom," Harper purrs. She puts a cat treat on the floor near each animal, close to each cat's nose. Never taking their eyes off us, they ignore them.

"Come on out," she continues, her voice smooth and serene. "There's nothing to be afraid of."

She reaches under the bed for Elsa, stretching her arm out before her. Before either of us have a chance to react, however, Elsa swipes at Harper, hissing, and scratches the back of her hand.

"Elsa!" I snap at the animal, but Harper tells me to hush.

"She barely got me," Harper says, looking at the thin red line forming from the base of her thumb to her index finger. "Don't get mad at her."

Beside Elsa, Alexis growls.

"I've never seen them do this before," I mumble. "Have you?"

"No, of course I haven't." She runs her lips over the small cut on the back of her hand. "But don't get mad at them, Bill. Something spooked them, and we should probably just leave them be."

"Oh, I agree."

Harper stands up, trying to be calm, to put her anger at me behind her. "I'm sure they'll come out when they're good and ready."

I nod, standing up with her.

"Should we take a bath?" I ask.

"Yeah, let's," she says, sighing. And then, as I'm turning out the light, she adds, "I'm sorry I lost my temper. I really am. But just because our cats were rattled by a little boy is no reason you should be too."

I have heard the howl before perhaps a half dozen times in my life, Alexis's high-pitched shriek. Beside me, Harper is already sitting up in bed, listening and alert. The howl came from downstairs.

When Harper can feel by the way I have moved that I too am awake, she asks, "What do you think she sees?"

"Probably a barn cat at the kitchen window. Or maybe it's the Glovers' cat," I answer, enumerating the stimuli that in the past have elicited from Alexis this sort of malevolent and prolonged squeal.

"Think we should shoo it away?"

"Or thank it," I suggest, yawning. "Whatever it is, it did manage to lure Alexis out from under our bed."

"Do you think Elsa is with her?"

I stretch my legs down to the foot of our bed, the flannel sheets soft and warm against my skin. There doesn't seem to be a cat on the blankets above us. "I don't know. She may still be under the bed."

The yowling continues, and may in fact actually be getting louder. Each cat bellow lasts a second or two longer than the one before it, and seems to become more enraged. Any second now I expect to hear the sound of her paw swatting the windowpane.

"Any idea what time it is?" I ask.

"Almost three-thirty."

I yawn again, savoring the momentary light-headedness I feel in the back of my neck and my head. "If it is the Glovers' cat, we might want to tell them it's not real smart to let him stay out all night."

Harper swings her legs over the side of the bed, and reaches for the bathrobe she keeps by her lamp. "I'm going to go downstairs," she says. "I'll never fall back to sleep with her crying."

Crying. It is a mother's word. It is certainly not the word I would have chosen to describe the shrill scream Alexis uses to protect her turf from interlopers. Especially now, as the standoff increases and Alexis gets madder and meaner, and her howling becomes more furious.

"I'll go with you," I tell Harper, curious whether it is indeed the Glovers' cat, or one of the wild things who race among the barns at the edge of town.

Harper switches on the hall light, and together we head down the stairs. I realize as I grip the banister that I have left my eyeglasses on my night table.

"I'll be right behind you," I tell Harper, turning around and bouncing back up the steps two at a time.

As I put on my glasses and the world comes back into focus, in the kitchen below me Harper screams out Alexis's name. Her voice sounds more confused than afraid, but I find myself running in any event, running as if my wife and my cat were somehow in trouble.

I expect to see Alexis pressed flat against the front porch window, howling, when I open the kitchen door, but she's nowhere near it. She is instead crouched in the middle of the floor, her fur once again at attention, prepared to pounce upon and attack something just out of view. From where Harper stands, however, about three feet behind Alexis, she can see clearly whatever it is.

"What is it?" I ask Harper, raising my voice so she can hear me over the horrific shrieks of our cat.

She motions me to her side with her hand, stirring the air with her finger, and I tiptoe across the kitchen in a wide semicircle around our cat. "What is it?" I ask again, worried by the way Harper's eyes are so wide, and the way she watches the cat from a distance.

When I am beside her I turn toward Alexis, and in disbelief I remove my glasses and rub my eyes. For a split second it looks to me like a mouse, but as I stare at it more carefully I can see that it is only a small piece of white cloth, a rag of some sort.

I am astonished: our cat is screaming unnaturally at a small piece of cloth. Moreover, directly opposite Alexis, helping her to surround the rag, is her sister Elsa. And although Elsa is quieter than Alexis, she is no less disturbed by the enemy between them: she too is prepared for attack.

I turn to Harper and try to smile. "They lead quite a fantasy life," I mumble, trying to find for her humor in the fact our cats have both lost their minds. "That must be the world's fiercest rag."

Harper stares at me, perplexed. She shakes her head. "That's no rag," she says slowly, her voice so flat I am reminded of her tone the night our son died, and she asked over and over and over, "Is he still with us?"

I stare at the object, trying to see if I've missed something. If I have, I can't tell what it is.

"If it's not a rag, then what is it?" I ask quietly, disturbed and frightened by the numbness in Harper's voice.

"It's that . . . that thing you wear on your wrist to keep sweat away," she explains, trying desperately to remember its name.

"A sweatband?"

"Yes, a sweatband. It belongs to the boy. . . ."

The boy. I look back at the floor, and see that indeed lying between our two cats is Lucky Diamond's wristband. "Why does it make them so angry?" I ask, regretting the tone of my question immediately. I'm afraid that I sounded more sarcastic than confused.

Harper looks at me as if I've just accused the boy of arson. Ignoring me, she kneels behind Alexis, whispering the animal's name in her soft, high-pitched voice, trying to soothe the cat. But Alexis only screams louder, never taking her eyes off the wristband.

"This is ridiculous," I tell Harper, trying to sound calm. "Let's put an end to it right now."

I wander over to the wristband, and reach down to pick it up. As my hand touches the terry cloth, however, Elsa starts to howl with Alexis, and together the cats attack. They fall upon the wristband in one churning tornado of fur and razors and spit, howling with a hate I've never heard before in my life, scratching and clawing and tearing at the wristband and—for no other reason than because it is in their way—at my left arm as well.

I try to yank my arm free, but eight claws are caught in the sleeve of my pajamas, and I hear myself yelling when I feel nails like barbed wire gouging away at my skin, and I see the light gray cloth of my sleeve turning red. Behind me Harper screams too, and reflexively I swing my arms over my head, the pain stinging in waves from my wrists through my ears.

"Let it go!" I hear Harper shouting at me from someplace very far away, "Drop it!" and for some reason I know what she means. The wristband is still clenched in my fist, so I toss it away from me as best I can and fall to the floor, the cats falling with me, and then, with the speed and violence of a runaway buzz saw, they cut across the floor after it.

"I'm getting a towel!" Harper yells, her feet pounding through the kitchen and into the bathroom.

I roll after Alexis and Elsa, afraid they're going to kill each other in their desperate attempts to shred Lucky's wristband. I have no idea how I can break them up with my bare hands, but I have to try, because I know if I don't they will die. In seconds, they have left a trail of blood and urine and fur in a swath from one corner of the kitchen to the far corner of the living room.

It's as if they're rabid, as if they're crazy with hate.

Before I can reach them, however, Harper is beside me with a beach towel, the one with the neon-bright starfish and seashells. She hands it to me and I dive upon our cats, fighting to hold them still under the material, trying to pull one writhing mass of fur apart from the other.

"Stop it!" Harper is screaming at them, "Stop it!"

Disoriented by the dark and half smothered, Alexis lets go of the wristband, and it falls between her and her sister. In the split second that she dives after it, trying to recover it, I am able to pull Elsa away in the towel, and whisk her into the kitchen. Behind me Harper falls upon Alexis, grabbing her under her front legs and hoisting her up and away from the wristband.

"She's bleeding!" Harper yells to me, crying. "She's bleeding everywhere!"

I carry Elsa into the bathroom and shut the door, separating Elsa from Alexis. I hold her firmly in the sink, surveying the damage. It is extensive. One of her eyes is cut shut, and she too is bleeding: in addition to the gash around her eye, there is blood trickling from her ear and from two wounds on her side.

I look down at my own arm, examining the scratches that could have been caused by a fork they are so straight, and the two, perhaps three, spots where the skin has been simply sliced away. I wonder for a moment where we should go first—the emergency room at the hospital or the veterinarian.

When I hear Harper's cries by the sink in the kitchen, however, I understand that my arm may last longer than Alexis. I know we'll go first to the vet.

Chapter 14

"What happened to your arm?" Mr. Godfrey asks me late Wednesday morning, as I arrive for the day at the college at about the time I normally wander outside for lunch.

"A bear got me," I tell him, strolling slowly across the street to the porch of the Trillium Extended Care Facility. The sun feels wonderful on my skin, even my bandaged left arm, and I am secretly pleased that for the price of a few stitches I have an excuse to wear a short sleeved sport shirt to work.

"A bear, eh?"

"A bear, yup."

He knows not to believe a word of what I am saying. "This time of year?"

"Just last night."

"What kind of bear?"

"A big one. It was dark, so all I know for sure is that it was big."

He nods thoughtfully. "I once bagged a bear, you know."

"No, I didn't know."

"Yup. Fact is, I bagged two of 'em in one day."

I am more than a little impressed. I have never heard of such a thing. "What kind were they?"

"Black bears, both of 'em. One weighed in just above three hundred pounds, one just below it."

I shudder just the tiniest bit. I don't normally think of bears in these woods, but of course they're out there. "Was this around here?"

"Yup. They were up top of Hogsback."

"You must have been pretty famous that day. It's not very

often that someone shoots six hundred pounds of bear in an afternoon."

"Shoot 'em? Who said anything about shooting 'em?"

"I thought you did, Mr. Godfrey. Didn't you just tell me that you bagged two bears?"

"I sure did. But it was Red Macomber who shot 'em. Crazy old Red Macomber. I just happened to be gettin' my dump permit, when Red drove up to the town clerk's office, and said he had somethin' to declare. Me, I just helped bag 'em, so Red could get 'em safely over the mountain to the taxidermist in Montpelier."

I smile at Mr. Godfrey. "Mr. Godfrey, you know it was no bear that got me last night. It was only a cat fight."

He rocks back in his chair, weighing what I have told him. "Must have been some cat fight."

"It was," I tell Mr. Godfrey, "it surely was." It was, I think to myself, a downright miracle that once all of the wounds were stitched and the damage assessed, neither I nor the cats were seriously hurt.

"Were they your cats?"

"Yup."

"What set them off? Another cat?"

"Sort of. The veterinarian said it was another cat's smell. Or maybe another animal's smell. A dog, perhaps. But he thought they must have smelled some other animal on . . . some clothing . . . someone left at our house."

He shakes his head. "You still gonna be able to coach your kids?"

"The Little Leaguers? Why sure."

"Good. Hilton Burberry doesn't take kindly to injuries."

I run a finger over the bandages on my arm. "You know Hilton?" I'm surprised, but I probably shouldn't be. Sedgebury is a small town in a small county.

"Nope. Never met the fellow. But I read him in the newspapers. And I remember him from his days with the Red Sox."

"I didn't know he was so famous."

"He wasn't. But his name used to pop up once in a while in the *Boston Globe,* or the *Herald.* Usually 'round spring training. He was ol' Tom Yawkey's mouthpiece, when Yawkey was runnin' the club."

"The Red Sox?"

"Right. When Yawkey was runnin' the Red Sox."

"And Hilton would become angry with the players when they got injured?"

Mr. Godfrey closes his eyes and smiles, allowing his ancient gray head to bob like a tennis ball. "He'd usually have a word or two for the press."

"Such as?"

"Such as? Let's see. Remember Johnny Pesky? Scrappy little infielder. Well, Johnny was a pretty durable guy, a pretty tough cookie. But once, I think it was 1950, Johnny had to sit down for a while. It might have been a knee, but I don't recall. What I do remember about it was the time Hilton was interviewed. A reporter asked Hilton how serious he thought Pesky's injury was, and Hilton answered, 'Well, sir, it's the sort of thing that's a pesky injury for most professionals, but it's a professional injury for Johnny Pesky.' "

When he is through speaking, he opens his eyes and looks over at me, as if to drive home the point of his story.

"That wasn't a very nice thing to say," I admit. "Are you sure it was Hilton who said it?"

"Yup."

"Well, Hilton's not really like that. He's actually an extremely nice fellow."

"Maybe."

"Would you like to meet him?"

He looks over my shoulder at the building that houses my office. "Oh, I don't think so. At my age, you have to be awful confident or awful stupid to waste time makin' new friends. And I don't think I'm either. . . ."

I hate the smell of a hospital. It smells of antiseptic and medicine and brown gravy. Institutional brown gravy that is prepared, I assume, with a meat fat substitute.

It is the brown gravy smell I recall most from the days (and nights) that Harper and I spent at the hospital with Nathaniel.

It was a week ago today that Donnie Casey fell into a coma when he was supposed to be on his way to the school bus, and never made it to school. In that week, Harper has visited the boy twice, two more times than me, so after work I grab my attaché case and drive up to Burlington to visit the child.

Or, more accurately, to visit his parents. I know without calling that John and Susan Casey will be by his bedside, waiting and watching and—because of who they are and how strong is their faith—praying.

As of last night, Tuesday night, Donnie Casey was still in that coma, and I have no reason to believe that his condition has changed. If, by some miracle, he had awakened, I imagine Harper would have heard, and she in turn would have told me.

The nurse at the front desk of the Medical Center remembers me, and I can tell by her horrified expression that for one brief second she fears I have forgotten my own son is dead. She is almost too happy when I tell her that I am there to see the little Casey boy, and she allows me upstairs without a yellow plastic visitor's pass.

Both of the passes are gone, she informs me without checking, and I am sure she is right.

I believe I know well the children's wing of the hospital, but I am still ill prepared for the memories that rain upon me when the elevator doors open. The Fisher-Price toys that litter the waiting room, bright blues and yellows and reds, plastic playthings that belong to no one in particular, and are treated accordingly by the transient children who come and go. The Naugahyde couches that straddle a tired end table from another era, its wood veneer chipped, its chrome legs beginning to rust. The *Scholastic* magazines with their torn pages and dog-eared covers, tossed randomly by tortured parents looking for anything, anything at all, to read.

And—of course—the smell of the brown gravy.

I am made a little sick by it all, and consider briefly turning back toward the elevator, and then going back home. But I catch a glimpse of Susan Casey midway down the corridor, leaning against the counter at the nurses' station and drinking a can of soda. I can't tell for sure, but it looks as if she may be speaking with an older nurse named Lorraine, one of Nathaniel's favorites.

"Susan, I'm so sorry," I say to her, putting down my attaché case so I can hug her, a tentative embrace between two adults who know each other but have never actually touched. Pulling away I look at her more closely, noticing how gaunt and tired her face has become. Her skin looks pale, and her brown hair black, indications, I know, of a scared and anguished parent.

She shakes her head, acknowledging that she too is sorry, and, more than that, confused. If she is anything like me, she is wondering right now why there is such a thing in the world as a virus that can attack a little boy's heart and drive her strong, precious son into a coma.

I turn to the nurse and start to say hello to her, but before I can open my mouth, she says to me, "It's Bill, right? Bill Parrish?"

I smile for her, commending her on her thoughtfulness and her memory. "That's right." I stand there awkwardly for a moment, reading the word *Lorraine* on her name tag, reminded of all the times she gave my son shots, changed the intravenous tubes in his arms, and talked with my wife about quilts.

She and Harper would talk about quilts for hours.

"So how have you been?" I ask. "Have you finished the quilt you were making for your grandson?"

"Oh, yes. Months and months ago. I'm off and running now on a new one—this one's for the contest this summer at the Champlain Fair!"

"Harper will be pleased to hear that."

Susan finishes her soda and puts the can down on the counter. "Is Harper with you?" she asks me.

"No, I came alone tonight. Is John here?"

She nods toward the door, a little more than halfway open. "He's in with Donnie. Reading, I guess. I just came out here to stretch my legs."

"Is there any change?"

Susan shakes her head no, afraid that she'll cry if she speaks.

"Is it okay if I put my head in and say hello?" I ask, directing the question first at Susan, but then at Lorraine as well.

"Sure, it's fine," Susan tells me. "I'm sure it'll mean a lot to John." She pushes the door to her son's room slowly open, the tips of her fingers barely touching the wood. Before we can walk in, however, John appears in the doorway, a huge man with a huge belly, wearing blue jeans and a plaid flannel shirt. He still has hooked onto his belt the tape measure he must use everyday as a site manager for a local construction firm.

He takes my hand, smiling broadly, and says, "Ain't this a dandy surprise! How you doin'?"

"Can't complain."

"What the hell did you do to your arm?"

"I tried breaking up a cat fight at three-thirty in the morning."

"Pretty ornery cats, eh?" He releases his grip on my hand, and then puts both of his own hands in his pockets, almost bouncing up and down on his toes.

"I just told Susan how sorry I am," I tell him. "She said there hasn't been much change yet."

"Nope, not yet, but it's only a matter of time." He looks past me at his wife, sensing her fear and frustration, and continues, "The doctors think he's going to wake up any day now, and it'll be like he took one hell of a nap, nothing more. Just like he took the world's longest cat nap."

"I'll bet they're right," I agree, having no idea whether John is lying to me or merely to himself.

Lorraine takes the soda can Susan left on the counter and throws it into a recycling bin against the wall. "We have a lot of optimism about Donnie," she insists, although I have a feeling her comments are directed more at the boy's mother. "We have a lot of confidence in the boy. He has been out of intensive care for two full days now, his brain activity is normal, he's responding well to the respirator—"

"His heart is beating like a big ol' conga drum!" John interjects, pounding his fist into his palm.

"So there really is room for optimism," Lorraine concludes.

I recognize John's hope and cheerfulness well. I saw it in myself, manifested with perhaps less bravado, with perhaps more subtlety. But it was the same essential thing. Blind, desperate, punch-drunk hope.

"I brought something," I tell both the Caseys, leaning over to open my attaché case, "a sort of get-well card. It's for Donnie when he wakes up." I hand to John Casey the game ball from last night's victory, slightly grass-stained and smudged with blue ink.

"It's signed by all of Donnie's friends," I continue, "the whole team. They dedicated the game to him."

Chapter 15

T he pitcher's mound on a Little League diamond is actually very low, little more than a small dirt bump in the grass. It's neither as high as the mounds at major league stadiums nor as perfectly proportioned, and there is always a huge divot missing directly in front of the pitching rubber.

No one, not even Hilton Burberry, bothers to fill in the divot hole between games, or even between seasons.

I stand on the Havington mound Thursday evening tossing batting practice to the team, considering myself extremely fortunate. I can't swing a bat, but I can throw and—if I don't strive for heroics—catch. Had Alexis and Elsa sharpened their claws on my right arm instead of my left, however, there would be absolutely nothing I could do tonight, other than wander aimlessly back and forth around the field, reminding kids to get in front of ground balls or to race into the outfield for relays.

I had discovered at an earlier practice that I was indeed capable of hitting baseballs around an infield; tonight I find that pitching batting practice is also deceptively easy. My left arm curled against my chest, both to protect the stitches and because this is how I was taught to mimic power pitchers as a boy, I rear back with my right arm, and then throw the baseballs in easy lobs over the plate.

It never ceases to amaze me how much of baseball little boys learn merely by mimicking their major league heroes. This is probably a reason, if only a small one, why boys are still so much better at the game than girls. Boys watch baseball, they watch it a lot. Nathaniel, although a dedicated Mets fan, would always watch whatever game was televised on Saturday by the network, even when the contest was between teams like Texas and Kansas City, or Cincinnati and Houston. When the game began early in the afternoon and he wanted to be outside, he would use the VCR to record it, and then watch the game at the end of the day, while Harper and I prepared dinner.

As a result, many of the basics I merely have to reinforce with the boys on the team, I have to explain in great detail to the girls. I think that's why Melissa Edington and Cindy Fletcher are at such a disadvantage. They haven't spent three or four years watching first basemen stretch toward the shortstop to scoop a throw out of the dirt. They haven't seen catchers block home over and over, to prevent sliding base runners from roaring past them and grazing the plate with their toes. They haven't stood in their family rooms or dens with the television on and pretended to be the center of the universe, a pitcher, and glanced over their shoulders to hold an opposing runner close to first base.

And until they do, until girls start reenacting home run swings and pick-off moves in slow motion, I doubt they will ever be major league prospects.

Lucky Diamond takes his last swing at batting practice and hits a sharp grounder right at Cliff Thorpman at short. Cliff bends his back and his knees, scoops the ball into his mitt, and throws the ball cleanly to Carl Northrup at first. It's a nice play all around.

"Well done, guys," I shout. "Lucky, most of those will be hits. Most kids don't have Cliff's hands," and I smile in the Thorpman boy's direction. He smiles back.

Lucky tosses the bat onto the ground beside the rest of the team equipment, and Roger Wheelock walks up to the plate, clutching his own personal bat, a neon green aluminum thing. Out of the corner of my eye I watch Lucky wander over to a small pile of three or four gloves just off the first base line. He picks one up, gently nudges another with his toe. He places his hands on hips and pivots in almost a complete circle, staring at the ground around his feet. I wonder, is he looking for ticks?

"I'm ready, Mr. Parrish," Roger informs me, and I turn back to the little boy at the plate.

"Attaboy, Roger," I hear myself shouting for no apparent reason. My father used to shout this expression at me, also for no apparent reason. It is, evidently, a genetic abnormality in a Parrish chromosome: we shout "attaboy" at small children when we have no idea what else to say. I grip the baseball against the seams, rock back, and throw him a waist-high pitch that he pops into the air behind home plate.

While Joey Fenton retrieves the ball, I glance over at Lucky Diamond, still milling around near the pile of gloves in foul territory. He bends over and reaches inside the canvas baseball bag, and then stands up and surveys the field. His eyes move slowly, systematically, from the left field line to the right field line, moving with the precision and assurance of a second hand on a clock.

"Eye on the ball, Roger," I tell the boy, throwing him a second pitch. This one he hits solidly, rapping it between first and second base. "That's a base hit!" I shout encouragingly, "That's a base hit in any league!"

From the corner of my eye I see Lucky walking across the infield toward me. He is chewing nervously on a nail, his finger poised just inside his lips. When he reaches the mound he removes his pad from his pocket, and scribbles quickly,

My glove's gone!

I catch the baseball Mike Harris throws in from the outfield, and then put my hand on Lucky's shoulder. "Do you know where you left it?" I ask.

He nods, and I realize he is on the verge of tears.

"Where?"

He points toward the pile of baseball gloves near first base, the pile he had been searching a moment before.

"Well, I'll bet someone took it by mistake." Around us, practice has become quiet. And perhaps because there is a pause in the batting cage, because Roger is standing with his bat against his leg at home plate, Pete Cooder and the outfielders have turned their attention toward the infield as well. A dump truck rumbles over the bridge near the firehouse, and against the sound of its three- or four-ton thumping I realize that even the birds and late afternoon peepers have become silent.

I turn to face center field, and smile. "Okay, team, time for a glove check!" I shout, trying to sound light. "I want you all to check the mitt on your hand, and make sure it's your own!"

"Who's the retard who lost his glove?" Dickie Pratt yells toward the outfield from third base. "Which one of you guys is the puke-brain?" he continues, laughing.

I ignore Dickie. Clearly he knows who has lost his glove, since Lucky is standing unhappily beside me. I watch the rest of the children glance halfheartedly at their mitts, and then look up at me. Evidently, they are all using their own.

"You're all okay?" I shout. "You've all got the right gloves on?"

"Come on, Mr. Parrish," Roger whines from the batter's box. "This is boring!"

Lucky looks down at his sneakers, imitation Nikes from the local discount store. He puts his pad back in his pocket and bites at his lip.

"Well, I want you all to keep your eyes open for Lucky's glove! He put it down behind first base, and now it has disappeared."

Dickie puts his own glove in front of his face, and my heart sinks when I realize that behind the leather the boy is laughing. I can tell by his eyes, and by the way his shoulders are rising and falling just the tiniest bit. I look over at Dickie's best friend, Cliff Thorpman, and—as I might have expected—the boy wipes a grin off his face and looks quickly away.

I hand Lucky my own glove, an antique not much younger than me, and say to him softly, "Use mine until yours turns up."

I then shout at Roger, still waiting for me to pitch to him at home plate, "You're a rightie, aren't you?" When he nods that he is, I continue, "Toss me your glove."

Lucky puts on my glove, tentatively at first, and then runs toward Pete Cooder and the outfield, his head down. He must know that Dickie Pratt hid his glove, he must have known it the moment his mitt disappeared.

"I brought you something," I tell Lucky as we walk toward the firehouse after practice. I wish that something now were a new glove.

Lucky looks straight ahead, and I am afraid it is because his eyes are red. Pete Cooder has already told me that he thought Lucky was crying a little bit while he was shagging fly balls.

"You left one of your wristbands at our house Tuesday night, and our cats sort of took it over. A wristband makes a great cat toy, you see."

Behind us I hear Bobby Wohlford's mother picking up her son

and Jesse Parker, reminding the boys to kick the dirt off their cleats before piling into the station wagon.

"Anyway, I felt bad that our cats got cat spit all over your wristband, so I thought I owed you a new pair." I reach into the pocket of my windbreaker and hand him the present, a gift that seems to me now pathetically small, pathetically useless.

The wristbands, white and orange and blue, are in a clear plastic package. He stares at them for a long moment, and then looks up at me and nods approvingly. He tries to smile, but it is a manufactured smile for my benefit only. As I had feared, his eyes are indeed red and moist.

"Try them on," I suggest. "Go ahead."

He tears open the top of the plastic, and stretches one over his right hand and one over his left. He flexes his hands, and rubs his wrists.

He tries again to smile, and gives me an okay circle with his thumb and forefinger.

"I have a feeling your mitt will turn up," I tell Lucky, hoping my anger toward Dickie Pratt has not crept into my voice. I squeeze his shoulder to reassure him, and then repeat myself stupidly: "I'll bet your mitt will turn up before you know it."

Chapter 16

I had sat for hours with Nathaniel in the hospital and played dice baseball, rolling the dice on the tray table that could be extended over his bed. When he felt up to it, we would move to the table by the window, watching the snow come on some days, and go on others.

We invented our own combinations with the dice, structuring the game so that home runs were more common in our league than in the majors, and each of our contests as high scoring as a Little League confrontation. We could hit home runs with a pair of sixes as well as fives, and doubles were slammed with pairs of ones, twos, or threes. Nathaniel was always the Mets, and I was always the Cardinals or the Cubs—his favorite rivals.

He seemed to be keeping fairly elaborate statistics for his players, and one day, about a week before we left Vermont for the bone marrow transplant, he shared them with me. I was astounded. My son, a boy only ten years old, was sufficiently comfortable with mathematics, sufficiently facile with fractions and percent signs and division, to calculate a pitcher's earned-run average and an outfielder's on-base percentage. On his yellow legal pad were columns and columns of numbers, with everything from a player's game-winning RBIs to his batting average, from his strikeouts to his saves.

Nathaniel had even taken the liberty of deciding that some of our contests were night games and some were day games, and then determining who were his best players "under the lights." And when he was through with numbers, he scribbled short managerial notes about his team, four- and five-word observations about each player's strengths or weaknesses:

"All field, no hit."

"Likes to steal a lot."

"Best smoke in the league."

"Plenty of home run power, but strikes out sometimes."

And while each comment was pure fiction, an observation wholly unrelated to the daily and literal throws of our dice, they were in their own way and in their own universe as accurate as the reports turned in by any professional bird dog or scout.

"I wish you would be more careful," Harper says unhappily, staring at my arm. "Those stitches look awfully nasty to me. I worry about you throwing a baseball around like a ten-year-old."

Her feet are bare and small at the base of her jeans, a pale but pretty white. We are sitting on the living room floor after practice Thursday night, sipping wine while the chicken finishes baking.

"You make me sound so old," I tell her. "I can still keep up with ten- and eleven-year-olds."

"I know you can. But I still worry."

The cats lie curled up like throw pillows on the couch, two little balls rolled into kitty croissants.

"Well, don't worry," I insist, although I know that she will. And I know from years of marriage and years of being in love that there is more on her mind than merely my arm, as "nasty" as the stitches on it may appear.

"Did you get Lucky a new wrist bracelet?" she asks.

"Wristband. I got Lucky a new wristband. If I got him a new wrist bracelet, it would mean we were going steady."

"You know exactly what I'm talking about."

I nod. "I do."

I reach up onto the couch behind me, and pet Alexis softly between her ears. She opens one eye warily, unsure after the other night what to expect. "I made some phone calls today," I continue.

"Oh?"

"Yup, I did indeed. Want to know what I found out?"

"Of course."

"I found out that there's no school for handicapped children in Granville. No school at all."

"Who did you call?"

"Oh, I phoned a number of people. I called the board of education, I called the state commissioner on education. I even called the governor's office."

Harper sips her wine, thinking. "I guess Lucky was mistaken," she mumbles finally.

I raise an eyebrow, aware of how theatrical my gesture must appear, but unable to stop myself. "You're kidding me, right?"

"No, I didn't think I was." She shakes her head and shrugs, trying to be noncommittal.

"Sweetheart, you can't really believe he was mistaken," I tell her, reaching over and patting her knee through her jeans.

She looks down at the spot on her leg where I touched her. There are still flecks of white paint on these jeans, remnants from the bookcase she was painting this past Sunday.

"I thought I'd gotten most of the paint out," she says, ignoring me. She puts her wineglass down on the floor, and scratches at one of the dried splotches with her nails.

"The boy wasn't mistaken," I continue, my voice becoming more urgent. "You know that."

"I guess," she answers softly, not looking up from her knee.

I take her hand and hold it in mine, rubbing the back of it with my thumb. "You guess? What do you mean, you guess?"

Outside our house a warm spring breeze knocks a branch from the hydrangea against the bay window, and its twigs click over and over against the glass.

"I guess I've known all along that he made the school up," she confesses. Verbalizing her suspicions, verbalizing what she has probably feared from the moment I told her Lucky wrote down the word *Granville* and she thought of a town thirty mountainous miles away, makes her sad.

"Me too," I agree, but there is no sadness or disappointment in my voice. "I didn't confront him about it tonight. But I will."

The hydrangea branches, small and sharp and clustered like talons, scratch at the window like they want to come in.

"Confront him?" Harper asks. "He's an eleven-year-old boy! How in the name of God are you going to 'confront' an eleven-year-old boy?"

"I don't know. But he lied to me. He lied to us. It seems to me, I should do something."

"Why? You're his Little League coach, not his father. I can't see why it's any of your business where he goes to school."

I sigh, closing my eyes and rubbing them with my fists. "Don't you think we should do something?"

She chuckles, the noise somewhere between a laugh and a sigh. *"Do something,"* she says, imitating me. "Do something. Sure, we can do something. There's nothing wrong with wanting to help the boy, Bill, there's nothing wrong with that at all. But don't 'confront' the child. He's eleven years old!"

"Then what? What would you do?"

"If you really feel you have to do something, then why not see about getting the boy into a proper school? Why not talk to his father? Maybe he needs some help with transportation. Maybe he needs a social worker to jump in a day or two a week. Maybe the boy needs some extra help with his homework—"

"We're not talking about just any child."

"I know that."

"No, I'm not sure you do. I'm not referring to his handicap. I'm referring to the fact . . ."

Harper crawls across the floor and sits beside me. She tries again to smile. "What is it about that child that makes you so damn weird? Will you please tell me that?"

"It's not me. It's him."

"Uh-huh."

I am tempted to push Harper away, angered by her refusal to take my fears seriously, frustrated by her inability to see in the boy whatever it is that disturbs me and frightens our cats. "I'm referring to the fact that Lucky Diamond scares every little boy and girl on my team!"

"Of course he does," Harper says, her tone sweet, patronizing. "He's different. He has a handicap. Trust me, there's no better way to scare a ten-year-old than to show him a kid with a physical problem. Blind kids. Kids in wheelchairs. Kids without arms. Bill, they scare the poop out of other little kids!"

"Melissa Edington and Cindy Fletcher are not scared of Lucky because he can't speak; it's something else."

"Now how do you know that?"

"I just do. He frightens them."

"He's different—"

"You bet he is!"

I'm suddenly raising my voice and I don't like it, I'm yelling at her over a mute little boy in a trailer.

"So what's your point?" she asks, refusing to yell back at me, refusing to raise her voice at all. "Why do you want to confront him?"

"I want to confront him," I hiss, "because I want to know what he's up to. I want to know why . . . I want to know why he's here."

Among Goddette Construction's half dozen projects in the county this year is the new IGA, a supermarket going up near the old bobbin mill in Sedgebury. It's about two miles east of the college.

As I approach the school on my way to work Friday morning, the sun rising into an already blue sky, I decide to veer left at the Sedgebury Inn instead of right, and head up to the site. I am fairly sure this is where Pete Cooder told me he's working these days.

Arriving at the site I do not immediately see Pete's truck, a huge red pickup with an extremely snazzy chrome horn and what Harper refers to in her best Southern drawl as "big and stupid tires." But I do see his friend Mike Boley, sipping what I assume is coffee from a silver Thermos, and chatting with two men I don't know.

About twenty yards behind them stands the squat skeleton of the supermarket, a series of beams and columns extending over a wide, flat hole in the earth.

"Goddamn, there was an accident," one of the men is saying, taking off his jacket and draping it over the pickup truck parked beside them. "Over on one twenty-five. That's why we're late."

"Some guy—I think it was Garnet Smithson, but I couldn't tell for sure—was hauling a backhoe on a flatbed, and he musta taken a turn too fast," the other fellow adds, gesturing with both hands.

Mike sees me and waves, but continues his conversation. "He hurt?" he asks.

"Nope, nobody got hurt, thank God. But it's one helluva mess. Backhoe's still on its side, half on, half off the road!"

I sidle up to the three men, feeling strange and conspicuous in my tie and blazer. They are all wearing jeans and sweatshirts and muddy brown shirts, uniforms of a sort for real work in Vermont, while I am dressed in the uniform of the flatlander that I am and will always be. I find myself wishing I had taken advantage of the stitches in my arm one more day, and worn a sport shirt this morning. I stand uncomfortably beside Mike, nod hello, and ask him if he has seen Pete Cooder this morning.

Mike points at the site trailer, planted into the mud about three trucks away.

"Is he in a meeting?" I ask.

"Cooder? Nah, he's just shootin' the shit. Go on over," Mike reassures me.

I thank him and wander slowly over to the trailer, simultaneously afraid to knock on the door and disturb whoever is in there, and afraid not to. I can feel the three men behind me watching me, wondering why I've come here to speak with Pete Cooder.

And it's a perfectly good question. I'm not altogether sure why I abruptly swerved left at the inn and drove here myself. I know I want to talk to Pete about Lucky: I want to get his impressions of the boy, I want to hear what he knows about his father. But I know also it could have waited until tomorrow, when I will see Pete in any event because we have a game.

Then again, surrounded by fourteen boys and girls, when would I have had a minute alone with Pete? Certainly not before the game, not when we will be desperately rounding the team up for the drive to Starksboro, and certainly not during the game itself. Perhaps we might have found a moment after the contest, when we were back in Havington and all of the children had been safely returned to their parents, but I can't be sure.

Besides, I don't want to wait until tomorrow. I want to talk to Pete now. I want Pete to tell me today that Lucky Diamond is a perfectly normal little boy, a child who is personable and hardworking and good. I want him to tell me, in essence, that I am . . . wrong . . . about the boy.

The trailer door is partway open, so I stand on the cement block that serves as a step into it, and yell softly, "Hello?"

Inside I hear the sound of men talking, debating. Evidently, the IGA's planned arch at the front door is a problem.

"Hello?" I call again, a little louder.

"Hello?" someone says over my shoulder, imitating me. As I turn around I see Pete Cooder behind me, smiling.

"I thought you were in there," I tell him, stepping off the cement block and shaking his extended hand.

"I was five minutes ago. But on a day like today, I just can't stay inside. Just can't do it. Don't you love days like today?"

"I do indeed. Especially Fridays."

"Yup. Especially Fridays. Boley said you were looking for me."

"Yeah, I guess I am," I say, trying to collect my thoughts, hoping it wasn't a mistake to have dropped by. When I resume speaking, I try hard to sound casual. "I have a question, something that's been on my mind the last couple days. It's no big deal, but driving to work this morning, I thought, What the hell? and came over."

"Good enough. What's up?"

"Do you know Lucky Diamond's father?"

"Nope. Don't believe so."

"I think he's a young guy. A logger."

Pete shrugs. "Damned if I know."

"So I'll bet you wouldn't know where I could find him . . ."

"Not offhand. Why don't you just ask Lucky?"

I sigh. "I probably will."

"Any special reason you're looking for him? Lucky's dad?"

"No, not really," I answer, pausing. "Can I ask you something else?"

"Why sure."

"I want your impression of somebody. I want to know what you think of someone."

He grins, waiting for me to go on.

"Lucky Diamond. What do you think of Lucky Diamond?"

He scratches the side of his neck. "You mean as a ball player?"

"No. I know what I think of him as a ball player."

"Me too. Excellent. Just plain excellent. Four or five years from now, when he's old enough for the Sedgebury Union varsity, he'll be all-county. Mark my words, he'll be all-county. You heard it here first."

"I agree. But that's not exactly what I meant. What I meant was, what do you think of him as a person?"

"As a person?"

"Uh-huh. As a person."

He looks down at the ground, watching the prints his sneakers make in the moist dirt. "Well, I'll tell you, Bill," he begins, not looking at me, "I try not to pass judgments on the bigger things in life. Know what I mean?"

"Sort of."

"Yup, I try not to. Seems to me a little boy who can't talk is starting out with a real bad break."

"I agree."

"Now I'm sure there's a reason he can't talk. 'Cause I believe there's a reason for everything. I really do."

I stand silently before him, unable even to grunt in agreement. I know with the cold logic of a father who has outlived his son that, no, there is not a reason for everything. "And?"

"Well," he continues, finally looking up from the ground and meeting my eyes, "There's no doubt about it, he sometimes spooks the kids. But I think that's just 'cause he can't talk. That's all. I don't think he's a bad kid. Do you?"

"No, of course not," I answer quickly. "It's just—"

"It's just that he spooks you too," Pete says, trying to finish my sentence for me. And before I can correct him, before I can explain to him that this isn't at all what I was going to say, he adds, "Well, you know what? He spooks me too. That little boy spooks me too!"

I watch an old man and an older man chatting. At moments, when the afternoon sun bounces off Mr. Godfrey's eyeglasses and hides the washed-out blue marbles that are now the man's eyes, the pair could be brothers. Hilton would be the natty younger brother, the dandy who went off to the city.

It is warm on the Trillium porch, but Mr. Godfrey sits in his rocking chair with a small quilt covering his knees. He's never done this before, and I can't help but wonder if it isn't a precaution demanded by the new floor nurse. The woman, a middle-aged storm trooper with jowls like dumplings, must have arrived in the last week because I've never seen her before. She has asked Hilton and me twice, phrasing the question differently each time, why we're here if we're no relation to Mr. Godfrey.

Clearly the idea that we're friends, at least Mr. Godfrey and me, doesn't hold much water.

I had expected that Hilton and Mr. Godfrey would have talked about baseball, reminisced about the Red Sox teams of the thirties, forties, or fifties. I had envisioned Mr. Godfrey asking Hilton inside stories about Ted Williams, and Hilton telling Mr. Godfrey the story of Mel Parnell's no-hitter. I had assumed that Hilton would regale us with tales about Luis Tiant's infamous, contorted windup, or Ben Slaughter's brief but mythic career.

In some ways, I'm still a very young man: baseball never comes up. Instead Hilton, who I have introduced as Mr. Burberry and who seems content to share my formality with Mr. Godfrey, talks about Eunice, his children, and his grandchildren.

It seems that one of them, a high school junior, plans on looking at Sedgebury College next fall. She's the star of the school's tennis team, and ranked in the top five in New Jersey.

Families. Children. Grandchildren. These are the memories that matter to these fellows, this is the stuff of their daydreams. Baseball is probably the farthest thing from their minds.

Mr. Godfrey surprises me by sharing stories of his precious wife, Abigail, and of a child I never knew that he had. The boy died with his own wife—Mr. Godfrey's daughter-in-law—in a house fire in 1962. Somewhere, Mr. Godfrey believes it is Arizona, his granddaughter is alive and well and raising a family of her own. She sends Christmas cards, but she has never been back east for a visit.

"You never told me you had a son," I hear myself saying to Mr. Godfrey before I can stop myself.

"You never asked."

And of course he never would bring the boy up on his own. In some ways, Mr. Godfrey is like me: a tragic aberration, a father who has outlived his son. I juggle some numbers in my mind, and guess that Mr. Godfrey was somewhere in his early sixties when his boy died, while his son was somewhere in his thirties. He might have been my age right now.

"What was his name?"

Mr. Godfrey pauses, and for a moment I am afraid that he has forgotten his own child's name. "James," he answers finally. "But I always called him Jimmy. Right up until the day he died, I called him Jimmy."

He then turns to Hilton, and continues in a voice that is soft with conspiracy, "And it used to anger the heck out of him too, let me tell you. There was nothing that boy hated more than being called Jimmy."

* * *

I plan to work late tonight, despite the fact I must be up early tomorrow morning for a game. This is commencement weekend. And although the actual ceremony is not until one o'clock on Sunday, two days from now, Saturday afternoon is filled with a variety of cocktail parties and receptions for the graduates and their families. Doug Bascomb and I will be—as he puts it— "working the room" at the president's open house from four to six o'clock, and then attending with our wives the special dinner for the inductees into the Sedgebury chapter of Phi Beta Kappa.

Frankly, I have always felt that Doug and I are wasting our time cultivating our premier scholars and their parents at this dinner. There is an unspoken belief in development that it is not the A or the A+ students who will grow into the sorts of robber barons and entrepreneurs who largely subsidize a small liberal arts college like Sedgebury. Instead, it is the B– and C+ students who will become tomorrow's feature stories in *Forbes* and *Fortune* and *Inc.,* and it is with these students that we should be building our strongest bridges.

Just after eight o'clock, I finally put aside the printouts of our endowment performance, and the construction estimates for everything from the new computer building to the proposed addition to the student center. With the last rays of light trickling in through the west window, I turn to something I find far more interesting these days, and examine the scorecard from the Triple-A Tigers' opening day victory. Our second game is less than fourteen hours from now, a nine-thirty away game against the very same team we beat Tuesday night.

The team we trounced. Even by the high-scoring standards of Little League, 15 to 4 is a healthy margin of victory. What was perhaps more impressive than our hitting, however, was our pitching. Jesse Parker allowed only one run in five exceptional innings, and Cliff Thorpman, our shortstop, allowed only three when he finished up.

I reach for a pencil in the far recesses of one of my desk drawers, and clean up the scorecard for posterity. I erase the coal-black smudges, I finish coloring in the black diamonds that represent runs, I note with small arrows into which fields our hits fell. Single to left. Double to right. Triple down the right field line.

The big hits? Lucky Diamond's home run early in the game certainly helped set the tone, giving the Tigers momentum they never relinquished, but his bases-loaded double in the fourth inning was what really put the game away.

Scanning the scorecard I am reminded of Melissa Edington's hit, and I smile. The infielders surrounded her, making a semicircle about fifteen feet from home plate, and she managed to tap a gentle pop-up just over the third baseman's head for a single.

I hadn't realized it at the time, but I see now that Dickie Pratt got on base every time he came up to the plate. He singled, walked twice, and reached second on a two-base error by the Starksboro left fielder.

I put the scorecard back in its folder, and the folder back in my briefcase, suddenly feeling just the slightest bit guilty. If any child on the team has a character flaw, if any one child has a mean streak, it sure isn't Lucky Diamond. It's someone like Dickie Pratt. Or a spoiled baby like Bobby Wohlford. It's the kind of kid who would hide another boy's baseball glove because the boy is poor, or different, or just can't speak.

Lucky's pad, the small spiral-bound tablet that I found the other day in the woods, has sat for days now in the top drawer of my desk. I have meant to return it to Lucky, despite the fact it seems too damaged by water to use, for the simple reason that I cannot bear to throw it away. I flip through it once more, staring again at the way Lucky scribbled the names Burberry, Pratt, Parrish, and Cooder, and then toss it into my briefcase. I'll return the pad to Lucky in the morning, I decide, as a prayer begins to form in my mind:

I hope to God Lucky's mitt is back by tomorrow. I hope it will miraculously appear somewhere in our canvas sack of bats and bases and balls.

Chapter 17

I hear in my mind the sounds of dice baseball, the rolling clatter Nathaniel's dice made when they bounced on the tray table on his bed. A series of small tinny thumps, the dice scratching against each other as they collide with Formica.

The noise has awakened me, drawn me from sleep and a dream of . . .

I no longer know what I was dreaming. Perhaps it was of dice baseball.

I sit up in bed, judging by the night sky that night soon will be over. For a brief moment I am unsure what day it is, and assume that it must be a weekday, and soon I will be off to work. When I am unable to remember what meetings I have before me, however, I realize that it is Saturday (although it is, in actuality, a Saturday in which I will indeed have to work, from four o'clock on). The alarm, set normally for 6 A.M., will not explode today until seven. I have instructed the Tigers to converge at the Havington diamond at eight-thirty sharp, and as a team caravan we will drive to Starksboro together.

I climb slowly and silently from bed, trying not to disturb Harper, and walk on my toes across the room to the clock. Squinting, I can see that it is just past four-thirty. The alarm will not go off for another two and one-half hours. I start back toward the bed, delighted by the idea of returning to sleep, when I hear from somewhere below me the noise. A small crackle like rolling thunder, far in the distance, but coming this way. It is the sound of two dice on Formica. And it is coming from the kitchen or the living room.

"Bill? Are you okay?"

Harper is lying on her side, the covers pulled up to her cheek. I stand perfectly still, listening.

"Bill?" she asks again, and I can see her beginning to move, propping her head up with her arm.

"Shhhhhh," I murmur, bringing one finger to my lips.

She becomes tense, her body alert. "Is someone in the house?" she asks, abruptly and completely awake.

A roll and a bang, a roll and a bang. That's what the dice sound like. A roll and a bang. I envision my little boy's hand filling in a scorecard drawn on a yellow legal pad. Single. Sacrifice. Groundout to second, runner advancing to third.

"Bill!"

I walk to the bed in three giant steps, three giant and silent steps, and sit on the edge of the mattress beside her. I massage her shoulder through the blanket, rubbing my hand slowly up her arm and across her back.

"Bill," she whispers urgently, "is someone in the house?"

"I don't know," I whisper, listening.

"Do you hear something?"

I nod, while below us the game continues, the dice thundering softly across a table or box top or floor. Groundout to first, pitcher covers. Error in right field, batter winds up at third. Suicide squeeze . . .

"What? What do you hear?"

She doesn't hear it, she doesn't hear it at all. I am relieved for her. Only I can hear the crackles and bangs that occupied Nathaniel's mind for days at a time one winter and spring, the sounds that would bounce up and down one small corridor of a hospital in Vermont.

"It was nothing," I tell Harper, kissing her cheek. "I thought I heard something, but I must have been mistaken."

"What? What did you think you heard?"

Suicide squeeze. The batter makes contact, dribbling the ball between the mound and third base, and the only play is at first. Runner slides into home, safe. All because the dice come up four and six, and any combination larger than seven scores the runner from third.

"Thunder. I thought I heard thunder."

"Is it raining?"

"No. It's a clear night."

One of the dice rolls off a table, bouncing onto a hard surface.

We have carpet in the living room, tile in the kitchen. The game is in the kitchen, the diamond our kitchen table.

"Do you think we should check to make sure no one is there?" Harper asks.

"Downstairs?"

"Anywhere."

"If you'd like," I offer. "Why don't you stay here, and I'll go check."

I pick up Alexis, asleep at the foot of the bed, and place her gently beside Harper. "Keep your mother company," I tell the cat.

At the top of the stairs I reach for the switch for the hall light. "Close your eyes," I warn Harper, before bathing the hallway in a bright and reassuring light. Below me, on the far side of the kitchen door, the dice continue to roll across the kitchen table, interrupted only by the time it takes to silently record the result.

The game, I expect, will disappear at any moment, and I walk downstairs with the faith that I will indeed find nothing—see no one—when I open the kitchen door. Nevertheless, I can feel my heart racing, racing because the noise on the far side of the door is as real as the sound of my wife's voice, or the sound of my cat's deep purr when I picked her up and placed her beside Harper only a moment before.

A roll and a bang, a roll and a bang. That's all it took for Nathaniel to see men diving headfirst into third, or poking opposite-field singles to right. That's all it took to bring his scouting reports to life. "All field, no hit." "Likes to steal a lot." "Best smoke in the league."

I open the kitchen door, and in that brief second between when the door swings open and the light from the hallway pours inside, shadows come and go, shadows of a son and his father playing dice baseball together.

At least that's what they looked like. The shadows. But even as they receded into the darkness of the dining room at four-thirty, quarter to five in the morning, I knew they could be the shadows of . . . anything. The light fixture over the hutch. The plants that hang near the front windows. The short, squat candlesticks that rest in the middle of the kitchen table, alone there except for a pepper mill.

I turn on the kitchen light and stand in the doorway. There is no one in the kitchen or the dining room, no one at all. There is no dice baseball scorecard on the kitchen table, no pencil, no dice. The three chairs that surround the table, our three straight-back colonials, are tucked in their places beneath it.

And the thunder? That rolling and distant crackling of dice is gone too.

I sigh and cup my hands before my mouth, blowing warm air upon them. Light is beginning to form just above the mountains to the east. Game time, nine-thirty, is still close to five hours away.

I notice my attaché case is standing by the wall behind the table, in exactly the spot where I place it every night when I return home from the college. In that case are my Little League folders, and the incomplete lineup for today's game—incomplete because I have still not decided whether to replace Dickie Pratt for the day with Joey Fenton. It is a question for me of discipline, not talent. I want to punish Dickie because I believe that he hid Lucky's glove; unfortunately, I am not absolutely positive that Dickie was the culprit.

I open my attaché, and reach inside for the folders, ignoring at first the large envelope with the articles about Little League I have clipped, and Lucky's tablet that I found in the woods. I glance at the Tigers' roster, wondering if perhaps I should start Mike Harris in place of the Pratt boy. Mike only played one inning on Tuesday night, while Joey Fenton played three.

This seems like a sound solution. I'll start Mike Harris.

I pencil the Harris boy's name into the lineup, and toss the scorecard back into my briefcase. I drop the large clasp envelope with smudged newspaper clippings on top of the scorecard, and push the pocket-size tablet off to the side to ensure that the brief-case will close.

And then I pause, and reach back almost reflexively for the tablet to glance through it, rippling through the pages with my thumb and index finger. I glimpse my name again, and try to imagine who it was who told Lucky that someone named Mr. Parrish was going to replace someone named Mr. Pratt as coach of the Triple-A Tigers. Hilton Burberry? The boy's father?

I hope Lucky's father shows up at today's game. I wonder if the man—whoever he is, whatever he's like—understands how fortunate he is to have a child. How blessed. How . . . lucky. The fact that the man's never there makes me angry.

"Bill? Is everything okay?" Harper calls from our bedroom.

My heart begins to race with an idea, a vision.

"Everything's fine," I respond. "I'll be right up!"

Using my own blue felt-tip pen I begin to write in the pad, jotting down names as fast as I can, scrawling positions in a penmanship that is barely legible, afraid if I pause I will realize . . . I am somehow out of control. . . .

So I write, pulling the names as quickly as I can from my memory and tossing them down on the pad like dirt on a brush fire, doing all that I can not to think. Thorpman. Wohlford. Parker. Pratt. Wheelock . . .

I make sure there is a catcher, one shortstop, three outfielders . . .

One first baseman.

In minutes—in, perhaps, one minute—I am through. I stare down at my handiwork, on one level appalled at what I have done, on another astonished that it took me so long to try this. Other men, I tell myself, would have tried this much sooner. Other men—other fathers—would not have waited this long to find a place in their lineups for their own Nathaniels.

I place today's date at the top of my lineup, making it feel that much more real to me, and savor it one last time:

C. Thorpman—SS
B. Wohlford—P
N. Parrish—1B
L. Diamond—CF
J. Parker—LF
D. Pratt—3B
M. Lamphere—RF
R. Wheelock—C
M. Edington—2B

I curl my arms against my sides, against the chill that I know is inside me, a chill that I know has nothing to do with the cold. If Nathaniel had lived and if I had coached, I would have placed him third in the batting order. Today he would have hit right before Lucky Diamond, and right after Bobby Wohlford. He would have been our starting first baseman, he would have played most innings of most games, he would have wound up an all-star. . . .

Upstairs I hear Harper rise from our bed, the wood creaking slightly as she swings her legs over the side and sits upright. She takes her bathrobe from the back of the door, and starts toward the stairs. She is worried about me, wondering what has kept me so long in the kitchen.

I close the notebook, shaking, my fingers barely up to the task. I know I cannot let Harper see this, I know I cannot let her see that I have been writing our son's name as I sat alone at our kitchen table. N. Parrish, Nathaniel (never Nathan, never Nate, never Nat). Our son. I cannot imagine what it would be like for her to discover that I have not let him go, that I insist on placing him back at first base.

I drop the notebook back into my briefcase, and flip the brief-case shut as Harper enters the kitchen. In her eyes there is worry, concern, perhaps even fear. I want to reassure her that all is well, everything's fine. But I know I can't. I know the words just aren't there.

I know that right now, in the perpetual 5 A.M. sadness that surrounds me, a 5 A.M. world of fathers without sons, a 5 A.M. world where the thin bands of light in the east are always a mirage, that the only word I could speak is my little boy's name. Nathaniel.

Chapter 18

In my family's case, the Little League genes evidently skipped a generation. Nathaniel was a better Little Leaguer than I was, and so was my father. My father was actually a star of sorts in the Yonkers Little League. Yonkers, New York. He never told me this, but both my godfather and my uncle did. They grew up with him.

They told me that my father was a Little League pitcher, and by far the best in the league. Among the boys that he played with a half century ago, my uncle assures me, he is still something of a legend. This is because my father threw to left-handed batters with his left arm, and right-handed batters with his right. He could throw a big lollipop curve with either arm.

I had always known that my father was ambidextrous, but until my uncle told me this one day while he flipped hamburgers at a family barbecue, I hadn't realized that my father was the only pitcher in the history of the Yonkers Little League—perhaps all Little Leagues everywhere—who threw ambidextrously in game situations.

Saturday morning, I listen to my son's voice as I shave.

It is on a small cassette that I store on the top shelf of my armoire, the shelf that holds my wallet and car keys and change. It is a two-hour tape of a radio talk show, one of those call-in programs that come on in the middle of the night.

On this particular talk show, people talk about nothing but sports. The callers are not merely insomniacs, they are insomniacs who are also sports fanatics. They are the type who, I am afraid, live alone for good reason.

"You gotta be able to wing it inside. If you conk somebody on the head, that's tough titty," I hear one caller growl from the portable cassette player set up now on the counter beside the sink. As I recall, the caller was explaining to the host why an umpire has to give a pitcher the inside corner of the strike zone.

"Point noted," the host says diplomatically, before switching gears abruptly. "Tonight's call-in poll is about the instant replay. Where do you stand?"

"Oh, man, you gotta kill that thing," the caller says.

"So you're opposed to the rule?"

"Oh, yeah, you gotta—"

"Thanks much," the host says, hanging up and moving on to another caller.

My son, of course, was the exception to my belief that only social misfits call up sports talk shows at two in the morning. There was a two-week period just after Christmas when a drug called Cytoxan, a drug every bit as nasty as its name, kept him awake at night.

"You wanna get the play right, that's what mattas," someone growls, voting in favor of the National Football League's instant replay rule. The kinds of people who listen to this kind of talk show feel very, very strongly about things like the instant replay. "So I say, keep the replay," the caller concludes.

At least Harper and I told ourselves it was the drug. The doctors said it was probably the cause, but there was no way of knowing for sure. In any case, for two weeks either Harper or I would sit up with Nathaniel, playing backgammon, checkers, or —when it was me—dice baseball.

"Hey, Mike, this is Richie, calling from Queens. First time on your show."

"Welcome aboard, Richie. What's on your mind tonight?"

"Two things. First of all, I'm voting against the instant replay . . ."

Nathaniel and I would listen to the radio, usually this particular sports program out of New York City. (Although Havington is almost three hundred miles north of New York, we are able to receive the city's more powerful AM stations after sundown.)

Sometimes Nathaniel would listen impassively, tossing the dice that controlled the destiny of his dice baseball league, and sometimes he would roll his eyes and groan, astonished even at age ten by the obstinance of the program's callers.

"You gotta fire him," Carl from Long Island insists.

"You gotta trade him," Gerald from New Jersey demands.

"They jus' don't get it, you gotta use him in long relief," Sal from Mount Vernon proclaims.

It got to be a joke between Nathaniel and me: "You gotta, you gotta, you gotta."

"I don't gotta."

"You gotta."

Finally, one night, Nathaniel decided he had to call in. He had to add his voice to the chorus of armchair quarterbacks and couch potato pitchers who told New York City's football coaches and baseball managers how to run their teams.

"I gotta," he said, giggling.

From the phone in the kitchen we started calling the program about two in the morning, and got through somewhere around our thirtieth try. Nathaniel dialed the telephone number once, and then just kept pressing the two little buttons on the phone that said reset and redial. Busy signal. Reset. Redial. Busy signal. Reset. Redial. When he did get through, the receiving operator at the station took his name and put him on hold, and I dropped a cassette into the tape machine in the den.

And then, together, we waited. Evidently, there were a great many insomniacs and fanatics tuned into the show that night. Nathaniel sat on hold for close to an hour, listening to the Carls from Queens and the Larrys from Lindenhurst argue about the NFL's instant replay rule, or explain how to rebuild the Mets.

That was another of that night's topics: how to rebuild the Mets.

"You can't win if you're weak up the middle, and the Metsies are about as weak as you get," one fellow hisses.

"You gotta toss him. You gotta get rid of him," urges another, referring to the team's manager.

"They gotta get a fifth starta," a third caller suggests. "You can't make powa pitchas go on three days' rest."

Through it all, Nathaniel waited patiently. He sat at the kitchen table in his bathrobe, drawing baseball diamonds on a yellow legal pad, and writing down what he wanted to say.

All of a sudden, he was on the air.

"Next up, Nathaniel," the host begins, speaking to my son on the phone. "Where are you calling from, Nathaniel?"

Nathaniel looked up at me and laughed, his eyes wide. I

turned off the kitchen radio, as we had planned, so there would
be no on-air echo, and signaled okay with my hand. I glanced
into the next room, the den, to make sure that in there the radio
was still on and the tape machine running.

"Vermont," Nathaniel says, as I run my razor under water. He
sounds to me now just the slightest bit tentative.

"Vermont!" the host exclaims. "I think you gotta win the prize
tonight for furthest call. What's on your mind, buddy?"

"I'm calling about the Mets," he continues, his voice revealing
to the host that he's just a small boy.

"You are, are you? Well, let me ask you something first, Nathaniel. You sound like a smart young man: what the heck are
you doing up at three-oh-five in the morning?"

"I *gotta* listen to your show," he answers.

Mike the host laughs. "Oh, a wisenheimer, eh? A smart al-
eck?"

"Yup!"

"You got all the answers?"

"I got 'em," Nathaniel says playing along.

I was very proud of Nathaniel that night. Only ten years old,
and he was bantering with a New York City radio talk show host.

"Okay, let me have it," Mike says. "Rebuild the Mets."

Nathaniel looked down at the roster of his dice baseball Mets,
and the statistics he had amassed of the team.

"First of all, the Mets need a catcher," he begins. "You see,
they've got all these young pitchers, but no one they can, you
know, look up to . . ."

The next night, for whatever the reasons, Nathaniel fell instantly to sleep.

I have no idea whether I will confront Lucky Diamond. At least
this morning. As I told Harper Thursday night, I am not in the
habit of confronting eleven-year-old boys.

And, in the case of one Lucky Diamond, I'm not even sure that
I should.

When I arrive at the Havington ball field Saturday morning,
most of the kids are already there, including Lucky. Some of the
children are lightly tossing baseballs back and forth, and some are
sitting in a small circle behind the backstop with Melissa Edington and Cindy Fletcher. The boys are approaching that age in

their lives when the fact that Cindy Fletcher is arguably the worst baseball player in Vermont no longer matters; they are discovering that she has other attributes.

I stroll past the small group by the backstop, my Little League folders secured in the clipboard under my arm, and holler good morning as I pass them.

"Think the rain will hold off?" Mike Harris asks me.

"Better hope so," I tell him. "You're starting today."

I walk up the first base line to the corner of the diamond where Lucky Diamond is playing catch with Mark Lamphere, kicking at the wet, dewy grass with my feet. Lucky smiles up at me as he backhands the ball, and then throws it back to our right fielder. He is still using the glove I lent him at our last practice, indicating that his has still not turned up.

"How you doing today, Mark?" I yell to the other boy.

"Okay, Mr. Parrish."

I give him a thumbs-up signal, and put my arm on Lucky's shoulder. Perhaps now is as good a time as any to ask Lucky whether he really believes there's a school for him in the little town of Granville, and when I might be able to talk to . . . to meet . . . his father.

"Give us a quick minute here," I shout to Mark, careful to smile as I say it, and I begin to steer Lucky off the diamond and toward the outfield. I had initially planned on walking toward the river, but the high grass there has been christened by our team the "minefield," an off-limits area where deer ticks might live.

"I have something to talk to you about," I begin, hoping my voice sounds even but not unduly stern. Behind us Pete Cooder arrives in his pickup truck, tooting the horn for the team. "Something that confused me a little," I add.

His body tenses, but he continues to look down at the grass as we walk.

"I learned the other day that there's no school in Granville other than a public elementary school. And you have to live in Granville to go there."

He looks up at me as we walk, raising his eyebrows politely and nodding. It is as if I am describing to him the weather in Georgia.

"Didn't you tell me that you would be going to school in Granville this September?" I ask firmly.

He shrugs, a gesture that could mean any one of a number of things: I don't remember. Maybe. So what?

"Did I misunderstand you?"

He reaches into the back pocket of his uniform for his notebook, identical to the one that now sits locked in my attaché case (and will remain there until I have the courage to delete one certain page). In a matter of seconds he has scribbled,

I guess so.

I discover that I have been tapping my clipboard against my hip, and I stop. Although I have not raised my voice, I have a feeling that if I were to turn around right now I would see the children watching us with interest, wondering what is happening. The air has felt to me strangely electric since I left the house, and I tell myself now that it just feels like rain.

"Well, I'm curious. Where *will* you be going to school in September?"

He writes quickly, biting his lip.

Did I do something wrong???

There is an urgency in his question marks, a fear. "No, you didn't do anything wrong. It's just that . . . it's just that I want to make sure you're getting the best possible—"

He cuts me off, holding up his notebook like a billboard, putting it squarely in front of my face.

Cause maybe I was just mistaken!!!

"Maybe. Or maybe I was," I tell him, staring at the word *mistaken*. It strikes me as an odd word for Lucky to choose. I would have expected him to use *wrong*. Or simply *mistake*. *I made a mistake*, I can imagine him writing. But he has used *mistaken* instead. *Just mistaken*. This is the way a schoolteacher might speak, these are in fact the words Harper had used Thursday night when we were discussing Lucky.

I guess Lucky was mistaken, she had said.

I try to think, I try to clear from my mind the image of the little boy before me writing frantically in a small notebook, or the sound behind me of Pete Cooder's voice. I shouldn't be doing this, I shouldn't be standing here now. An eleven-year-old boy is standing in front of me blinking madly, blinking, I am afraid, to hold back tears.

Maybe its not Granville, but I know it begins with a G. I know it!

"It's okay, it's not a big deal," I tell him, trying to calm and reassure him. "It's not a big deal. I was only asking these questions because . . . I was only asking because I was worried."

From somewhere behind us Pete Cooder shouts at me, "Yo, Captain Bill, shouldn't we be gettin' these all-stars to Starksboro?"

"I'm riding in the back of the truck!" Bobby Wohlford yells, starting a chorus of cries to ride in Coach Cooder's truck. "I call the back of Pete's truck!"

Lucky opens his mouth into a little o, wishing desperately he was able to speak, before jotting down one final plea:

You got to believe me!

I stand by our bench at the Starksboro field, and stare at first base. I try to watch the other kids warm up, but I'm unable to concentrate on anything other than the padded white square that rests on the ground, and the child whose name I've forgotten who stands right beside it. I know the boy's name will come back to me any moment, so I half close my eyes, I squint, hoping to further blur the boy's image. I don't want to recall his name, I don't want to see who he actually is. I want to see instead my boy, my son, the child whose name I jotted down last night in the little blue notebook. N. Parrish. N. Parrish, today batting third and playing first base. N. Parrish, leaning forward on his toes, tapping his glove against his thigh in anticipation . . .

"That was nice of you to give Mikey a start," Pete Cooder says to me, suddenly standing beside me.

"He didn't play much on Tuesday," I answer.

"Give your infielders a few more warm-ups, Carl," Pete calls to the boy at first base. Carl, he called him. Carl Northrup. I watch Carl Northrup throw a soft grounder to Mike Harris at third. Mike looks up at the last second, and allows the ball to roll through his legs and into foul ground.

"Head down, Mikey!" I shout at the boy, trying to wake myself up. "Remember, head down!"

"Any special reason you put him at third?" Pete asks me quietly. "Every once in a while he'll catch a fly ball. But I don't think he's ever managed to field a grounder in his whole life."

"I wanted to bench Dickie Pratt."

"How come?"

I glance over my shoulder, making sure the boy isn't within earshot. I see him a good twenty-five yards away, sulking by our canvas bag of baseball bats.

"I think he's the one who took Lucky Diamond's glove at practice the other night."

Pete nods thoughtfully. "You think so?"

"I do. I think it was Dickie Pratt."

"No. I mean, you really think someone took the kid's glove? You don't think Lucky just lost it somewhere, or dropped it somewhere?"

"Nope."

Mike retrieves the baseball from underneath the Starksboro team's bench, and throws a pathetic fly ball across the diamond to first base. It bounces five feet in front of Carl and dies there.

"You've seemed a little edgy this morning," Pete continues. "You feelin' okay."

"I didn't sleep well last night."

"Boy, I did. This time of year, I sleep like a baby."

I glance at my watch and see that it's almost nine-thirty. "Okay, guys," I holler, "time to bring it in!" and Pete starts clapping beside me.

"Is your dad at the game today?" I ask Lucky while he waits for his first turn at bat. There seems to be a pretty good crowd in the row of bleachers behind us.

The boy stops windmilling the bat with his arms, and shakes his head no. He never takes his eye off the opposing pitcher, he never makes eye contact with me.

"Well, it's not a very nice day for a ball game," I say. "It looks like it's going to pour any minute."

Lucky nods, but he continues to watch the pitcher. I am not sure if he is trying to concentrate or ignore me.

"Someday I'd like to meet him—your father. Think I will?"

Behind us Carl Northrup hits a sizzling line drive, but it is directly at the shortstop. The little boy catches the ball in front of his face, saving his parents thousands of dollars in dental reconstruction, and holds Bobby Wohlford at first.

"Two outs!" the Starksboro catcher shouts to the infielders, holding two fingers high.

Lucky finally looks over at me and nods noncommittally. He then starts toward home plate.

As he steps into the batter's box Dickie Pratt says, in a voice loud enough for Lucky to hear, "That kid can't find anything, can he? First it was his glove, and now it's his dad. Unbelievable!"

For a moment the two boys watch each other, Dickie trying his best to look tough, but his facade withers quickly under the fury in Lucky Diamond's gaze. The loathing. His eyes two blue lights of malice and hate, Lucky glares at the Pratt boy and stares him down.

"That's enough," I tell Dickie, my own voice quiet but firm. I then turn to home plate and call out, "Let's go, Lucky, let's get a hit!"

At ten minutes to ten, raindrops begin to fall. The rain is light, not even what I might call a drizzle. Just enough that some of the players and a few of the spectators extend their hands before them, palms up, confirming that it is indeed raining.

Bobby Wohlford throws a pitch, his fastball, and the Starksboro batter hits a fly ball to the middle of the diamond. Cliff Thorpman calls for it at shortstop, wanders in a few feet to catch it, and the first inning is over without either team scoring.

"Super inning," I yell at Bobby as he jogs past me.

"The ball's gettin' wet and slippery," he tells me. He takes off his glove and places it palm down on his head like a skullcap. "Rain hat," he explains.

"This inning we got Mikey Harris, Mark Lamphere, and Roger comin' up," Pete yells, pointing at each of the three children scheduled to bat this inning, "six, seven, and eight! Now let's go get some runs!"

The Starksboro pitcher, a boy with the last name of Beattie, is the kind of pitcher who scares Little Leaguers. He is tall and heavy—just plain big for his age—and the mound makes him appear even larger. Hilton Burberry has told me that he throws harder than any boy in the Sedgebury league, perhaps any boy his age in all of northern Vermont. Yet Beattie is only Starksboro's number two pitcher, because his control is abysmal. He is wild, even by Little League standards.

This combination, speed and inaccuracy, is what frightens my team. They're all convinced he is going to bean them. As I watched him pitch in the first inning, however, I realized that they had little to fear. Beattie knows he throws hard, and that is exactly why he is wild: he is evidently scared to death of hitting someone, so he pitches outside. Way outside.

"All his strikes are on the outside corner of the plate," I mention to Pete, referring to Beattie. "He rarely even grooves one down the middle. Have you noticed?"

Pete nods. "He's probably a nice kid. With that fastball of his, he could really ring somebody's chimes."

Beside me Mike Harris takes his warm-up swings, whipping his little aluminum bat through the air.

"Don't forget this," I tell Mike, reaching down and handing him one of our monstrous blue batting helmets.

"Thanks, Mr. Parrish."

Pete looks down at the boy. "You been watching him pitch?" Pete asks him, and points at Beattie.

"I guess."

"You guess? Well, I got a tip for you. He's gonna pitch you outside. His first pitch is either gonna be a ball, or it's gonna be on the outside corner of the plate. Got it?"

"Uh-huh."

"Good. Remember: head up, watch the ball, and expect it to be on the outside part of the plate."

Beattie finishes his warm-up tosses, and the Starksboro catcher rifles a practice throw down to second base. He too has a pretty fair arm, although the ball bounces in front of the base and skids underneath the second baseman's glove into center field.

Mike Harris, standing in the on-deck circle, looks up at the sky and shakes his head. "The bat's all wet," he says to no one in particular, and tries to dry it off on his uniform pants. He then walks into the batter's box, and prepares for Beattie's first pitch. I glance at my watch, knowing that it is three minutes to ten.

Mike bats right-handed, so I am able to watch his face as he digs in. I can see that he's frightened. I probably shouldn't have let him bat sixth, but I wanted him to have Dickie Pratt's place in the lineup as well as his spot at third base.

Abruptly he backs out of the batter's box before Beattie can throw his first pitch, stalling. He leans the bat against his legs and rubs his hands on his shirt, trying to dry them, and then for the second time in a minute he tries to wipe the raindrops from his bat on his pants. It is clearly a losing battle, especially since the rain has begun to fall harder.

Any minute now the umpire may call time-out and stop the game until the storm passes.

Finally Mike returns to the batter's box. He looks over at Pete and me, and I try to mouth the word "outside" to him, reminding him where Beattie is most likely to pitch.

The boy at the plate raises his bat off his shoulder, plants his right foot, and bends both his knees. The boy on the mound looks in at his catcher, reading the signal for the pitch in the number of fingers the catcher flashes between his shin guards, (although all Beattie has thrown today are fastballs), and he begins to wind up. He brings his hands together over his head and rocks one step back, twists his leg around, rearing back for momentum, and then abruptly kicks forward. He is perhaps the only boy on the field more afraid of hitting Mikey than Mikey himself, and he never takes his eyes off the batter. His leg leads first, dragging his body and arm forward with it, and the ball appears suddenly at the top of his right hand, surging over everyone toward home plate.

Or, more accurately, just off home plate. The ball is coming outside, a good foot outside, almost to the spot by the plate where Mikey Harris would be standing if he were a left-handed batter.

Mikey is not a leftie, however, he is a rightie. He is standing far from where the ball is pitched. Perhaps because both Pete and I have told him to expect the ball outside, however, and technically that is exactly where the ball has been thrown, Mickey decides to swing anyway. He begins to whip his aluminum bat around, well aware on some level that the ball is too far from him to hit it with a conventional swing.

And so he lunges at it, stepping onto home plate at exactly 9:58 in the morning in his effort to reach it.

I will never know whether it is the fact that Mikey lunges at a pitch far outside of the strike zone that causes him to lose his grip on the bat, or whether it is the rain, which has now been falling for almost ten solid minutes, that makes the bat handle so slippery he is unable to control it. It may even have something to do with the fact that—at least in my life—9:58 is a cursed time of day.

But the bat takes off. It explodes from Mikey Harris's hands like a helicopter's runaway propeller, slicing through the electric air like a razor. . . .

Maybe it is too soon to be here. Maybe it was a mistake to have offered to coach. I'm writing my son's name in mock batting orders, I'm accusing a little boy who can't speak of lying. . . .

I'm punishing Dickie Pratt for stealing, although I have no proof at all that the boy really did anything wrong. But I have benched him just the same, I have sat him down in the wet grass of the Starksboro diamond. . . .

I yell. I yell instinctively the second the bat leaves Mikey Harris's hands and begins to cut through the air, a whirling aluminum missile. I yell one word, and I yell it loud and hard and in fear.

"Dickie!" I yell as loud as I can, trying to warn the little boy twenty-five feet from home plate, a little boy sitting with his head down, staring intently at something in the damp grass beneath him.

He looks over at me, looking up in the general direction of the voice that has cried his name, moving his head perhaps one inch, perhaps two.

But it is enough. Barely. The bat zooms past Dickie Pratt's ear, so close to the boy that he can hear it, perhaps feel its wind, and he whips his neck around to see what has just flown by like a bullet.

The bat crashes into a tree stump with a loud metal clank, and falls harmlessly to the grass. For a moment not a soul on the field or in the stands says a word. The only noise is the sound of the rain *plink-plinking* onto the empty spots on the wooden benches and onto the metal cage over home plate.

Finally Pete Cooder nods his head and says to me in a very quiet voice, "Nice goin' there, Captain Bill. Nice reflexes." We watch Dickie Pratt try to stand, but his legs have suddenly become wobbly, weak, and so we rush over to him.

From the corner of my eye I can see Lucky Diamond pounding his hand into my glove, slamming his fist into its palm. He looks up at us as we surround Dickie Pratt, impassive and unmoved, and looks away only when his eye catches mine.

Yes, it is indeed too soon to be here, it was a mistake to have offered to coach: I am sure that I saw in the mute boy's gaze a disinterest that looked almost cruel.

Chapter 19

Harper looks up from the Sunday newspaper's magazine, the publication open to two pages of recipes for chutney. "You know what?" she begins.

"What?" I look up from the sports section. We are both sitting on the living room floor early Sunday night, insulated from the rain that began yesterday morning and hasn't stopped for more than ten minutes ever since. The storm not only rained out Little League games across the county, it caused the Sedgebury commencement ceremonies today to be held inside Halberstam Hall, the first time in almost three decades that the exercises weren't conducted in the immaculate quadrangle before the school library.

"I've been feeling a little funny for about three days now," Harper continues. "I probably shouldn't tell you this, because we won't know for sure for weeks."

"Yes?"

"Well . . . I feel maternal."

"Honestly?"

"Honestly." She is smiling her broad Southern smile, a smile that I have loved for years, but have seen only rarely for two. I crawl across the carpet and kneel beside her. I kiss her once on the forehead, and then pull her toward me, holding her as tight as I can.

"Now don't get all mushy," she says, and although I cannot see her eyes I know she is rolling them. "I probably shouldn't even have told you yet. Because it just might be some sort of biological false alarm."

"I doubt that. You're the one who has told me that a woman just knows when she's pregnant."

"Well, this one does."

"Why don't I pick up a pregnancy test kit tomorrow in Sedgebury?" I whisper, my mouth close to her ear. "So we can be absolutely positive." I nip gently at her earlobe, and her body ripples in my arms.

"No, please don't. I'm really only a day or two late. When we're a little farther along, maybe. But not now. I don't want to get all clinical right now."

I nod, knowing exactly what she means, and I too start to smile—a smile of joy, of relief, of anticipation.

I sit on Nathaniel's bed later that night while Harper is taking a bath, pounding my fist into Nathaniel's old glove. The sharp pops sound very much like a baseball being caught squarely in the pocket. Perhaps that's why little boys (perhaps that's why everyone who plays baseball) like to do it. It's one of baseball's most common, most harmless rituals. It's like a tennis player bouncing a ball on the court before serving, or a basketball player dribbling before attempting a foul shot.

And yet it had looked so evil to me when Lucky Diamond was doing it Saturday morning. Perhaps because it seemed the entire world had stopped moving at that moment, everyone except Lucky. Perhaps because everyone on and off the field had stopped breathing when the bat flew from Mikey Harris's hands, everyone had stood perfectly still. Everyone except Lucky.

An aluminum bat slipped from a little boy's hands on a rainy Saturday morning. That's all that really happened, I remind myself. Bats slip from little boys' hands all the time, especially in the rain. I am sure that bats, the antique wooden variety, slipped even from mine.

It is possible—no, it is likely—that what I perceived as Lucky's almost heartless indifference to Dickie Pratt's close call was in actuality shock. Bewilderment. The boy had been stunned.

Had I not seen that brief exchange between Lucky and Dickie Pratt only minutes earlier, that moment when Lucky's blue eyes went dark with hate, I probably wouldn't have given the incident a second thought. It probably wouldn't have stayed with me the way it has, the images passing before my eyes with astonishing clarity each time that I close them.

I have not told Harper about the incident, because I know it would upset her. Or rather, I would upset her. The incident itself? She wasn't there, she wouldn't think anything of it. But I would upset her, my response to the incident. She would shake her head and tell me again that Lucky is an eleven-year-old boy who needs my help, not my paranoid misgivings. And I know she would be right. Her instincts are good. Just as I trust her when she tells me that she feels maternal, I know I should trust her when she says I am overreacting, when she says I am not thinking straight.

After all, what has Lucky done to deserve my distrust, to arouse my suspicion? Certainly nothing I—nothing anyone—could prove. He wasn't the one who threw a bat at Dickie Pratt, he didn't personally attack my cats, he didn't put Donnie Casey in a coma.

It isn't Lucky Diamond who obsesses for a little boy long gone, writing his name into lineups at five in the morning.

"Bill?"

Lucky is, essentially, a little boy very much like Nathaniel. He too reads biographies of Custer and Lafayette and Lee, he too scorched his name into his baseball glove with a wood burner. . . .

"Bill?"

I look up and see Harper standing in the hallway in her nightgown, her arms wrapped nervously around her chest.

"What are you doing?" she asks.

I remove my left hand from Nathaniel's baseball glove. "I was just thinking. Daydreaming, I guess."

She is frowning. The sight of me alone in Nathaniel's bedroom has upset her. "What about?"

"Nothing special."

She wanders into the room and sits on the bed beside me, resting her hand on my knee. "You were thinking about Nathaniel."

"Not really. Not exactly."

She takes back her hand. Something in my tone has tipped her off. "Don't tell me you were stewing over Lucky Diamond again. Please, Bill, give that child a break, won't you?"

"Someone took his glove," I explain, trying to sound casual.

"I know. You told me Thursday night when you got home from practice. And then again Saturday morning."

"I wish I knew who did it."

She leans against the headboard, curling her legs up beneath her. She runs two fingers absentmindedly over the swirls in the bedspread, as if she were following directions on a road map. "Can I make a suggestion?" she says finally.

I nod.

"Give him that one. Give him Nathaniel's old glove."

By the way Harper turns her full attention upon me and shakes her head, I must look appalled. And I am indeed surprised. After Nathaniel died, neither of us were able to give away any of his things. We just didn't know where to begin. That's why his clothes, his books, his toys have sat in this room like museum pieces, gathering dust. Now, however, Harper is suggesting we give away one of our son's most cherished possessions.

"Oh, my lord," she says, her voice light, "the idea must have been in the back of your mind! You can't tell me you didn't think of it first! Why else would you be sitting here now with the damn thing on your hand?"

"I don't know," I answer, although I do know. I do know that on some level she's right, and I must have had the idea first. "I guess you're right. I guess I did figure this was a better loaner than my old glove."

"Loaner? I really think you should give the poor boy the glove, Bill. *Give* it to him. He needs it more than you do. Don't you think?"

She's right again, of course. There is no reason in the world not to lend—not to give—the boy the glove. And there are at least a dozen reasons to do so, including my own guilt for accusing the child of lying.

"You're not keepin' your eye on the ball!" Pete Cooder reminds Roger Wheelock Tuesday night as the boy finishes his swing and misses another pitch, the bat twisted so far around him that it taps the back of his helmet. "Find it when I'm startin' my windup, and then keep your eye on it," Pete continues, rearing back and throwing the boy another practice lob.

"No batter, no batter, no batter!" Dickie Pratt cries from third base.

When Saturday's game was rained out, I scheduled a practice for tonight. It wasn't that I believed we needed the practice (although I am indeed finding that Little Leaguers always need practice), as much as I could tell that the children wanted to practice. They were very disappointed when we didn't get to play two days ago, and the idea of not getting back onto the field until this Thursday's game against Lincoln seemed to them an impossibly long time.

Practice has been going on for a good half an hour by the time I arrive at the ball field, a little past six. Fortunately, I warned Pete Saturday morning that I would probably be late, and to plan to begin without me: with the first Sedgebury alumni weekend occurring this weekend, it is a miracle that I escaped the office by five-thirty.

"Evenin', Bill," Pete says to me, smiling, as I wander out to the pitching mound to join him. Most of the Havington Tigers are scattered in the field behind him, shagging the batting practice flies and grounders until it is their turn to bat.

"Looks like you have everything under control here."

"Must be some mistake then," he says. "An optical illusion, maybe. I don't think I ever have anything under control." He then rears back and throws Roger another pitch. The boy steps toward the ball, and hits a grounder to Cliff Thorpman at shortstop.

"That's better," Pete yells at the boy. "You were keepin' your eye on the ball." He turns to me, looking at the baseball glove under my arm. "New glove?" he asks.

"Nope. A good four years old."

"Didn't look new. But it didn't look like yours either."

"Good memory."

"Lousy memory. Just a good eye."

I put the glove on my hand, flexing the webbing with my fingers. "It was Nathaniel's."

Pete nods solemnly, but says nothing. It will never cease to astound me the way that even the most talkative people become quiet when I mention my son. They just have no idea what to say.

Pete looks at the infielders and outfielders surrounding us, and shouts, "Look alive out there, stay in the ball game!" He is referring primarily to Cindy Fletcher, who—while Mark Lamphere watches hypnotized from a dozen yards away—is performing ballet pirouettes in slow motion in right field.

In center field, standing with his hands on his knees, is Lucky Diamond. He is still wearing the glove, my glove, that I loaned him.

I would like to march out there right now and give him Nathaniel's glove, but I know that I can't. It would remind the team that the child probably can't afford a new glove of his own, it would remind them that Lucky is different.

"Why don't you keep tossing batting practice, and I'll work for a while with the pitchers," I suggest to Pete. "That will spread out the action a little bit."

"Sounds okay to me."

I scan the field briefly, and holler for Jesse Parker, Bobby Wohlford, and Cliff Thorpman to join me in right field. And then, with a sudden inspiration, I yell for Lucky Diamond and Carl Northrup, telling them to join us as well. I have an idea that I will teach our staff how to hold runners on base, a skill these kids know little about: Triple-A is the only level in the Sedgebury County Little League in which leading is legal.

"Carl, you're going to be our first baseman, and Lucky, you're going to be our base runner," I explain.

It will be much easier to give Lucky my glove discreetly in a small group of five than it would be smack in the middle of batting practice.

"Well, it was just gathering dust in our house," I tell Lucky casually, trying to downplay the significance of the gift.

Despite Harper's argument that the child would have more use for the glove than me, until this moment I hadn't decided for sure whether to tell Lucky the mitt was a loaner until he had a chance to buy a new one, or whether I should tell him it was a gift he could keep. Perhaps unconsciously, I have opted for the latter. Baseball gloves aren't cheap, and by telling the child that the glove is his, there is no pressure on him or his father to find the money for a new one anytime soon.

"That was a real nice gesture," Pete says to me after practice, shutting the rear gate of his pickup truck.

"Giving Lucky my boy's old glove?"

"Yup."

I carve a small avenue in the gravel of the firehouse parking lot with the toe of my sneaker. "Was it obvious? Do you think the kids noticed?"

"Nah. Maybe Jesse knew what was happenin', maybe Carl. But they're good kids. They understand."

"I hope so."

"You know, I couldn't a done it."

"Sure you could."

"Nope, I couldn't. That's why I know how hard it probably was for you. You took a memory of your boy that musta meant a lot to you, and you gave it away. That's a real hard one."

I smile, but not because I am flattered. I smile because I am proud of Pete Cooder.

"I can do it now, but I couldn't have done it a month ago. I couldn't have done it even a week ago," I hear myself saying, surprised. I know where this conversation is going—I know where I'm leading it—and I wish I could tell myself to calm down, change the subject, simply be quiet.

Ever since Harper told me Sunday night that she feels maternal, every time I think of the idea that we will again be parents, I am filled with so much joy that I feel I must let some go, I feel I must share the news with someone. Nevertheless, until now I have not told a soul, because we won't know for weeks if she's right. I have not told my brother, although I spoke to him today on the phone, I have not told Doug Bascomb, although we were in the office together all afternoon.

I have not told a soul that Harper thinks she is pregnant because I would hate to jinx it. Now, however, standing in the twilight with a man I hardly know, I know that I am about to open the safety valves of my heart and let some of that joyous steam escape.

Because otherwise, I just might burst.

"Nope," I repeat, "I couldn't have done it even a week ago."

"Because you didn't know Lucky good enough?"

I shake my head, grinning. "Nah, it doesn't have anything to do with Lucky. It has to do with me—with me and Harper."

"Really?"

"Really." I am truly astonished that I am telling Pete Cooder this, but I can't help myself. I've been dying all day to tell someone, and I simply can't keep it inside me any longer. I find myself rationalizing the fact that I am about to share the news with Pete

Cooder instead of my brother or Doug Bascomb by telling myself that I am actually doing those people who are close to me a favor by shielding them from the information: if Harper is incorrect, if it is—as she put it—a "biological false alarm," they will be spared the disappointment.

"You've got to keep what I'm about to tell you a secret. Harper and I haven't told anyone this, and we probably won't for at least a month."

"Sounds like a mystery."

"Nothing of the sort," I reassure him. "This is only good news. Great news. Harper and I decided after Christmas that we were ready to start a family again—that we wanted to start a family again. So for a couple months now, we've been trying to have a baby. And the other day, Sunday, Harper told me that she thinks she may be pregnant."

"Serious?" Pete asks, digesting the news for one short moment.

"Serious."

He laughs, one loud bellow of joy for me, and slaps me hard on the back. "All righty! That's the kinda news I like to hear!"

"Now we don't know for sure," I tell him quickly, "and we probably won't know for sure for a while, so you have to keep this a secret."

"You mean I shouldn't tell Hilton to write a story for the *Sedgebury Independent?*"

"No, not yet."

He laughs again. "Goddamn, I'm happy for you. I'm real goddamn happy for you." He looks over my shoulder, still smiling from ear to ear, and says to someone behind me, "Now, remember, you too got to keep Mr. Parrish's news a secret. Understand? Just the three of us know."

I turn around to see who is there, and my happiness is drowned in a wave of nausea that jolts me. I lean against the side of the truck for support, telling myself that I have no reason to be frightened, that to think for even a moment I do is an indication of how unstable I have become.

I rub my eyes, trying to find within me the courage to plaster back onto my face a smile. But I can't, I can't, the smiles are gone, and I am left with only a blank vacant stare for the boy who can't speak.

Chapter 20

How sure is Harper that she is pregnant?

When I return home from work Wednesday night, I see she has been cleaning out her lingerie drawer, finding all of the body briefers and body stockings, teddies and tap pants that she believes she will soon no longer be able to wear. The lingerie is spread out on our bed in haphazard piles of black and purple, red silk and lace.

"I figure I have about four months until I pop," she says to me, smiling. "So I might as well go wild with this stuff while I can."

"Keep the ball down, Bobby, keep the ball down!" Russ Wohlford screams at his son Thursday night. Bobby removes his cap and wipes the sweat off his forehead with his sleeve, and stares at the runners on base behind him. Lincoln has men on first and third, with nobody out. We are already trailing 6 to 2, and it's only the third inning; a big hit here can pretty much put the game away for Lincoln.

"Bear down, Bobby, for crying out loud, bear down!" Russ Wohlford yells from somewhere behind me.

Pete Cooder wanders over to me and whispers, "Bobby's old man has one strong pair of lungs."

I nod. "He's known for being a little too verbal at these games."

The boy gets into the stretch position on the mound, and stares in at his catcher, Roger Wheelock, looking for the signal for his next pitch.

Pete and I sometimes play a game together as we stand by our bench, something we call, "What if?" The premise, essentially, is to ask each other how we would coach our team in specific situations if the Triple-A Tigers consisted of professional athletes instead of ten- and eleven-year-old boys and girls.

"Okay," Pete asks me, "What if: would you play for two, or would you bring the infield in and try to cut the run off at the plate?"

"With nobody out, I'd play for two. I'd rather give them one run, then risk a real big inning by bringing the infield in."

Pete shakes his head. "Five runs is a pretty big lead, Captain Bill."

Bobby glances over at first base, trying to look the Lincoln runner back to the bag. The runner doesn't budge, he holds his lead a good twelve or fifteen feet away from the bag. For a second Bobby looks back at the plate, but only for a second. Before we—me, Pete Cooder, any ball player on the field—know it, he whirls and pretends to whip the ball to Carl Northrup at first base.

"Balk!"

The word is screamed simultaneously by both the home plate and field umpires, two heavyset teenagers who I have been told are twin brothers from Vergennes. I shake my head, surprised at Bobby. It was only two nights ago that we spent an hour practicing how to hold a runner on first base, studying both the legal and illegal moves.

The Lincoln side of the field explodes with cheers and applause, and the third base coach starts waving the runner in from third, and shouting for the runner on first to advance to second.

"Ah, so much for strategy, Captain Bill," Pete mumbles, smirking.

"What are you talking about? That wasn't a balk!" Bobby yells at the home plate umpire, walking halfway in from the pitching mound. "No way! That was no balk!" He is joined by Roger Wheelock, who has heaved his mask into the dirt and begun to scream too.

I hand Pete my clipboard and jog out onto the field, quickly steering both Bobby and Roger back to the pitching mound.

"Tell him, Mr. Parrish," Bobby hisses at me, "tell him he's a jerk and that was no balk."

"Oh, I don't think so," I say to the boy calmly when we arrive back at the center of the diamond. "That was a balk. You can't keep your foot on the rubber, and fake a throw to first base."

"I took my foot off the rubber!"

"Didn't look that way to me or Pete. And that's beside the point. Both umps called it at the same time, so there isn't a prayer of our winning any argument. What you—what you both —have to do, is put the balk behind you and start concentrating on the batter. Okay?"

Bobby shakes his head, furious at one more of life's petty injustices.

"Okay?" I ask again, a little more enthusiastically this time.

"Okay," Roger says, pulling at one of the leather knots holding his catcher's mitt together. I take an okay from one of the two as sufficient confirmation that the tantrum is over and the game will go on, and jog back to our bench.

When I arrive, I see immediately that Pete has been joined by Russ Wohlford. He looks like a man who has just had his tires slashed.

"Evening, Russ," I say, taking back my clipboard from Pete.

"Is that all you're going to do?" he says to me, his hands on his hips. Everything from the way Russ is standing to the indignant tone of his voice reminds me of Dan Brodie, the Little League dad who accused me before the entire world of kicking dirt on home plate when I was nine.

"Yup."

"That call stunk. And I got news for you, if Wes Pratt were coaching, he would have stood up for my son."

"Well, Wes isn't coaching. I am."

Bobby stands still on the pitching mound, despite the fact the umpire has yelled to resume playing. Evidently, he is waiting for some signal from his dad that it is okay to pitch.

"You're setting a lousy example for the kids, you know," Russ continues. "You're telling them it's okay to get stepped on. You're telling them it's okay to—"

"Find me after the game, Russ. We can talk about it then. Okay?"

"It just stinks. And your taking it like this stinks too!"

I shrug, and turn away from the man. It is a good thing I don't have in my hand a paper cup full of Coca-Cola. If I did, I might really set a bad example for the team.

*   *   *

At first I am not sure where I have seen the truck before. It even crosses my mind that perhaps it is not this specific truck with which I am familiar, but merely this type of truck: a tremendous, blue and silver four-by-four pickup, a little rust around the doors, a white cab on the back.

It is in the top of the sixth inning, while Cliff Thorpman is setting down Lincoln in order for the first time in the game, that it dawns on me why I know the truck. I saw it last week, beside Lucky Diamond's trailer, when I drove the boy home after dinner.

Now it is parked at the Little League field here in town.

I spin around to look into the stands as the top of the sixth comes to an end, and the Triple-A Tigers race off the field. Somewhere in those bleachers, perhaps wandering somewhere behind me, is Lucky's father. The logger. I begin in the upper left corner of the small wooden stands, my heart racing, and I stare up at each row of seats, my eyes moving from left to right as if I were reading a book.

In the collage of faces and clothes—windbreakers and work shirts, sweaters and sweatshirts—there are few I do not know. Such is life in a small town where everyone is related to someone. I may not be able to attach a name to each face, but each is a face I have seen at one time or another in my travels through Havington, or Sedgebury, or Lincoln.

Even the elderly couple in lawn chairs, their legs spread, their identical pear-shaped bellies rolling onto the nylon webbing of their seats, is familiar. It may have been at the IGA, it may have been at a Christmas Eve service at the church, it may even have been at the Trillium Extended Care Facility, when—perhaps—they were there on a visit, but I know I have seen them before.

"Batter up!"

I turn to my team and tell them who's up this inning, bellowing out the names Pratt, Fletcher, and Wheelock. Dickie Pratt already has his batting helmet on, and is swaying three bats in slow motion, trying desperately to follow through on his practice swings. My eyes glance past the boy and across the infield, studying the Lincoln side of the diamond for a single male I don't know: a male who appeared, in the split second and dim light that I saw him, to be no more than thirty, to have had what might have been light brown hair.

A male who looked neither large enough nor heavy enough to be a logger. A male who I do not believe had a beard, but who might have had a mustache.

There are perhaps three men I don't recognize in the Lincoln bleachers, and while any one of them could be Lucky Diamond's father, I don't believe any one of them is. Two appear to have wives beside them, and one of those men has a thick black beard. The third fellow has the build of the man I saw briefly in Lucky's trailer, but he looks too old. He looks like he's my age. He is also wearing a navy blue blazer and loafers, and has a briefcase leaning against his shins.

Nothing about him suggests he's a logger.

"If we can get two or three back this inning, I think we still got a chance," Pete is saying to me softly. "Five runs is a lot to make up in one at-bat, but if we can narrow the gap a bit right now . . . well, you never know."

"I think Lucky's father is here."

Pete looks into the stands, squinting. "Where?"

"I don't know, I still haven't met him. But I think his truck is that blue and silver pickup."

Pete glances over at the truck, and then says, "It could be his truck. I wouldn't know. I wouldn't know the guy if he drove that rig through my front door."

Dickie Pratt hits the first pitch into right field for a bloop single, and when the right fielder boots the ball in her attempt to scoop it up, Dickie races to second base.

The Tigers start to cheer, and some of the boys at the top of the order begin to realize that they may have a chance to bat this inning. "Get a bat, you're on triple deck!" Cliff Thorpman reminds Bobby Wohlford. "And I'm on double deck!"

I see Hilton Burberry across the diamond, talking with one of the Lincoln coaches. At one point he gestures toward the Lincoln shortstop, an excellent athlete and an excellent infielder. Already tonight he has handled perfectly five ground balls and a pop-up.

"All righty, Cindy, a walk's as good as a hit, a walk's as good as a hit!" Pete shouts at Cindy Fletcher, clapping his hands and encouraging the little girl.

"Anybody here you don't recognize?" I ask Pete.

He scratches the back of his neck. "Sure. Some of the crowd from Lincoln. I don't know all of them."

Over on our bench Lucky Diamond is sitting with Jesse Parker, sipping a paper cup full of Gatorade. He appears to be staring at the ball game, concentrating on the opposing pitcher, or perhaps on Dickie Pratt at second base. If he knows that his father is here, he is not now paying attention to him.

"Move in, move in!" the Lincoln coach yells at his team, waving his arms frantically at the outfielders. Word must have gotten around the league that Cindy Fletcher is not exactly a home run threat.

"I really would like to meet him," I tell Pete.

Pete nods, only half listening. "Wait for your pitch, Cindy, wait for your pitch!" he reminds the girl.

After throwing two pitches that were balls just off the outside corner, the Lincoln pitcher tries to sidearm one past Cindy. He doesn't succeed. The ball slams into the small of Cindy's back with a thud, and the child falls to the ground in tears. Hit batsman.

Pete and I race out to home plate simultaneously, and kneel beside her. From our side of the field, someone—I believe it is Bobby Wohlford—screams, "It's only a flesh wound!"

"I said to get a walk, not to get hit," Pete tells Cindy lightly, trying to smile.

"I didn't do it on purpose," she sniffles, leaning up on one arm and rubbing her lower back with the other.

"Did he hit you on your backbone?" I ask.

She shakes her head no, and sits all the way up. She is going to be fine. "He got me right here," she answers, rubbing a spot on her back that I believe is below her kidneys.

"Think you're going to live?" I continue.

She rolls her eyes, disgusted with me, and clicks her tongue against her teeth. This mannerism will serve her well in three or four years, when high school suitors have stupid suggestions for dates. "Of course I'm going to live."

"You feel up to staying in the game?"

"Yes! This might be my only chance to run the bases this year!"

Her candid analysis of her potential surprises me, and I lie to her automatically. "Nah, you'll be on base a ton this year. But if you want to stay in the game, go get 'em!"

She stands up and wipes some of the dirt from home plate off her uniform pants, and then runs to first base. The spectators in both sets of bleachers applaud for the child, and I think it is at Jesse Parker that she sneaks a small smile.

When I start back to our bench I look toward the spot where I had seen the blue and silver pickup truck parked, and my shoulders sag and my heart drops: the truck is gone, leaving behind an empty parking space between the Wohlfords' and the Parkers' station wagons.

Lucky Diamond comes to the plate in the bottom of the sixth with two out, and the tying runs on base. Dickie Pratt has scored, Cindy Fletcher has scored, even Melissa Edington has scored. We are within two runs, with Bobby Wohlford on third, and Carl Northrup on first.

"We're gonna win this right here. You know that, don't you? We're gonna win this one right here," Pete tells me. "Lucky's going to poke a screamer over the left fielder's head."

I nod, not wanting to get my hopes up for the boy. He has hit the ball well tonight, and has two solid doubles to show for it. Now, however, the Lincoln outfield is playing the boy so deep they might just as well be in the next county.

The first pitch to Lucky is bounced in the dirt for a ball, scooting past the catcher to the backstop, and Carl advances to second base.

"Little bingo, Lucky, little bingo!" Pete shouts, clapping his hands. "A single's worth two!"

The second ball looks low too, but Lucky surprises us all by swinging at it, stepping into the pitch, and tapping a slow roller toward the middle of the diamond. This looks to be the end of the inning, especially given the hands of the Lincoln shortstop. The boy glides almost effortlessly to his left, watching the grounder into his glove. He stands up, staring over at the first baseman, the ball securely in the webbing of his mitt, while Pete Cooder mumbles "darn it" faintly beside me.

The shortstop rears back to throw, and then, perhaps in his haste to end the inning, proceeds to heave the ball a good fifteen feet over the first baseman's head. Bobby Wohlford comes home, Carl Northrup comes home, and Lucky Diamond winds up on second base.

Although these two runs only tie the score at nine, I realize by the way the Lincoln pitcher slams his glove into the ground in anger that the game is as good as over, and we are about to win.

On second base Lucky Diamond looks over at me, and for one brief second raises his hands over his head, his fists clenched, and smiles.

It's a great smile.

I can't believe that his father didn't stay here to see it.

Chapter 21

"Twenty-two thousand dollars, eh," Mr. Godfrey says to Harper and me Sunday afternoon, repeating the cost of one year at Sedgebury College in disbelief.

The rain taps steadily on the roof over the Jensen House porch, as the last of the alumni leave the college for—in most cases—another five years. Some will return in the fall for homecoming, but not very many: the alumni who were with us this weekend are from the older classes, with the youngest bunch being the forty-six-year-olds back for their twenty-fifth reunion.

Some of these alumni will, of course, never return. I don't imagine many of the six fellows from the sixtieth reunion class will make it back for their sixty-fifth.

"It's amazing, isn't it, Mr. Godfrey?" Harper agrees, her eyes following a tree swallow as it dives under the Trillium porch across the street to escape the rain. "I don't know where parents get the money these days!"

Mr. Godfrey, who has been standing the whole time since he walked over to us to say hello, finally sits down for a change in one of the small Adirondack chairs on our porch. "What do you get for that twenty-two thousand dollars?"

I think for a moment, my arms crossed. "Well, you get room and board for about nine months. You get to use all of the college facilities whenever you want to. And you get access to eight classes. Four each semester."

"How many classes you got? You know, to choose from?"

I flip through the blue and yellow Sedgebury course catalog in my mind, trying to calculate how many courses are listed on a page, and how many pages there are in the book. After a moment, I tell Mr. Godfrey, "About one hundred and fifty. But that's a guess. There might be a few more, maybe a few less."

Mr. Godfrey rests his wooden cane across his thin and fragile legs, thinking. Finally he looks up at me, his eyes appearing just a little tired, just a little sad. "That's really not such a bad deal, when you think about it. They make me pay more than that to stay over there," he says, nodding across the street at Trillium. "And the closest thing we ever had to a class was the time Dr. Ravich showed us all how to push the new emergency call buttons by our beds."

"Well, Hilton, this is indeed a surprise," I tell Hilton Burberry Tuesday afternoon as I emerge from my office. Kim Swanson, Doug's and my secretary, is handing the fellow a cup of coffee, no doubt convinced he's a high-roller from the class of '36 who forgot something here this past weekend. He's wearing gray slacks and a summer-weight blue blazer, a uniform more common on Sedgebury alumni than sportswriters for the local newspaper.

"Family who used to live here was named Furman," Hilton tells me, sipping his coffee and glancing around the reception area. "This room we're standing in was the little girl's bedroom."

"I hadn't realized the house was so well-known."

"It's not. I wrote a story for the *Independent* eight or nine years ago, something like, 'The Great Homes of Sedgebury.' This was one of them."

"That's a far cry from sportswriting."

"Writing is writing. Up until I started getting tired a few years back, I used to write a good many feature pieces."

"You'll have to show me some. I'm sure I'd enjoy reading them."

"Oh, I wouldn't be so sure of that. Feel free to withhold judgment until you come across a couple."

I smile, surprised when he fails to smile back. "So what brings you by this afternoon?"

"I didn't know if you had heard about the accident yet. The one up near the notch."

"No, I hadn't heard about any accident," I tell him, shaking my head.

Hilton looks at the couch behind him. "Want to sit down?" he asks. "I think I do."

I nod, and together we sit. I reach for the coffee table and pull it closer to us, allowing him to put down his cup if he desires.

"What accident?" I ask again.

"I didn't think you could have heard yet. I don't think most people know about it. I only heard because Eunice and I were just down at the newspaper, dropping off a pair of my articles."

"Well?"

"Well, there was an accident this morning, about nine-thirty. A pair of loggers were loading up a skidder, by that straightaway just past the Goshen Trail. No one knows yet if the grapple was broken, or if they didn't hitch the logs up properly. That really doesn't matter right now. Anyway, something snapped, and the timber—a good three or four days' worth of cutting—went pouring off the skidder like a tidal wave. One of the loggers died immediately. His entire upper body was flattened by the logs, completely flattened."

If anyone other than Hilton Burberry were telling me this story, I would feel pain for the loggers and their families, and I would say I was sorry. But I would view it as an accident in some ways as removed from my life as a train wreck in India or an avalanche in France. If anyone other than Hilton Burberry were telling me this story, I would assume the accident would have no impact on my life, that it would have nothing to do with me.

Because it is Hilton Burberry with the news, however, and because he has come by my office to share the news with me, I am afraid the accident will concern me. I'm not immediately sure how, but I know that it will.

It will, I realize suddenly, the hair on the back of my neck bristling, have something to do with Lucky Diamond. Instinctively I become worried about the boy, afraid for him, his father, and—on another level—afraid for myself.

"You said there were a pair of loggers. What about the other one?" I ask.

Hilton sighs. "He disappeared."

"He disappeared? What do you mean he disappeared? Is he trapped under the logs, or the skidder, or something?"

"No, nothing like that. He ran away. For whatever the reasons, he took off. There's some feeling down at the state police that the accident may not have been an accident, but I don't think there's much to that. I think that's just the talk of a couple young bucks looking to make a name for themselves in a murder investigation."

"Who discovered the accident?"

"Some hikers. They said they heard the rumble and the crash a good mile away in the woods."

"Would I know the loggers? Either of them?"

"Nope. They were both real loners, real off-horses. Hardly any friends, hardly any family. Especially the fellow who died. A guy named Jeff Grout."

I shake my head. As Hilton had predicted, I don't know him. I've never even heard the name.

"Doesn't seem to have any family, at least none around here. Came to the area sometime in the winter, and lived for a while in one room above a bar in Bristol. No one in town is sure where he was living the last few weeks. Only people who ever talked to him were some of the people who worked in the bar and a few of the regulars."

"Young guy?"

"Yup. Maybe twenty-seven, twenty-eight years old."

"And the other one? The one who disappeared?"

"It doesn't seem likely you ever met him either. But you do know his boy. He's on your team."

"Lucky Diamond," I volunteer, nodding. "As soon as you told me there was a logging accident, I had a feeling Lucky's father was involved. A bad feeling."

Hilton puts his coffee cup down on the table and leans forward, his hands on his knees.

"Eunice is picking the boy up from the state police right now, and then she's going to swing by for me."

"He doesn't have a mother, you know," I tell Hilton. "At least, I don't think he does."

"Nope, it was just Lucky and his old man. Always had been. His mom died in childbirth."

I remove my glasses and close my eyes, massaging the bridge of my nose. "You know a lot about the boy, don't you?"

"Not really. A few facts I just got at the newspaper."

"Do you—do the police—think Lucky's father will return?"

"He'll return all right. The state police have already issued a bulletin on the fellow across New York and New England. I think the question is whether he'll return voluntarily, or whether it will take the authorities to bring him back."

"If you don't think murder was involved, why do you think Lucky's father ran away?"

"Panic, maybe. Maybe Lucky's old man was the one who hitched up the logs, and he feels responsible. I don't really know. Only thing I'm sure of is that I don't think there was a murder."

I nod, not sure whether I really do agree. "Well. I thank you for the news, Hilton, as bad as it is. I appreciate your sharing it with me." I start to stand, but Hilton remains anchored to the couch. Evidently, he has something more to say.

"I was wondering about something, Bill. You got one more minute for an old fellow?"

"I do for you. If you stop calling yourself old."

Hilton smiles just the tiniest bit. "Back in December, when you first came to me for a Little League team, you told me something. You told me you needed to coach real badly, to help you cope with the loss of your own son. Nathaniel."

"I remember."

"How is that going? The coaching. Is it working?"

I shrug. "On some level. I enjoy the kids, I enjoy being around the kids. But I don't think I ever expected that a Little League team alone would make the hurt go away completely."

"No, I wouldn't think so," Hilton says, pausing for a brief moment. He then takes a deep breath and continues, "What I'm about to suggest is a real wild card, a real long shot. And I'm only suggesting it because I was just down at the paper, and everyone there was buzzing about the accident, and the little boy all alone at the state police barracks."

"Yes?"

"Well, if I hadn't sent Eunice over to get the boy and bring him home with us, who knows how long he would have sat there? I imagine a social worker would have showed up eventually, and someone would have found a foster home to take the boy in for a couple of days or a couple of weeks."

"He doesn't have any family? Aunts or uncles or grandparents?"

"Evidently not a one. Someone asked the boy who they should phone for him, and he said there wasn't anybody. I meant it when I said it was just him and his old man. And now it looks like it will just be him."

"Unless his father returns."

"Even if the fellow returns, there's going to be a lot of hard questions for him to answer, and a lot of discussion about how fit the man is to raise the boy. And between you and me, I'm not sure the man is fit at all. I found out this morning that Lucky's not even enrolled in school this spring!"

I stretch out my legs before me, watching them disappear at the shins beneath the coffee table.

"So I think the best the boy can expect right now is to shuttle from one foster home to another for the next seven or eight years," Hilton continues.

"Oh, I don't know, Hilton. He's a pretty good kid. Why don't you think he would hit it off with one family, and stay there the whole time?"

Hilton shakes his head. "With his handicap? Come on, Bill, you know what I'm saying here. You know the system. There's not a chance in the world it will be just one family. A boy like Lucky is too much work for most people. I'd expect most families in the foster care program will take him for one year, maybe two. But that's all."

I pull my legs back from under the table, and lean forward on my knees. The crash position. The position in which I sat listening to Nathaniel's doctors and interns and specialists: attentive, alert, and prepared for the worst.

"So I was wondering, Bill," Hilton continues, drawing out the *L*s at the end of my name, "if maybe you and I could put our heads together and come up with a solution that's better for the boy than some state foster home."

I remain silent, aware of where Hilton is taking this conversation (it is no longer *our* conversation), and refusing to go there on my own. If Lucky were any other boy in Vermont, any other boy in the world, it would be different. If Harper didn't believe she was pregnant, it would be different. If there wasn't something about the boy that disturbed me, our cats, it would be different.

If Donnie Casey weren't ill, if I hadn't seen a rain-soaked bat fly from Mikey Harris's hands . . .

"Listen to me, Bill. Listen!" Hilton says, pounding his fist on my knee, "Don't you think you just might be able to make that ache of yours go away with another little boy? A boy who needs you just as much as you need him? Don't you?"

I return Hilton's gaze, surprised at how old his eyes seem to me right now. His voice had sounded so strong only a second earlier that I might have thought I was sitting beside a forty-five or fifty-year-old man.

"Why are you so interested in Lucky Diamond?"

"I'm no more interested in Lucky Diamond than I am in Roger Wheelock. Or Cindy Fletcher. I'm interested in—"

"You're interested in Lucky Diamond. Right now you're interested in Lucky Diamond," I tell Hilton, cutting him off with more vehemence than I had intended. "We're not talking about Roger Wheelock or Cindy Fletcher. We're talking about Lucky Diamond."

"And William Parrish! This is about you too."

"No, I don't think so."

"Well then, you're kidding yourself, son. You're just plain kidding yourself." He shakes his head sadly, disappointed in me.

"Hilton, why are you doing this?" I ask lightly, trying to smile. "Why are you putting me in this position?"

"I didn't think I was putting you in any position."

"You were."

His breathing tired, he says, "Will you think about it?"

"Yes. I'll think about it," I tell the commissioner. When I formulate the words in my mind they are meant as a lie to pacify the man; when I speak them, however, when I hear the sound of my voice, I tend to believe them myself.

"And you'll talk to Harper?"

"I'll talk to Harper."

"Would you do one more thing?"

"Perhaps," I answer cautiously.

"The boy thinks the world of you. I've seen him watch you at ball games, a couple practices. He just thinks you're the greatest. Would you come by our house tonight and say hello? Would you spend some time with him?"

There is no way I can refuse; there is no way I should want to refuse. I would have to be a ghoul to say no. "Sure. I'll be happy to," I tell Hilton, rising. "I'll stop by on my way home from work."

Hilton grasps the armrest of the couch, and pushes upon it to stand. "Well, I thank you for your time, Bill. I appreciate it."

"No, I appreciate your stopping by."

He takes my hand to shake it, and then says to me something I know I have heard once before. "Just remember," he says, "nothing in this world happens by accident. If you look deep enough, you'll find there's a reason for everything."

Chapter 22

Did you ever notice that the crew of the space shuttle *Challenger* typified our fourth-grade conceptions of a melting pot nation? It did. Blacks and whites and Orientals fell ten miles into the Atlantic Ocean with equal opportunity, women demonstrated they could fall from the sky as well as men. It was a multiracial, multigender catastrophe, and I think this is part of the reason why it made such terrific television, why it was such an endlessly watchable tragedy.

Harper doesn't agree. She thinks it was the teacher that made it all so stylish. Of course, as I used to remind her, she's biased.

Used to remind her.

We haven't discussed exploding space shuttles in well over a year.

Can there be anyone in the world more alone than Lucky Diamond?

I ask myself this question when Eunice opens the front door of her home and gestures toward the living room, where she says Lucky is watching *Jeopardy* on the color television set.

That's what she calls it. The color television set. It sounds to me as dated as if she had referred to the movies as moving pictures.

"Where's Hilton?" I ask. The house smells like baked potatoes.

"He'll be right back. He just had to go to the store for me to get some cocoa and butter. I'm making the boy brownies."

"How is Lucky doing?"

Before Eunice can answer, the boy emerges from the living room, with the faintest trace of a smile across his face. It is a smile that tells me he is glad to see me, a smile that says so more eloquently than words.

Sometimes I am surprised at how expressive the boy's face is, but there is really nothing surprising about it. Lucky has lived, I

have assumed, his entire life without speaking. His ability to tele-
graph his emotions with his eyes, his mouth, his shoulders, is a
survival mechanism of sorts, a means of adapting. It is one of the
many ways he has found to overcome just one of his many dis-
advantages.

"Come on in," Eunice says to me, and I meet the child before
the large picture window facing to the west.

I crouch slightly so that I am at eye level with him.

"So, champ," I begin unconvincingly, tapping my fingers on
my knee. "So . . . I heard there was an accident. And I thought
I'd drop by."

I squint as I look at him, because I am looking also into the sun
in the window behind him, beginning to set now over the
Adirondack Mountains across Lake Champlain. For a second he
meets my gaze, his eyes red from . . . red from crying.

The idea of Lucky Diamond crying surprises me, as it had
when I realized he had been crying after Dickie Pratt took his
glove. It just never crosses my mind that the boy might cry. But
of course he does. He is, after all, an eleven-year-old boy, and
boys his age still cry.

Especially right now.

What is it about Lucky Diamond? What is it that leads me to
see again and again in the boy things that cannot possibly be
there, why is it I am surprised whenever I see traces of normalcy
rise from the silence that surrounds him? Why do I find myself
fascinated—frightened, obsessed—by conspiracies that cannot
possibly exist?

Wes Pratt, suddenly and surprisingly promoted at work, tells
Hilton Burberry that he no longer has time to coach the Triple-A
Tigers. A new boy appears in town and joins my team, arriving in
time to play baseball . . . but not, in his father's eyes, to go to
school. That father, a man I have glimpsed only briefly and never
met, witnesses—perhaps causes—an accident and abruptly disappears off the face of the earth.

Is the point of it all, the point of this conspiracy, simply to
provide Harper and me with a boy who would have been Nathaniel's age right now? Is the point of this conspiracy merely to,
as Hilton said, replace the child we lost?

If that is indeed the object of some great and mysterious plan,
if there is indeed a reason for everything and giving to Harper

and me a child is the object in this case, then there are certainly more evil conspiracies in the universe, ones that should scare me far more.

"They think Donnie Casey might have pneumonia," Harper tells me over dinner, her voice tired, partly because of the news she is sharing, partly because of the hour of the day. It is already nine o'clock, and we are only now sitting down to eat.

I watch Harper push a snow pea around her plate with a chopstick. "What happened?"

"Patty Glover didn't know all the details. All she said was that it has something to do with the respirator. She said that it's actually fairly common to get pneumonia from a respirator."

"How are John and Susan doing?"

"I can't imagine they're doing very well," Harper says, no doubt reminded of her own feelings, her own depression, when Nathaniel's condition would deteriorate.

"No. I guess not."

"And I think what's probably most frustrating for them is that the hospital is putting the child through one test after another, when all they're really doing is treating the boy's symptoms. That's all they say they can do with viral myocarditis: treat the symptoms."

Elsa rubs up against the side of Harper's chair, reminding her that she is there. "Did word of the logging accident get around the school today?" I ask.

"No, I don't think so. I didn't hear about it until you called me this afternoon."

"Hilton told me more of the details when I was up at his place this evening. It just sounds grisly."

"You can spare me."

"But Lucky seems to be doing okay."

Harper reaches down and strokes the cat between her ears, eliciting a small purr. "I'm glad."

"Hilton doesn't think the boy's father will get to keep Lucky when he returns . . . or when he's brought back."

"That's probably in the child's best interest," Harper says, without looking up at me. "From all that you've told me, he doesn't sound like much of a father."

"No, I don't think he is." I pause before continuing, unsure exactly how I should raise the idea that Hilton has implanted inside me. Finally I begin: "Hilton had a bizarre idea today. Completely bizarre. Out of nowhere he asked me if we'd be interested in taking the—"

"Don't even ask it," Harper says quickly, her voice quivering with sadness. "Please, don't even ask it."

"You don't know what I was about to say," I tell her helplessly.

"I do. And you know I do."

Slowly and deliberately she captures a water chestnut between the wooden prongs in her hand. And then, instead of eating the vegetable she drops it back onto her plate and discards her chopsticks onto the dining room table. "I just can't believe what kind of day it has been," she says, a shudder in her voice, on the verge of tears herself. "I just can't believe how much . . . how much sadness there was."

Harper and I curl up together, making love on our sides in a ball. Her legs, her knees, wrap around my shoulders, and I press my thighs against the small of her back as we push against each other in slow motion. No thrusts, no pounding, no ramming.

She holds me with both of her arms as tight as she can, not so much hanging onto me as she is pressing us closer and closer together.

Sometimes we're not even moving, except for our mouths. I nibble at the skin on her shoulder and her neck, allowing myself a small moan each time I feel Harper's tongue in my ear, wet and warm and bathed in the sound of her breath.

Her bottom is damp with perspiration, soft and firm as a small throw pillow, and I cup each cheek with my hands, massaging them in rhythm with her hips, allowing my fingers to probe the crack between them.

"Too deep," she starts to murmur at one point, before changing her mind. "No, not at all . . ."

We keep our eyes shut tight, because even with the lights out and the shades drawn, our eyes become used to the dark and we are able to see.

Abruptly Harper reaches behind me and pulls the sheet up over our heads, protecting us for a few more moments from a world full of pain.

Chapter 23

Early Wednesday morning, while Harper is still asleep, I cut three daffodils from the small patch in our front yard, wrap their stems in a moist paper towel, and then drop them discreetly in the front seat of the jeep. I then return to the house to shower and shave, and prepare for work.

Just after six-thirty, Harper appears downstairs, her hair wild with sleep. She is wearing her red cotton bathrobe—her summer bathrobe—for the first time this year.

"You were up before the alarm," she says, yawning, and putting on water for tea.

"I was indeed," I agree, clicking my briefcase shut and placing it beside the front door so I won't forget it.

"Do you have a busy morning?"

"A little." I pull her close to me, holding her, and in a moment I am out the door and headed, in Harper's eyes, in the direction of the college.

Nathaniel is buried in a cemetery on the Havington-Lincoln line, in a plot very close to the woods.

It is, by New England standards, a fairly new cemetery, dating back only from 1872. A flu epidemic that year decimated Sedgebury County, especially the hill towns, and the Havington elders realized that a few more good-sized natural tragedies would fill up the existing cemetery by the turn of the century. And so they purchased some land belonging to a farmer named Dunlap, and built another cemetery.

Nathaniel is therefore buried in what is referred to by the locals as simply the "other," the county's term for the second cemetery. It is a term that when used by the locals expresses no value judgment, no condescension. The fact is, the vast majority of people who have died in Havington for the last seventy-five years lie now in the other.

Harper's and my families, however, have never been wild about the second cemetery's nickname, and so we are careful never to use the term around them.

Perhaps because there are no markers in the other dating back to the seventeenth and eighteenth centuries, the most interesting headstones may belong to young people who were buried there in the 1960s and 1970s, when individuals were evidently taking a fair amount of liberty with their epitaphs. Harper found one marker with a sports car carved into the solid Barre granite, and the poem,

> *Life went fast,*
> *Like this car,*
> *Because Derek passed*
> *On slippery tar.*

Derek lived to be eighteen.

Another grave has a peace sign in the stone and three simple words from an old Byrds song, "Turn, turn, turn." The woman, Shawna Patrice Bedulla, lived from 1951 to 1971.

And then there is the Bissette crypt, where David Bissette was buried in 1969. He died in Vietnam, and his family placed beside his marker his photograph, sealed in a special glass sepulcher. The picture they chose was his formal military portrait, and the boy looks in it a good five years younger than the twenty-three years claimed on the gravestone.

Nathaniel's marker is an arch-shaped slab of Vermont granite, light gray with small capillaries of black, that extends perhaps three feet above the ground. It sits facing south, deep woods of maple and birch and spruce beginning only ten yards behind it.

By the time I arrive there Wednesday morning, seven o'clock, the sun has risen high above Mount Ellen, and the dew in the grass has begun to dry. I place the daffodils at the base of the stone, and I tell Nathaniel that I know he never cared about flowers, but I like to bring them anyway. I do it for me, because it makes me happy, and I ask him to indulge me, to put up with his father.

The pollen count must be high today, and I find myself drying my eyes and blowing my nose.

I ask Nathaniel how he'd feel about a kid brother or sister, because there's a chance now that one's on the way, and I see him shrugging his shoulders in his green and white striped rugby shirt. He wouldn't mind. I think if it made Harper and me happy, it would make him happy.

I don't believe I ever met a child—I don't believe I ever met a person—as good-natured as Nathaniel.

I ask him what he thinks of Lucky Diamond, whether he would have been the boy's friend. I tell him that Lucky can't speak, and I am suddenly overwhelmed with the image of the two boys playing together on our living room floor with Nathaniel's plastic Food Fighters, my son handling all of the necessary sound effects for Burgerdier General and Private Pizza.

What, I continue, would you think if Lucky lived with us for a while? You wouldn't have to share a room with him, even after the baby arrives. You wouldn't have to hang around with him any more than you wanted to, you wouldn't have to look out for him every minute, you wouldn't have to let him have all of your toys. . . .

The tears begin to fall faster, and I no longer bother to wipe them away.

"Forgive me," I say to my son, aware for the first time of the sound of my voice, "for giving Lucky your baseball glove. I'm so sorry. It's just that he needed it so badly. . . ."

The *Burlington Free Press* has an article about the logging accident, a page one story in the second section. I read it as soon as I arrive at my office Wednesday morning.

HAVINGTON, VT—A Sedgebury County man was found dead yesterday morning, apparently the result of a logging accident on the Goshen Trail Road.

Jeff Grout, 27, was discovered shortly before 10 A.M. by two hikers near the Appalachian Trail, his body crushed underneath at least nine hundred pounds of timber.

Grout was pronounced dead on the scene by paramedics from Sedgebury County Hospital at 11:45. An autopsy is scheduled for this afternoon, but Dr. Richard Fullerton, deputy state medical examiner, said it is likely the cause of death was massive internal injuries.

According to State Police Officer Jamie Sturman, the first trooper to arrive at the scene, the accident may have been caused when a hinge collapsed on the skidder hauling the timber.

"It looked to me like one of the loading clamps failed," Sturman said, "but there will be an investigation. The company that makes the skidder is supposed to be in town tomorrow to examine the whole thing from front to back."

A skidder is a four-wheel-drive tractor with a special grapple for hauling logs over rough terrain. The particular model that Grout was using was built by the Hudson-Stockard Company of Portland, Oregon, sometime in the early 1980s.

The hikers, James and Melissa Cameron of Boston, Massachusetts, were visiting Vermont on vacation.

James Cameron said he believed that they were at least a half mile away from the accident when they heard the logs tumble off the skidder.

"It sounded a little like what I imagine an earthquake would sound like," Cameron said. "There was a lot of rumbling, and the ground really did feel like it was moving. But the sound came from the direction where we had seen this guy loading a bunch of logs, so we had a feeling that there was an accident."

Grout was logging on private land just off the Appalachian Trail, owned by Hilton Burberry of Havington.

He is survived by his mother and father, Eugene and Vanessa, and two sisters.

I toss the newspaper on my desk, dizzy with rage, managing only a feeble nod for Kim Swanson as she arrives at the office and calls hello through my door. No sooner have I come to believe that I understand why Lucky Diamond is here, no sooner have I come to believe that I know why things happen, than I discover that once again I have been deluded. Or, worse, deceived.

I no longer know the difference.

I know only now that I want once again to control my life, that I want once more to know I can believe what I see, and to know that all that I see is real.

I breathe deeply, trying to calm myself, and rub at the pain in my temples. I feel now as confused and frustrated as I have in my worst moments since Lucky Diamond came into my life, as filled with dread as the moment I saw my cats stalking a terry cloth wristband, or the moment I realized that Lucky had overheard me telling Pete Cooder that Harper might be pregnant.

I reach for the *Free Press* and read the article a second time, hoping that I have skipped one paragraph, perhaps misread another. Of course, I haven't.

There is no mention anywhere in the article of a second, missing logger named Diamond; there is no reference to any state police "bulletin" for the second fellow. The hiker in fact referred to "this guy," as if there was only one.

And for reasons that I can only imagine, when Hilton told me about the accident yesterday afternoon, he chose not to mention the fact that the accident occurred on his land.

Chapter 24

As soon as I have hung up the phone, having found once again that there is no answer at the Burberry house, Kim Swanson buzzes me on the intercom to tell me that Jamie Sturman is returning my call. It is already almost lunchtime.

I thank Kim, reach for the receiver, and punch the button that flashes like a yellow warning signal.

"Hi, Jamie. Thanks for calling me back."

" 'At's okay, coach. What can I do for ya?" he asks, his accent even thicker on the telephone than it is in person.

"I saw in the newspaper there was quite an accident up by the Goshen Trail yesterday. On Hilton Burberry's property."

There is a long pause at the other end of the line. Evidently, Jamie assumed that I had called to speak with him in his capacity as the chief of the Havington Volunteer Fire Company, not as an officer with the state police. I can imagine him now lighting a cigarette with his disposable lighter, deciding carefully what he should say.

Finally he clears his throat, and says, "Ayup, there was an accident all right."

"Could I ask you a question? As a friend?"

"Ya could. I can't promise I'll answer it."

"That's fair. It's really pretty harmless."

"Uh-huh."

"I hear you were the first trooper there."

"Jus' luck. I was up at the firehouse when it happened, so I was right close."

"Sounds like it was a real nasty incident."

I hear him exhale. He probably did light a cigarette. "I've seen worse."

"Really?"

"Ayup. Good thing is Jeff never saw it comin'. Never had more 'n a second to be scared."

"Was he all alone up there?"

" 'Sume so."

"He wasn't helping anyone, he didn't have anyone helping him?"

"Far as I know—far as we know—he was workin' solo. Don't believe there's any evidence he was workin' with anyone else yesterday mornin'. Don't think it even crossed anyone's mind down here he mighta had a partner. But we'll be sure to ask Hilton."

"Is it normal to log alone?"

"'Pends on what you're doin'. Sometimes Jeff worked with Huey Sanders. But ol' Huey's got hisself a good job working a backhoe for Goddette, and spends as little time as he can these days loggin'. So Jeff's been goin' it alone a lot lately.

"Loggin' can be a right nasty business," Jamie then adds, an afterthought.

"I guess so."

"Why you wonderin' whether Jeff was alone up there? You heard otherwise?"

I have thought about this question, and I am ready for it. I have decided that I am not prepared just yet to tell a state police officer what Hilton told me yesterday: I want to speak first with Hilton. Besides, it sounds now as if the state police will soon be talking to Hilton in any case. So I answer instead with another question: "I was actually wondering if I knew this particular James Cameron. The one who came across the accident. He wouldn't be from Boston, would he?"

Jamie's whole tone changes, brightens, becomes less suspicious. My call and my questions suddenly make sense to him, and now he wants to help me. "He would indeed."

"How old was he?"

"Thirty-seven, I think."

I throw out a guess. "Dark hair?"

"Brown."

"Sounds like the Jim Cameron I knew," I tell Jamie, lying. All I know about James Cameron is what I have read in this morning's newspaper.

"It's a small world."

"Think I could talk to him. Say hello?"

"He's more 'n a little upset, you know."

"I'll bet he is."

"So go slow with him."

"Where's he staying?"

"He and his wife—real pretty gal—checked into the Full Spruce. Just offa seventeen."

"Well, I just might give him a call. Say hello."

" 'At might be a nice thing to do for the fellow right now. A mighty nice thing indeed."

"Full Spruce," a female voice answers, no doubt the desk clerk.

"Jim Cameron, please."

"Cottage six. Hold on and I'll connect you."

The phone rings once, twice, three times. I'm about to hang up when a tired and exasperated voice picks up.

"Hello?"

"Hello, Mr. Cameron?"

The exasperation turns immediately to anger. "Look, I don't want to give any more interviews. I've had it, my wife has had it. We're about to check out and return to Boston, okay?"

Quickly I reassure the man, "I'm not a reporter. I'm not calling for an interview or a story or anything like that."

"Who is this?"

In the background a female voice asks Jim, "Who is it, honey?"

"My name is Bill Parrish. I live in Havington. I was a good friend of Jeff Grout's," I murmur, lying again.

Cameron sighs. "I'm sorry," he says sympathetically. "I'm sorry you lost a friend. And I'm sorry I just jumped all over you. It's just that we haven't had a moment of peace since the newspaper published our names this morning."

"A lot of people want the story?"

It sounds as if Cameron is covering the mouthpiece of his telephone with his hand, but I can still hear the muffled sound of the man explaining to his wife that it is "some friend of the logger" on the phone. He then removes his hand and answers my question, telling me, "Two Burlington television stations, two Vermont newspapers, and an outdoor magazine published in Montpelier."

"Well, I just wanted to ask you one question. And the answer's just for me, for my own curiosity. I promise you, I'm not writing an article."

"Go ahead."

"Was Jeff alone up there?"

"Was he alone up there?" Cameron says aloud, repeating my question. He sounds incredulous, astounded that this is the reason I have bothered him. "Yes," he responds firmly, "the man was alone up there. If there was someone with him, we never saw him. And neither did the police."

I pull into the driveway at close to five-thirty, less than ten minutes before practice is scheduled to begin. Harper is sitting on the front porch in shorts, her legs dangling over the edge. Judging by the red and blue Magic Markers beside her, she is grading her students' homework or exams.

I kiss her on the forehead as I race past her and into the house, telling her that I am running late, and tonight of all nights I must be on time. Pete Cooder has a league softball game, so Russ Wohlford—Bobby's dad—is planning to help me.

Harper stands up and stretches, and follows me inside and upstairs to our bedroom.

"How was work?" she asks. "Did you ever track down Hilton?"

"Nope," I answer, ignoring for the moment her first question. "I tried him all day, and never got an answer."

"I didn't think so. I ran into him about four o'clock at the Grand Union. He was shopping with Eunice and Lucky."

I stand still, only one leg in my pants. "Did he say where he had been all day?"

"He did. He—they, the three of them were together all day— spent all morning at the Department of Human Services up in Burlington, and most of the afternoon with some child welfare people. The three of them looked kind of cute together. Even Lucky. A boy and his grandparents."

"Did you tell Hilton I was trying to reach him?"

"Of course. He said he would call you at your office as soon as he got home."

"He didn't."

"He probably missed you. He probably just missed you. By the time he got home, you were probably out the door yourself."

I look at my watch, frustrated and angry that I don't have the time to call him right now. I finish pulling on my jeans, and reach deep into the closet for my sneakers. "I'll have to call him when I get back."

"Or he'll call you. He said if he missed you this afternoon, he'd call you tonight or tomorrow."

"Did you tell him why I wanted to speak to him?"

"Sort of. I hinted that it was about the accident. But I had to be discreet, because Lucky was there. Oh, that reminds me: Eunice said Lucky won't be at practice tonight. One of the child welfare people—a psychiatrist, I think—told the Burberrys that Lucky should have a quiet night tonight. Just take it easy and watch television."

I remember that my clipboard is downstairs in my briefcase, and make a mental note to grab it on my way out the door.

"I made a doctor's appointment," Harper continues, hopping onto the edge of the bed, smiling.

"Oh?"

"Uh-huh. I couldn't wait anymore. I bought a test kit yesterday, an e.p.t., and I tested myself this morning."

The fact that Harper has made a doctor's appointment, the fact that she is sitting on the side of our bed and smiling, tells me the answer. Hilton and Little League and Bobby Wohlford's dad no longer seem very important, and together we start to laugh. I wrap my arms around her and then push her down onto the bed, falling gently on top of her and kissing her on her lips and cheeks and nose.

"Do you feel maternal?" I ask.

"I feel very maternal," she answers. "I feel about as maternal as you can get."

"I love you," I tell her joyfully, my voice soft with love, rich in thanks. "I love you so much."

"I love you too," she says, whispering. "I love you too."

"Four more, four more!" Russ Wohlford is screaming, his voice slightly hoarse, when I arrive at practice.

The children are lined up along the third base line, preparing to run as fast as they can to the equipment bag perhaps sixty yards away in deep center field.

"Go, go, go, go, go, go!" the substitute coach suddenly yells, clapping his hands, and starting the children off on another dash.

"Wind sprints, Russ? Don't you think that's a little excessive?" I am fairly confident that the children are too far away to hear me, but I ask the question softly nonetheless.

"These kids—Bobby too—just don't have any wind. They don't have any wind at all. We're becoming a nation of couch potatoes," Wohlford says, indicting me for my role, before returning his attention to the outfield. "Look sharp, team, we got three to go! Line up and look sharp! Now go, now go, now go, now go!"

The line stampedes toward us, thirteen children pounding the ground with their Nikes and Reeboks and Converse and Keds. Some of the boys pull ahead, athletes such as Bobby Wohlford and Jesse Parker, while slower kids like Joey Fenton and Mark Lamphere agonize behind them, their faces contorted by exhaustion and cramps.

"Don't ever be late for practice again, Mr. Parrish, please," Roger Wheelock mumbles, standing beside me for a brief moment while he catches his breath.

"You're not telling me that a couple of wind sprints have done you in, are you, Roger?" I ask the boy, trying to smile.

"A couple? Yeah, right."

"In line, in line, in line," Wohlford bellows. "You got ten down, you got two to go. Ready . . . set . . . now go, go, go, go, go, go!"

"You have to anticipate the play," I tell the infielders, focusing on my second base platoon of Melissa Edington and Cindy Fletcher. "You have to know exactly what you're going to do with the ball if it's hit to you, before the ball is pitched. *Before.* That's what I mean by anticipation."

Spending time with the infielders tonight is a rebellion of sorts, an attempt to undermine Russ Wohlford. Or at least contain and minimize the damage he can cause. As soon as Wohlford had finished putting the kids through boot camp, I clapped my hands exactly as he had been clapping his, and brought the team together around me. I asked all of the infielders, including our pitchers and catcher, to gather with me by home plate, while I asked the outfielders to work with Mr. Wohlford in right field. As a result, I have ten kids with me, while Russ only has three with him.

"For example, Cindy: suppose there are runners on first and third, and only one out. We're winning by two runs, and a ground ball is hit to you. What will you do with the ball?"

"Kick it into left field!" Dickie Pratt shouts, smirking, answering for the child.

"Beat it to death," Carl Northrup adds.

Cindy starts to stick her tongue out at Dickie, but stops herself: she is at the age where such a response would only elicit more abuse, and abuse of a far more suggestive and threatening nature. Instead she simply glares at the boy, before answering, "I'd toss the ball to second base."

"Exactly right. Now suppose we were only winning by one run?"

She looks down at her sneakers, thinking. This is a hard decision for a little girl, a hard choice. "I guess it would depend on how hard the ball was hit," she says finally.

The Pratt boy groans loudly, shaking his head in disgust. "I hope I'm never pitching when you're playing second base."

"I hope so too," she shoots back.

"Okay, we're going to play this game for real," I tell the team. "Go to your positions, and take turns. I'm going to tell you where the runners are and what the score is, and I'll want all of you to think about what you should do with the ball. Remember, anticipate. Got it?"

A few of the kids nod, but most simply race for their positions around the diamond.

I turn toward the backstop, surprised to see Harper sitting on the grass beside it. She smiles and gives me one small, unobtrusive wave.

Behind me I hear Roger Wheelock telling his mother that he hasn't had to run so much in one day since soccer practice in the fall, and that as a result, tonight "practice sucked." Mrs. Wheelock squeals her son's name, and slams the car door shut as she chastises him for his choice of words.

I put my arm around Harper's shoulder as we walk past the firehouse, the sun now well below the Adirondack Mountains.

"I like it when you come by practice," I tell her.

"You don't get self-conscious?"

"About how I coach Little League?"

"Uh-huh."

"Maybe a little."

"I thought so." She reaches into her pants pockets and removes her keys to the jeep. "Are you in the mood for a Creemee?"

"Is the ice cream stand still open?"

"Till nine o'clock now."

"Well, sure. I can always be talked into a Creemee."

"I'll drive. Want to bring Lucky?"

Abruptly my legs feel as brittle as balsa, and I stop walking so that I can look at Harper. Reflexively my arm falls away from her shoulder as I stare into her eyes, trying to read her thoughts.

"What?" she asks, her voice light but nervous. "You look like you think I've lost my mind."

The Lampheres drive past us over the bridge and wave, followed closely by Mrs. Wheelock. Each car is filled with three or four Little Leaguers.

"I'm surprised. I thought you told me the child was supposed to have a quiet evening in front of the television set tonight."

She sighs, curling her lower lip. "I don't think there's a child psychiatrist in the world who would object to a soft ice cream cone."

"No, I guess not. It's just . . ."

Her eyes linger on me, then on something above and behind me. In my head I know that something is a tree branch in the twilight, the rising moon, or perhaps a plume from a silent jet plane; in my heart, however, I am convinced that the something she sees is something more devious, something in the darkening sky that is there just for her. "It's just what?"

"We'll have to drive all the way up to the Burberrys' farm to get him, you know."

"I know." She taps her fists lightly on my chest, drumming her hands there for a long moment. "Lighten up, you," she tells me, smiling. "All I said is we should take the kid with us for an ice cream cone. I didn't say I wanted to adopt him, for God's sake."

Chapter 25

I lie in bed awake that night, my heart pounding the way it does when I have drunk too much coffee too late at night. It is without question odd that Hilton was gone when we stopped by his place to pick up Lucky Diamond for a Creemee, but it certainly was not unpredictable. Of course he was gone: it made confronting him tonight impossible.

And the fact he was watching two adult softball teams go at it in Sedgebury for a newspaper story made all the sense in the world, because it meant that he still wasn't home when we brought Lucky back almost an hour later, his mouth covered with peanut butter ice cream and chocolate sauce.

I roll over and curl up against Harper, pressing my face as close to her back as I can without waking her. I can recall a thousand images of Harper kissing Nathaniel, I can recall her kissing his forehead alone a hundred different ways. She kissed our son with joy, she kissed him with concern; she kissed him to check for fever, she kissed him with lips filled with forgiveness.

And she kissed him the way she kissed Lucky Diamond tonight, a simple see-you-later kiss filled with maternal wistfulness, a good-bye kiss smack on top of his head, her eyes averted because she was going to miss the child more than she thought was fair.

Finally, Thursday morning, I track down Hilton Burberry. I call him at his home a little past eight o'clock, as soon as I arrive at my office.

"We need to talk," I tell him, making no attempt to hide the anger that has crept into my voice.

"I think we do," he agrees, surprising me. I had anticipated a variety of answers from Hilton Burberry, ranging from defensiveness to feigned innocence, with whatever response he chose cloaked in histrionics. What I had not expected was agreement, an answer that was simple and honest.

"Well. Shall I begin?"

"Nope. Are you free for lunch?"

"You don't believe we can discuss this over the phone?"

"Oh, I believe we could. But I'd prefer not to."

"Okay. I can make myself free for lunch."

"I appreciate that. You have any idea where you'd like to go?"

"How about the Maple Tree?"

"The Maple Tree will be fine."

"Noon? Will noon work for you?"

"Son," Hilton says, taking a breath so deep it sounds as loud as his words, "at my age, most any time works."

The Maple Tree sits across the street from the Sedgebury Inn, in a restored village house with fish scale woodwork and two cupolas. The house was probably built about the same time as Harper's and my house in Havington, just before the turn of the century.

When I arrive, Hilton is seated at one of the tables in the room that I imagine was once the parlor, concentrating upon the menu as if it were a novel. He has placed his straw hat on the corner of the table and draped his blue and white cord sports jacket over a third chair.

"Good afternoon, Hilton," I say formally, as Debroah, one of the two owners and the hostess today, hands me a menu and seats me across from the older man.

He looks up at me over his eyeglasses, and then rolls his eyes toward Deborah. "I want you to know, Deborah, I'm going to order this special shrimp and strawberry soup today because I trust you. But it better taste a whole lot better than it sounds."

The owner smiles at him. "Have we ever let you down, Mr. Burberry?"

"Can't say that you have."

"It's a wonderful soup. Richard invented it himself," she adds, referring to her husband and partner and chef.

I order a glass of wine to be polite (it really doesn't matter to me right now what I eat or drink), while Hilton asks for a glass of ice tea.

"I hope you didn't have to juggle too much of your schedule to meet me for lunch," Hilton says, dropping the menu back onto the table.

"I would have juggled hand grenades to get here today."

He shakes his head. "I suppose you would have at that."

There is a tape of Vivaldi playing somewhere behind us, music that I believe is from the *Four Seasons*. I watch Hilton as he begins to slice a piece of bread from the small, freshly baked loaf on the cutting board between us. His hands move gingerly, and he slides the serrated-edged knife back and forth in agonizingly slow motion.

"Eunice and I probably love the bread here most of all," he tells me. "Honey oat, you know. If you give a damn about cholesterol—and at my age, you probably should, but I don't—oats are supposed to be a good food for you."

I nod, uninterested. "I didn't come here to talk about bread or cholesterol. You know that."

"I do." He tears the slice of bread he has cut from the loaf, ripping the crust along the bottom like paper. "You came here because I'm slowing down, because I'm not as sharp as I used to be."

"I came here because you lied to me."

"Same thing."

A young woman appears at our table in a white blouse and dark skirt, the Maple Tree uniform of sorts, bringing with her my wine and Hilton's ice tea. She introduces herself and describes to us the specials in detail, although the moment she is gone I can recall neither her name nor a single entrée she mentioned.

"Why did you tell me that Lucky Diamond's father was with Jeff Grout when he died?"

He chews a piece of bread without butter. "You're an odd one, Bill, you know that?"

"You're not answering my question."

"It wasn't the question I expected," he says, swallowing his cherished honey oat bread. "I was sure you would ask me why I *didn't* tell Jamie Sturman or any of his buddies from the police barracks the day of the accident that Lucky's old man *was* there."

I sit back in my chair, trying to concentrate. Hilton Burberry may talk of being old, his mind and memory as porous as those of the Trillium residents, but it's all an act. His mind is as sharp as

when he negotiated the baseball contracts of major league baseball players or dealt with the unions for forty-plus years at
Fenway Park.

"No. You lied to me the other day, Hilton. Lucky's dad wasn't
there. Jeff was all alone. I spoke to James Cameron, one of the
hikers who reported the accident, and he said Grout was all
alone."

"You also spoke to Jamie Sturman," Hilton says, his eyes
glancing randomly at the three other tables in this part of the
restaurant. "As a result, I had to spend a good hour with the state
police yesterday afternoon. In their offices."

"You're not answering my question. When you came by the
college the other day, the state police hadn't connected the accident to the Diamonds. There was no 'bulletin' on Lucky's father,
and Lucky wasn't sitting around the police barracks, twiddling
his thumbs."

Hilton stretches across the table for his coat, still hanging on
the empty chair beside us, and reaches inside it for a handker-
chief. "You're right," he says simply, after blowing his nose.
"Lucky wasn't there."

"Want to tell me where he was?"

"No place mysterious, Bill. He was home. That's where. He
was home. Eunice and I went up and got him at his old man's
trailer."

"And his father? Where was he? Because he sure hadn't been
with Jeff Grout."

Hilton stares at me, trying desperately to look sincere, straight,
honest. "You have every right to doubt me. But on this one
point, you have to believe that I'm telling you the truth: when
Jeff Grout died, Lucky Diamond's old man disappeared. That's a
fact, a bit of history that will not change."

I keep my voice even. "A fact? Then why did you hide this
'fact' from the police on Tuesday?"

"I hadn't figured out yet what to do with the boy."

"I don't believe you," I tell Hilton, sighing and shaking my
head.

"Why, because it's so stupid? It is, indeed. As soon as I told
you the truth Tuesday afternoon, I should have told Jamie. You'll
be happy to know, I have now."

"No, I don't believe Lucky's father was ever there."

The waitress returns to take our orders, and I confess that I have not even opened the menu. She smiles, tells me there is a lot to choose from, and agrees to return in another few minutes.

"Son, I've told a good many . . . expedient exaggerations in my day. I've told a lot of white lies and a lot of big lies. But what I just told you is the truth. You can either accept it or not, there's nothing I can do about that."

I fold my arms across my chest. "Hilton, the guy who reported the accident said Grout was alone!"

"Perhaps the fellow was wrong."

"How can you think that? Because it was your land?"

Hilton runs a finger along the brim of his hat, circling the small red and blue band around the straw. "I wish the newspaper hadn't mentioned that. The only time I like to see my name in a newspaper story is when I write it."

"How do you know that Lucky's father was working with Jeff Grout?" I ask again.

"Well, let me see. I could tell you that it was because I was the one who hired him. I could tell you that he was working for me. But I'd wager those answers wouldn't be good enough for you."

"You're right, they wouldn't. Just because you hired him doesn't mean Lucky's father was there Tuesday morning."

"You're absolutely right, Bill. Unfortunately, that's the best I can do for you."

"Is that it?" I ask, raising my voice for the first time. "You're just going to keep lying to me? You're just going to keep saying he was there?"

"He was there!" Hilton insists, hitting the table hard enough with his fist that other diners turn to stare. "I'll swear it to you, I'll swear it on any life or Bible or icon you goddamn want!"

"But you won't tell me how you know that, how you can be so sure?"

"No," Hilton says, lowering his voice. "There are just some things in life you have to accept on faith, Bill, and this is one of them. I know what I know, and you have to trust me. But I will swear to you, I will swear it to you any way that you want: when Jeff Grout died Tuesday morning, Lucky Diamond's old man disappeared."

* * *

Hilton will swear, Hilton will plead, Hilton will promise. Hilton also will hint. In the word games that matter to an attorney like Hilton, the semantics that are in some way his life, somewhere he has hidden the truth. It crosses my mind that Jeff Grout was Lucky's father: the newspaper said that the man was only twenty-seven years old when he died, which was about the age of the man that I glimpsed one night in that trailer. But could Lucky's father really be that young? It is of course possible . . . but it doesn't seem likely.

No, the truth lies in Hilton's use of the term "old man." He has never said to me exactly that Lucky's father was at the accident, choosing to use instead the expression, "Lucky's old man." It is a choice of words that is either extremely vague or extremely precise. In either case, however, it is a choice of words that I am sure Hilton made carefully.

Chapter 26

"I asked Eunice if she knows why Lucky can't speak," Harper tells me over dinner Thursday evening.

"Was this yesterday at the Grand Union?"

"Oh, no. This was this afternoon. I ran into her in the kitchen at the town hall, when I was dropping off the ice cream I promised for the strawberry supper Saturday night."

"What did she say."

"The poor child was born without a larynx. He just has no vocal cords. Isn't that awful?"

I push a thin stalk of asparagus around on my plate. "It is."

"She also said that the boy's mother died when he was born. He has never, not for one day in his life, had any kind of maternal influence. Not for a single day!"

I nod. "I think Hilton told me that."

"Well, I had an idea. Your game this Saturday is in the morning, right?"

"Uh-huh."

"Let's go to Lake George in the afternoon. To that huge amusement park you can see from the expressway. You know, Volcano Park. We'll take Lucky, and the three of us will spend the afternoon there."

"Was this your idea or Eunice's?"

Harper looks at me, perplexed, holding her empty fork in midair. "What does that mean?"

"I was just wondering whether Eunice gave you the idea to take Lucky to Volcano Park. After all, it had never crossed either of our minds to take Nathaniel there."

"It had crossed my mind."

"Oh. I didn't know that."

"Are you angry with me?" she asks, her voice a combination of confusion and hurt.

"No." But I am filled with anger, an indefinable rage that wells up from the belief, true or untrue, that things are happening around me that are out of my control. That I am being used, that my wife is being used, that the strings of our hearts are being pulled because someone knows that those hearts were broken the March before last.

"Good. Because it was my idea."

I squeeze my fork in my hand, unable to shake the fury inside me, and then press it hard against the place mat before me.

"Sure. Let's take the boy with us. That's a fine idea," I agree, but without much conviction.

Harper looks down at my hand, and then up at me, her eyes wide with worry.

"You scare me when you get like this," she says. "I'm afraid you're going to give yourself a stroke or something."

I let go of the fork and sit back in my chair.

"I'll be fine," I insist, sighing, as together we stare at the way that I bent my dinner fork into a *U*.

I want desperately to believe that things happen for a reason.

I want desperately to believe with the faith of Pete Cooder that life is a series of rational causes and effects, of purpose and fore-sight and planning.

I want to believe that the strings that pull me—that pull us all —are guided by hands that are loving, by a mind that is good.

And I want to believe those hands are not Hilton Burberry's.

Mark Lamphere stands in left field Saturday morning, a warm and magnificent day in June, crossing and recrossing his legs. Occasionally, I see him hopping up and down, jumping in one place.

Meanwhile, Jesse Parker continues to labor through a very long inning on the pitching mound. He has already walked two batters, struck out one, and thrown at least a half dozen pitches to the little boy now at the plate. It is possible he has thrown twenty-five pitches this inning without a single fair ball resulting.

Working from the stretch, he looks in at Roger Wheelock, catching, and gets his signal. He glances once over at the runner on first base, and then rears back before exploding toward home plate.

The ball sails high and outside, well beyond Roger's reach, and both runners advance, giving Sedgebury men on second and third with only one out.

Pete Cooder shouts to Jesse that he doesn't have to give in, there's room on the bases. He then turns to me, and motions with his head toward Mark Lamphere in left field.

"See that?" he asks me. "See what Mark's doing?"

"Uh-huh."

He smiles. "Looks to me like someone's got to go to the bathroom big time."

The boy wraps his right leg so tightly around his left that his legs look like rope. He is standing essentially on one leg, looking very much like an ostrich with a baseball glove.

"Count is full, three balls and two strikes," the umpire bellows for the benefit of the pitcher and batter.

Jesse again pitches from the stretch, although it is unlikely that the little boy on third will attempt to steal home on anything other than a passed ball or a wild pitch. The Sedgebury batter swings at Jesse's next offering, getting just a small piece of the ball and fouling it into the backstop behind him.

"Look sharp, you guys, look sharp," Pete yells at the infield, trying to keep them alert, or—at the very least—awake. "Let's hear a little chatter out there!"

Mark Lamphere folds his arms across his chest, and shakes his head in disgust at the foul ball. Another pitch, and he's no closer to the end of the inning and his chance to race into the woods for relief.

"No batter, Jesse, this guy stinks!" Dickie Pratt shouts at our pitcher, his attempt at moral support.

Jesse stares in again at Roger, shakes his head in agreement with the catcher's suggested pitch, and then throws a big lollipop curveball. The batter swings well above the ball, missing it by a good two feet, and strikes out.

"You gotta love that kid," Pete says approvingly. "It's not every eleven-year-old who'll throw a curveball on three-and-two."

I can almost feel our left fielder breathing a sigh of relief when Roger shouts at the team, "Two outs! We got two outs! Play's at first base!" For the first time in a dozen pitches, he actually stands still on two legs in the outfield.

The next Sedgebury hitter bats left-handed, and I glance down at the score book in my hands to see where he hit the ball his first time up. As I had suspected, he hit it the opposite way, to the left side: a line drive in the gap between Mark in left and Lucky in center, that rolled for a two-base hit.

"Cliff, Mark," I yell at our shortstop and left fielder, "on your toes! Ball's probably coming your way!"

Sure enough, Jesse's first pitch is an outside fastball that the batter slams into left field, a sinking line drive down the third base line. Mark Lamphere takes off for the ball the moment it leaves the bat, racing as fast as his legs and his bladder will allow him. Across from us the Sedgebury crowd stands and cheers, anticipating that two more runs are about to cross the plate.

Mark digs across the dry outfield grass, however, his legs churning like baby pistons, and then throws his body at the falling liner, diving with his glove outstretched before him. His body slams hard into the ground, bounces and slides, and the ball is swallowed up by his mitt.

It is an astonishing catch, especially given the fact that Mark isn't the sort of boy who makes astonishing (or even expected) plays. There is a brief moment of silence when the cheers migrate from the Sedgebury side of the diamond to the Havington bleachers, and then behind us the parents stand and whistle and clap.

Mark lies on the ground in the outfield for an extra couple of seconds, and for a moment I fear he has hurt himself, injured himself with his dive. Pete Cooder and I share a glance, concerned. Slowly, however, the Lamphere boy gets to his feet, and both Pete and I notice that the front of his pants are soaking wet —as wet as if he had just dove on his belly into a puddle.

But of course there was no puddle in left field, not on a hot sunny day like today. Together Pete and I clap for the boy as he races in, races past us, and then—in a stroke of little boy genius— tells his teammates that he's never been so hot and sweaty in his entire life. We watch as he proceeds to pull the top off the water cooler, hoists the cooler over his head, and then douses himself from head to crotch to foot in the wet stuff. He empties literally half the cooler on his uniform, and the wet spot across the front of his pants disappears in a flood from above.

It is a very impressive solution, indeed. I doubt now that even a trained dog would notice the price Mark Lamphere paid for perhaps the best catch of our season.

No one in the bleachers appears to think anything of the fact that a green state police car has appeared in the parking lot by the firehouse, and a state trooper has sauntered up toward the bleachers.

The car, after all, was driven by Jamie Sturman, and it is a safe bet that everyone at the game simply assumes that Jamie is there as a fan of the Havington Triple-A Tigers.

I know otherwise. At least I believe otherwise.

"Couldn't find anyone from Jersey to take a ticket, eh Jamie?" Pete Cooder yells at the officer, smiling.

Sturman smiles back, and walks slowly up into the stands, surprising me by sitting beside Harper. I watch from the corner of my eye as the officer and my wife appear to exchange pleasantries, but there is no doubt in my mind that Sturman is here on business.

On the field, Bobby Wohlford takes his lead from first base, preparing to steal second. In Little League, stealing second base is almost a given, especially for a speedy kid like Bobby. Bobby represents the tie-breaking run, the run that would give us the lead going into the last inning.

The Sedgebury pitcher throws Carl Northrup a change-up of sorts, a slow pitch, and Carl flails wildly at it, missing it by far. Meanwhile Bobby Wohlford races for second base, and goes into the bag standing up when the Sedgebury catcher doesn't even venture a throw.

I turn toward the bleachers, noticing that Harper is grinning at something Jamie has said. When she sees me watching, she waves. She then motions toward Bobby Wohlford at second base, and gives me a thumbs-up signal with her right hand.

"Okay," Pete asks, initiating a quick round of our game of hypothetical baseball management, "What if . . . We now have the go-ahead run on second with nobody out. Does Carl bunt him to third, or does he try and hit behind him, maybe drive him in?"

"No question: Carl hits away. We have our number four and five hitters coming up. This could be a big inning."

Pete nods in agreement. "Okay, then. We're all set."

Carl takes the next pitch, a ball outside.

In the on-deck circle Lucky Diamond is swinging two bats in slow motion, letting the bats glide back and forth in small arcs. Occasionally he looks up into the stands, and it crosses my mind that he is staring at my wife and Jamie Sturman, watching them with interest.

"You can do it, Carl, a single puts us ahead!" Pete yells at our batter. "Little single's a big hit right now!"

Carl swings at the Sedgebury pitcher's next offering, tapping a weak grounder to shortstop. Bobby has to remain at second base, while Carl is thrown out at first.

"That's okay, Carl, that's only one," Pete screams across the diamond, before whispering to me, "Guess we should have bunted."

Behind me I see Jamie Sturman nodding his head in agreement with something Harper is saying. At least that's what it looks like. The man takes off his teardrop sunglasses and rubs the bridge of his nose. I realize by the gesture that it might not be that Harper has said something he agrees with, so much as she might have said something that didn't surprise him.

Lucky Diamond drops one of the two bats he was swinging, and walks into the batter's box, windmilling his remaining bat in anticipation.

"Come on, Lucky!" I hear Harper cry behind me. It is perhaps the first time I have ever heard her yell anything at a baseball game. She is not normally a boisterous or vocal fan; in fact, with Nathaniel she tried to be as unobtrusive as possible.

The pitcher comes to a full stop in the stretch position, and then throws Lucky a fastball inside. Lucky ignores it for ball one.

"Good eye!" Harper yells behind me.

The second pitch is a thirty-five-foot curveball, a classic Little League wild pitch that bounces ten feet in front of the plate and skids to the backstop. The pitch is ball two, and Bobby goes into third base standing up.

"Think the kid will groove one down the middle?" Pete asks me, wondering if the Sedgebury pitcher will now make the mistake of trying to get a quick strike on Lucky.

"Good chance."

And we're correct. With Bobby Wohlford on third base, the pitcher goes into a full windup, and throws his next pitch right over the center of the plate. I cannot see Lucky's eyes from where I am standing, but I imagine them big as coffee cup saucers when he sees this batting practice lob approaching. He waits, steps into the pitch, swings, and then pounds the ball perhaps two hundred seventy-five feet into the high grass in left field for what will undoubtedly be the game-winning home run.

It goes without saying in Little League that it is as important to be a team of good winners as it is to be a team of good losers. After our victory, I push the team across the diamond to greet the Sedgebury team, and thank them for a good game.

No sooner have the high-fives and handshakes begun than I am joined near our bench by my wife and Jamie Sturman.

I give Harper a small squeeze around her shoulders, the sort of public display of affection that is almost (but not quite) acceptable in small hill towns in Vermont. I then shake Jamie's hand, smiling.

"Nice game," Sturman says. "Congratulations."

"Wish I could say I had a whole lot to do with it."

"Your boys haven't lost yet, have they?"

"Boys *and girls.* You can't forget Melissa Edington and Cindy Fletcher. But you're right, so far we haven't lost a single game. The Havington Tigers are off to a three-and-oh start."

"'At's not shabby. 'At's not shabby at all."

"Nope."

"You enjoyin' the coachin'?"

Before I can respond, Harper rolls her eyes and grins, telling the officer and local fire chief, "He loves it. I don't think he's had this much fun since he was a Little Leaguer himself."

"'At's good. You oughta like what you do."

Harper turns to me and asks, "Did you talk to Lucky about Volcano Park?"

"No, I didn't have an opportunity."

"That's okay," she says. "I'll go ask him right now, before someone drives him up to the Burberrys'." She then looks at Jamie and adds, "I'll see you later. Give my best to Gayle."

He nods, and reassures her he will.

"So, did you enjoy the game?" I ask the officer.

"Ayup. That Lucky Diamond has a killer swing. It's a killer, all right."

"His home run was the longest shot this year. By far."

"It mighta been the longest shot this decade."

"He's a talented kid."

"Ayup. 'Course, I really came by this morning to talk about his dad."

"Business, eh?"

"'At's right." He smiles. "I'm here as Officer Sturman—not Chief Sturman or jus' plain Jamie."

I try to ignore the small wave of tension rippling across my stomach, and open the fists I have made at my sides. I have done nothing wrong, I have nothing to hide. There is no reason why the presence of Officer Sturman should upset me, no reason at all. "I figured. Little League is a lousy spectator sport if you don't have a child playing."

"Oh, I don't know about that. I had a nice time this morning."

I nod.

"I was wonderin'," the officer continues after a brief moment, "what you thought about Lucky's father."

Behind me I hear Dickie Pratt and Bobby Wohlford trying to chant something at the Sedgebury team, but unable to recite a line before their voices are lost in hysterics. The cheer has something to do with beanballs and farts.

"What I thought about Lucky's father?" I say, repeating the question reflexively while I gather my thoughts. "Well, it disturbs me that he never comes to practice, and I've never seen him at a game. I saw his truck at the field once, but I don't think I saw him. And I wish he hadn't kept Lucky out of school this spring, but I guess I'm a little biased in that direction. Harper's a teacher, you know."

"I know."

"But I should also tell you, Jamie, any opinions I have about Mr. Diamond are less than worthless. I've never met the man. I've never even spoken to him on the telephone."

Jamie reaches for a cigarette in the breast pocket of his shirt and lights it with his small disposable lighter. "'At's what your wife said. She said she didn't think you had ever met the fellow."

"That's right."

"'Cept once. She said there was one time when you mighta met him. Couple weeks ago, Lucky had dinner at your house, and you drove the boy home. It's possible, she said, you spoke to him then. Or at least saw him. She didn't think you had, but she said I might as well ask."

I shake my head. "No, I never spoke to him. I barely even saw him that night. I saw someone in the trailer where Lucky lives, but I didn't really get a good look at the man."

He inhales deeply the smoke from the cigarette, holding it for a long moment inside him. So few people smoke anymore, watching someone who does is almost fascinating. "It's mighty strange," he says finally, exhaling. "I did some nosin' around yesterday, and the state did some nosin' around yesterday. We talked to Lucky, we talked to social service people, we talked to school boards. And it's not what we found that's so peculiar . . . it's what we didn't find."

"And that was?"

Jamie reaches into his other breast pocket, the one without his cigarettes, and removes a folded sheet of yellow paper covered with names and dates and phone numbers. He flattens the paper as he says, "Lucky Diamond was born a little over eleven years ago, in April. He was born in Massachusetts, in Boston General Hospital. His mother was somebody named S. McCormick, and she died in childbirth."

Some of the children start to approach us, so Jamie whispers, "Walk with me up the first base line a bit."

I nod, and together we walk slowly toward right field. "Go on," I insist.

"S. McCormick was a minor. She may have been a runaway. The Boston police are doin' some serious checkin', but it looks like that's what she was, all right. A runaway."

"She wasn't married?"

Jamie shakes his head, and allows himself a small, derisive laugh. "Married? She was fifteen years old!"

"Did she say who the father was?"

"Nope. Maybe if she'd lived she woulda said something some-day, but she didn't, so there's no record—at least none we've found—of who the boy's daddy is. Or was."

"What happened to Lucky? Did he go to an orphanage? Was he adopted?"

"Nope, he never went to no orphanage," Jamie answers, glancing down briefly at the yellow paper in his hand. "Two days after he was born, a fellow came forward named Diamond and adopted him."

"Well, there must be plenty of paperwork on him. Adoption is a complicated legal process."

"You'd think so, wouldn't you?"

"I would."

"Well, most of that paperwork seems to have disappeared. The adoption services in Boston, the hospital, and the welfare people are diggin' through every old box and floppy disc they got, hopin' to find somethin'."

"What do you mean, it disappeared?"

Jamie stops walking and tosses his cigarette onto the ground. With the toe of his shoe he grinds it into the dirt, ensuring that it is out, and then reaches over for the butt. "Exactly that: the paperwork—if it ever existed—on the Diamond adoption has fallen off the face of the earth." I watch him as he places the remains of his cigarette in his pants pocket.

"In that case, how does anyone know that the boy was adopted by someone named Diamond?"

"Well, we don't know for sure. 'Cept a doctor in the delivery room and a woman with the state adoption services remember the little boy with no vocal cords. Separately, they both recalled the kid was taken home by some guy named Diamond."

"They must have pretty good memories. Eleven years is a long time to remember that kind of detail."

"Most times, yup. But they both remembered the fellow's name was Diamond because they were big baseball fans. Red Sox fans. And it seems this Diamond fellow said he worked for the Red Sox."

I pause, watching Pete Cooder and two of the boys toss our team bats and balls into our canvas bag. "What did he say he did for them?"

"Nothin' real exciting. And there's a conflict in their stories here anyway. The doctor thought Diamond had said he was an usher at Fenway during the season, but worked for a ski resort during the winter. The woman from the adoption group was positive the man did somethin' more impressive than that, some-thin' like public relations. She said he wore a suit. Right now we got the Red Sox checkin' all their personnel records, to try and find for us a guy named Diamond."

"How old was he?"

"Somewhere in his thirties. One said early thirties, one said late thirties. All they agreed on for sure was the guy's name. Diamond. And that was because they thought it was a real neat coincidence that a guy named Diamond worked for a baseball team."

"Is it possible that Diamond was Lucky's natural father?"

"Sure, it's possible."

Behind us, car doors in the firehouse parking lot are slamming shut and engines are starting. "We should start back. I shouldn't keep Harper waiting too long," I tell Jamie. "But I have to ask: why are you telling me this? Why do I need to know this?"

Slowly Jamie and I start walking back through the outfield. "Oh, I guess there are a couple reasons. I was hopin' you'd met the man. So far, I haven't found a soul who has. And I guess I thought of you 'cause you called me on Wednesday. Whether you meant to or not, you were the first person to make me think we better be pushin' around what happened up on the Goshen Trail a little more carefully."

Ahead of us, Lucky is standing with Harper, waving at me as I approach. They are both grinning from ear to ear.

"Have you spoken to Hilton Burberry?" I ask Jamie. "He knew Diamond, I'm sure of it."

"Twice now. I'm goin' up to his place again this afternoon."

"Does he know why you're coming?"

"'Sume so. You think tellin' him was a mistake?"

"Of course not," I tell Jamie quickly, lying.

"Yup. I'm gonna see Hilton in about thirty minutes. You probably don't know this, but he's a double-good person to talk to."

"Oh?"

Jamie nods enthusiastically. "See, he mighta known Diamond if the guy really was loggin' his land. But he also mighta known Diamond from when the fellow was workin' for the Red Sox. See, Hilton used to work for the Red Sox too."

"That's what I gather."

"Yup. It's possible they knew each other years ago."

"That's a good possibility, all right," I agree. And then, just before I am greeted by my wife and Lucky Diamond, just before I am close enough that either of them could hear our conversation, I add, "Assuming Hilton did know this fellow, you might also ask him why a baseball usher or public relations man decided to become a logger."

Chapter 27

I will never know for sure what Nathaniel thought most about dying. I will never know if his emotions were as simple as fear, as primal as terror. I do know there was a lot of that, I do know for a fact he was frightened of death; but what I will never know is whether he was cognizant of the injustice of his premature death, if he was aware of just how unfair it was. I will never know if he thought about missed opportunities, of all of the things he would never do.

I sat often by the side of his bed—his own bed in his own room, as well as a variety of beds in the pediatric wings and intensive care wards in hospitals in two states—and tried, sometimes desperately, to understand how a child his age viewed the increasingly short time before him, what he thought of the huge unknown he was facing. I tried to find the words that could make it explicable, tolerable, acceptable.

Once, on the insistence of one of the doctors at the Medical Center, we had a long talk about eternity and "the long run" with a child psychiatrist; another time, with the local minister beside us, we talked about heaven. Nathaniel tried to be stoic through these chats, he tried to be helpful and listen, but it was too much to ask of the boy; both conversations ended abruptly when Nathaniel exploded into sobs—wordless, inarticulate sobs that wracked his thin, frail body, but in their force and frustration were eloquent.

Harper rolls the tremendous swab of pink cotton candy against her tongue, and then wipes a tiny piece off her lip with her finger, smiling.

She is wearing green hiking shorts and a blue polo shirt, and her sunglasses are back on her head like a hairband. She looks to me as lovely today as she has on any day I have known her.

Behind her the line forms for the Volcano Park roller coaster, a little boy with the baseball cap of the Havington Triple-A Tigers working his way patiently to the front.

"You really don't think I should ride it?" she asks, tugging playfully at the sleeve of my shirt. "You really don't think it's safe?"

Because I know that she isn't serious, because I know that there isn't a chance in the world she would actually ride a roller coaster with our new baby growing inside her, I pretend to shrug nonchalantly. "Oh, why not?" I answer, "These things are safe," at which point she playfully bounces her cotton candy off my nose, and tells me she will next suggest skydiving.

Lucky and I each wave to Harper, still savoring her cotton candy on the ground, once we are seated on the roller coaster. Like most of Volcano Park, the theme of the roller coaster is dinosaurs, and there are small dinosaur decals along the inside of the seats and along the safety bar before us. Over our shoulder is the "volcano" that gives the park its name, a one-hundred-foot-high plastic model of a mountain that—the television commercials insist—explodes every night at ten-thirty, just before closing, and spews forth rivers of molten fire into the moat that surrounds it.

It is a spectacle that is, I am told, far more interesting than fireworks, and far more terrifying for small children.

From where we sit, Lucky and I can see in the distance real mountains, whole mountains of evergreen trees, with the interstate highway the only sign of civilization outside of the walls of Volcano Park. These are the Adirondacks.

I watch as the mute boy beside me removes his pad and his pen from his back pocket, and holds them securely in his lap. I keep expecting him to write me something before we start, to share with me some thought or observation. But he sits happily still, resting his chin on the safety bar, and grins.

Does he wonder where his father has gone, does he wonder why his father has left? He must. I doubt a minute goes by when he doesn't think about his father, perhaps wonder where the man is at that moment.

"You ever ridden one of these things before?" I ask him, the question driven in part by simple curiosity, in part by the mysteries that surround Lucky Diamond.

He nods his head that he has, and then turns his attention to the man who will start the ride, a tremendously heavyset but muscular fellow wearing the black and silver tee shirt of a heavy metal rock band I have never heard of. Lucky is staring at the tattoos on the man's forearms, a Freudian nightmare of mermaids and snakes.

"Where? In an amusement park in Boston?" I continue.

He turns to me, surprised that I know where he's from. It is as if I have just told him he need only open his mouth to speak. He gathers himself quickly, however, and nods his head yes.

"Did you like living in Boston?"

He flips open his pad to the first blank page, and answers,

It was ok.

"Did you live in the city itself?"

He nods that he did. One side of me wants desperately to resist asking the next question, but I can't, not after I have begun.

"I'll bet you lived near the ballpark. I'll bet you lived near Fenway."

He doesn't look at me as I make this statement, concentrating instead on the pad in his lap. He writes quickly, and then tilts the pad in my direction so I do not have to crane my neck to read it. I see instantly that he has ignored my supposition that he lived near the baseball stadium.

I like it here more than the city.
I like living in the woods alot.

I decide to repeat my question, this time with more authority. "So, tell me: did you live near Fenway Park?"

I follow his eyes to see what he's watching, and I follow them down to the man below us who will start the roller coaster. He is standing now behind a small metal podium of sorts, with a series of levers across its top. He spits the cigarette in his mouth onto the dirt beside him, and wipes his mouth on the black sleeve of his tee shirt.

All at once he yanks the largest lever toward him, and our car starts to inch forward, quickly gaining speed and momentum as we rumble down a long flat, straightaway—the runway of sorts.

I look around one last time for Harper, wanting to wave to her once more, but she has disappeared into the crowd of parents herding their children into the line before—and I notice the sign with the name of this ride on it for the first time—the Lava Coaster.

Holding his pad and pen tight against his chest with one hand, Lucky chews at the fingernails on his other.

We start our ascent up through a thin, tight, tunnel, the sky a blue dot impossibly far in the distance, while a sound system pipes in what are supposed to be the cries and bellows of the dinosaurs. Some are angry, some are scared, some are remarkably similar to the sounds of an elephant.

Imitating my father—imitating every father who feels compelled to tell a child the obvious for no discernible reason—I tell Lucky, "Here we go!" as we approach the top of the tunnel and prepare to fall over the other side.

For one breathtaking second we hover at the top of the roller coaster, higher even than the amusement park's infamous volcano, and I try to steal a glimpse at the lava-making machines inside the crater; before my eyes can focus, however, we stop teetering on the precipice, and freefall forward.

Instinctively, almost everyone on the ride begins to scream, especially the children. Every child but the one beside me, that is. His mouth is shut tight, although his eyes are wide and his free hand—the one free from the responsibility of protecting his pad and his pen—is now grasping the safety bar for what I presume is dear life.

I smile at the boy in sympathy, wondering what a mute thinks when everyone around him is yelling at the top of his lungs. I follow his eyes again, following them this time to the right of the ride below us, and, astonishingly, to the man in the heavy metal tee shirt, talking now with my wife.

My stomach turns for reasons that have little to do with our sudden descent. I want to know why Harper is standing beside a man with cowboy boots and a mermaid tattoo, I want to know why she is laughing, smiling, why it looks as if any moment she will offer him a bite of the cotton candy she has been eating.

I try to focus on the pair, but the Lava Coaster turns hard to the left, pulling us away from them, and races up another small mountain of track.

Beside me Lucky smiles, removing his hand from the safety bar, and sits back in his seat with confidence.

We start what I pray is our final descent, the Lava Coaster's last downhill slalom. I pray this not because I am frightened of the ride: I have become oblivious of the ride's dives and swerves, to the way it pretends to bring us all to the brink of catastrophe, and then safely back. I pray the ride is over because I want to find Harper and learn why she was talking with the operator. I want to know why she was smiling. I want to know what was so funny.

I have tried on the ride to convince myself that my emotions are jealousy, pure and simple. In my mid thirties, I have told myself, I have become a small-minded and jealous idiot.

But I know this isn't the case. I know Harper too well to think for one moment that she would be interested in an amusement park barker, a tattooed motorcycle geek.

No, my desperation for the ride to end is triggered by a vague but profound sense of danger, an unceasing fear for my wife. Something is going on, I know it; I know it with the same authority and passion that I knew I would find something behind a stone wall one Thursday afternoon up on the French Highway. I know it with the same gut-wrenching conviction that I knew a rain-soaked bat would fly from a little boy's hands at Dickie Pratt's skull.

I am scared to death for Harper, and I have to find her.

As the Lava Coaster careens down the final stretch of track, I scan the park as best I can, searching for a beautiful woman in green hiking shorts and a blue polo shirt, a woman wearing her sunglasses back on her head like a hairband. Unable to find her, my eyes keep gravitating back to the heavy fellow operating the ride, standing alone now by his podium, concentrating on slowing the roller coaster cars to a halt.

When we stop, the two teenage girls in the car behind us are the first off the machine, one screaming that the ride was radical, the other mumbling that she thinks she might puke.

"Let's go find Harper," I hear myself telling Lucky, pulling the safety bar up and over our heads.

There is tension in my voice, impatience that the boy detects. He looks at me and tries to smile, and writes quickly,

That was great! Thanks!

"No problem," I murmur, stepping up onto the boardwalk beside the tracks, aware for the first time of just how many people are crammed right now into Volcano Park. "Harper said she would meet us at that concession stand opposite the ride. The one with the dinosaur puppets."

As we circle back around the dozens of people in line for the Lava Coaster, I take a series of long, deep breaths, trying to calm myself. For all I know, I imagined the whole scene, I made the whole thing up; for all I know, Harper never said one word to the Lava Coaster operator, it was someone else that I saw. For all I know, this is one more false alarm, one more delusion, one more case of William Parrish scaring himself in his sleep. . . .

As soon as we arrive at the concession stand, as soon as we are underneath the yellow awning with the red volcano, I can see that Harper isn't here. I peer quickly inside to make sure, but the room is empty except for two small boys and an old man with a beer belly behind the counter.

"She's not here," I say more to myself than to Lucky. "Let's see if she's waiting for us by the roller coaster." I put my hand on Lucky's shoulder and guide him with me out of the small, musty concession stand, and start back toward the metal podium and the man with the tee shirt that looks downright violent.

"Any chance you saw a woman—a blond woman—with a blue shirt and green shorts?" I ask the fellow running the Lava Coaster. Despite the waves in my stomach and the throbbing at the front of my head, I am unable to take my eyes off the man's tattoo, and the two snakes that are sucking at a mermaid's breasts.

His head darts back and forth between the cars racing along the distant tracks above us, and the dials and levers on the machine before him. It is as if we are invisible, and he never looks up at us. This only makes the pain in my head worse, the fear for my wife more pronounced.

"Excuse me," I continue, speaking a little louder now, "I'm looking for someone, and I think you might have seen her!"

The rock and roll band on his tee shirt, a group with the surprisingly benign name of Bongo Bonne Bouche, evidently consists of a half dozen men with long silver hair and inordinate amounts of sharp jewelry. The operator looks at me briefly, sizing me up, and then asks in a voice dry from smoking, "You got a badge?"

"No. I'm not a police officer."

His eyes are bloodshot, the veins in them a graphic relief map of rivers and roads and state borders. With enough sleep and a case of Visine, they might someday revert to a blue that is probably not all that different from Lucky's.

"When the ride stops, ask me what you want," he says after a moment. "I shouldn't take my eyes off the cars till they're back on the ground."

Around us, around me and Lucky and the man with the mermaid, swirls the amusement park, images of extinct reptiles adorning everything from a miniature golf course to the rows of games along the midway. Graphic artists have taken grotesque liberties with the creatures, allowing a stegosaurus to rear up on its hind legs to do battle with tyrannosaurus rex; the triceratops, a pudgy vegetarian with a unicorn's horn on its nose and a pair above its eyes, is depicted on one tent canvas with the carcass of a deer or gazelle dangling from its teeth.

"I just want to know if you've seen a blond woman in a blue shirt!" I ask again, ignoring his request to wait another few minutes. I want to know where my wife is, and I'm not sure I am capable of waiting.

He scratches a small cut near the mermaid on his arm, and looks at me with a combination of condescension and disgust, while over his shoulder the Lava Coaster races past, the upraised and outstretched arms of the people upon it the cilia of a giant paramecium flying by at the speed of sound.

"Yeah!" he finally answers, shouting over the roar of the roller coaster. "I did see some blond babe. She was lookin' for dinosaur books."

"What did you tell her?"

"I told her to try a library," he says, smirking. He then turns away from me, looking up at the Lava Coaster's last car, and then down at one of the dials before him. Behind me I hear a midway barker screaming for small children to come inside his tent and see the bones of a brontosaurus, the only brontosaurus bones in Lake George (bones now covered with graffiti—the hearts and arrows of teenage lovers, their names scrawled in paint across spinal cord discs).

Anger and panic colliding within me, I reach for Lucky Diamond's shoulder, preparing to return with the boy to the concession stand where we were to meet Harper. When I look down, I see that he has written me a note.

Lets try the gifts shop. They got books there.

He holds the pad like a billboard, almost shaking with urgency.

"We were just there, Lucky," I remind him, but the boy is insistent, shaking his head that I'm wrong.

He pulls back his pad and scribbles,

**We were at the toy store!
The gifts shop is at the entrence!**

As I read and digest the words before me, Lucky points with his free hand toward the parking lot in the distance and the gate to Volcano Park. For a brief moment I am torn: one side of me is convinced that because Lucky has suggested the gift shop, the gift shop is indeed where she will be; that part of me that has felt besieged by conspiracies, however, surrounded by plots and plans and programs, worries that this suggestion is a ruse, an attempt to steer me away from my wife.

I suddenly have a vision of Hilton and Eunice Burberry riding the Volcano Park merry-go-round of dinosaurs, a knowing smile on Hilton's wrinkled face as he waves maniacally at me from the carousel's blue and yellow and fire red allosaurus.

I look down at Lucky. "Let's take a look," I agree, and together we start to jog through an amusement park full of dinosaurs.

From somewhere above us there is a large clap of fake thunder, a part of one of the Volcano Park rides we have not yet found.

We are perhaps thirty yards from the gift shop when I see Harper, and my entire body tingles with relief. She is fine, she is reading the plaque at the base of a twenty-foot-high metal model of a pterodactyl, while above her the Volcano Park Earthquaker shakes and twists and turns screaming children upside down. Her hands are behind her in the back pockets of her shorts, and the only part of her body that is moving is her head, bobbing back and forth as she skims the knee-level panel of information.

I yell hello and she looks up, smiling. Lucky, with the strength and energy of a child, continues to run toward her, while I slow to a walk.

I watch as she removes her hands from her pockets and waves at me, as she pulls her sunglasses up off her eyes and onto her head, using them once again as a hair band. Her engagement ring, perhaps her wedding band, sparkles in the high afternoon sun.

She starts toward me, a woman as lovely as any I will ever know, when abruptly she can sense what is happening above her, just as I can see it happening, unfolding, with my own eyes.

For us both there is a split second of disbelief, a moment when we—certainly when I—cannot believe that the sort of accident found only in tabloid newspapers is about to happen to us, to her, a moment when in our separate heads and hearts we pray that it's a nightmare, that it's not real.

But it's not a nightmare, not now, it's no delusion or dream or illusion. It's real, it's as real as the thousand-pound piece of tri-colored metal that has just flown from the tip of the Volcano Park Earthquaker, flown up and away with the centrifugal force of a rocket blast, a Mesozoic missile shaped like a boulder and trans-mogrified by carnival paints into a mammoth Peter Max projectile of death.

I scream my wife's name, a cry of love and panic and despair, a cry that cuts across the park and silences all other voices, while Harper stands frozen, unable to accept or fathom or understand that this is indeed how she will die, as much a statue as the flying reptile behind her, and almost as close to extinction.

As the metal debris is about to fall to earth and crush her, a ground-level blur cuts into her waist, driving her sideways with what might be the speed and force of a charging rhinoceros. The blur, a blur of a white tee shirt and blue jeans, drives Harper yards away and into the dirt, while the Earthquaker's prehistoric rubble crashes into the ground right beside them.

Around the pair there is screaming, the cries of an amusement park that has just witnessed a thousand-pound hunk of metal fall from the sky, missing—perhaps by inches, perhaps by less—a smallish blond woman who depends on her sunglasses to keep her hair from her eyes.

In a pile beside the piece of debris, a piece of metal as big as a compact car, lie my wife and Lucky Diamond, both of them shaking their heads in relief and astonishment, both of them crying like small children.

Chapter 28

Summers are slow when one works for a college. There is time for long lunches, there is no reason not to sleep late. In another few weeks, when June turns to July, Doug Bascomb, Kim Swanson, and I will even implement our annual summer schedule, in which two of us stay home every Friday, and one person remains in the office to put up a good front and answer the infrequent phone calls.

Today, the Monday after Harper nearly became as extinct as the graffiti-covered dinosaurs of Volcano Park, I sit at my desk at Sedgebury College, and stare at the names of the little boys and girls on my Little League team.

I stare most at the name L. Diamond.

But I read also names such as D. Pratt, J. Parker, and C. Thorpman—names of little boys who once played inside my house. They raced up and down our stairs, they dug up our yard, they sat at our kitchen table drinking Kool-Aid. They did everything that eight-, nine-, and ten-year-old boys do.

Once, Cliff Thorpman almost killed himself at our house, diving out a second story window. Evidently, he was a turtle with the powers of a superhero. For a variety of reasons, however, the powers of evil had stripped him of his unique talents, and he had become cornered in Nathaniel's bedroom: a turtle bereft of his shell, his adversaries only yards away, pounding up the stairs to his bunker.

His only hope of escape was to jump, and hope that Nathaniel and Jesse and Dickie wouldn't jump after him. And so he did. He jumped out of Nathaniel's window, landing squarely among the wild roses growing along that part of the house. He broke no bones, he needed no stitches; but Harper went through one and one-half bottles of Bactene, dousing and cleaning the myriad of cuts and scrapes all over the little boy's body.

Harper does not know the details, but she called me a few minutes ago to tell me that sometime this morning, sometime just before breakfast, little Donnie Casey woke up.

I wave to Lucky Diamond as my jeep rolls to a stop at the end of the Burberry driveway late Monday afternoon. He is standing in the front yard, aimlessly throwing a baseball high into the air, and then catching it.

"You do this a lot?" I ask him, smiling as I raise an eyebrow.

He shrugs his shoulders self-consciously. Inadvertently, I have embarrassed the boy.

"Well, you keep doing it," I say quickly. "I knew there was a secret to the way you catch everything. I just didn't know what it was." And then, so he understands that I am here to see Hilton, I continue, "Is Mr. Burberry around?"

He nods that he is, and so I knock on the metal of the screen door, and holler softly inside, "Hello?"

Alone, Hilton and I stroll down the hill in his backyard toward the woods. Ahead of us is a small clearing, the start of a trail or walking path, and beside that a gazebo.

"I built that," Hilton says to me, pointing at the gazebo, "over the course of two weeks. My son and one of my grandsons were visiting Eunice and me, and it seemed like a productive way for us to pass the time. That was probably eight or nine years ago. And you know what?"

"What?"

"I don't think I've sat in the son of a bitch three times since."

We walk up the steps into the gazebo, and then collapse into two of the three Adirondack chairs in its center. We are surrounded by the cries of the peepers and the crickets.

"Thank you for seeing me," I begin, surprised at how obsequious my words sound.

"Glad to," he says, reaching over to fix a cuff on his pants. When he looks up he continues, "I ever tell you why I worked for the Red Sox?"

"No. But I assume it's because you love baseball."

"Oh, I guess that's part of it. I do love baseball, you know."

"I know."

"I love the confrontations, the one-on-one confrontations. That's what baseball really is: a hundred head-to-head, one-on-one confrontations. Independent battles that demand from a man that he use his brain as well as his body. And those battles just keep coming. Pitcher versus batter. Catcher versus base runner. The right fielder's arm versus the legs of the man on third base. Every game, there must be a hundred of them. See, I never bought that sentimental crap that baseball is a team sport. It's just not true. Baseball is all about egotistical sons of bitches squaring off in man-to-man battles.

"Sometimes, a .220 hitter would tell me or Tom Yawkey that he wanted more money because he had 'sacrificed' himself for the good of the team seventeen times. I'd tell him, fellow, you'll get more money, but not because you 'gave yourself up.' I'd give him a raise because he'd won a one-on-one battle with the pitcher seventeen more times than his average indicated.

"That's what makes baseball different from every other sport. Football, basketball, hockey—they'll never replace baseball. No real 'team' sport could. There wouldn't be enough of the one-on-one, two bastards in a ring fighting that makes baseball special."

Perhaps fifty yards in the distance, Lucky is helping Eunice set the table on the back porch for dinner.

"I don't know, Hilton. Pete Cooder and I have spent a fair amount of time this year using Little League to teach children teamwork. We've worked pretty hard to build a team spirit."

"Little League baseball isn't real baseball. I know you understand that."

I nod.

"If he's any good, a ten-year-old who's taught about teamwork will outgrow the notion. He'll figure out it's more productive to win."

"If winning is so important to you, why did you stay with the Red Sox? In all the years you worked for them, they didn't win a single World Series."

He smiles wistfully. "But we were always so damn close. And if you added up the hundreds of one-on-one battles that occur in every single game, I'd bet—no, I know, I know it for sure—you'd see the Sox won most of them. Ted Williams sure as hell did. So did men like Luis Tiant and Dom DiMaggio. Bobby Doerr. Carl

Yastrzemski. Every year, after every disappointment, I'd tell myself that next year—next year—would have to be our year."

"It never came."

His look becomes stern. "It hasn't come yet."

I stretch my legs, chastised. For a long, quiet moment we sit together in silence, while he waits for the inquiries that he knows are coming. Finally I begin.

"I spoke with Jamie Sturman on Saturday."

"So I gather. He came here too. Matter of fact, he came here Saturday and today."

"Today?"

"'Bout three o'clock. He had some more information."

"I'm curious, Hilton: did you tell him who Lucky's father is?"

"Nope."

"Did you tell him who S. McCormick was?"

"He already knew a bit. He knew she was a runaway. He knew she was a kid. One of the delivery room doctors remembered the emergency surgery that saved Lucky's life." He pauses for a minute before continuing. Then: "Congenital atresia of the larynx. Born without a larynx. That's what Lucky's problem was. If the doctor doesn't perform a tracheotomy within seconds, the baby will die."

"Why couldn't they save Lucky's mother?"

"It was a fairly unpleasant delivery all around. She lost a lot of blood, and died right there in the delivery room."

"Did you know her? S. McCormick?"

"Susie? Not really. But I know she loved the Red Sox. Or maybe she just loved ball players. But she was just a child, and I don't think she had any idea what she was getting herself into," Hilton says, before falling silent.

When it feels as if he may never speak again, I ask, "Will you tell me about that? What she was getting herself into?"

He pushes his tongue into his cheek distractedly, thinking. Remembering something, perhaps, remembering an evening, a night, a moment.

"I doubt it. I don't think it's any of your business."

"If it's about Lucky, it is."

"Now why is that?" There is a sudden edge to Hilton's voice, a hint of anger.

"Because Harper and I are thinking strongly of filing papers to take foster care of the boy. And, if his father really has deserted him, to adopt him." The words sound strange on my lips, but I am glad I have said them. It makes the idea real, it makes it something I can wrap my arms around and use to help fill the breaks in my heart.

"So you changed your mind, did you?"

"Yes, as a matter of fact, I did."

"Well, for all we know," he tells me disgustedly, "by now it's too late. This is becoming, so to speak, a federal case."

"Is that what Jamie told you today? That the federal authorities are involved?"

"That's part of it." He runs a finger over one of the boards on the gazebo's low side walls, perhaps trying to calm himself by examining how well the wood has survived this last decade. He then looks up at me. "It seems the Boston Red Sox have never had a person on their payroll named Diamond. Imagine that. At least that's what Jamie said. Not an usher, not someone in public relations. No one. Evidently, the memories of the doctor and the social worker who thought Lucky had been adopted by a man who worked for the Red Sox were faulty."

"Or the man was lying."

From the porch, Eunice cries across the yard, "William, should we set a spot for you at the table? We're going to eat outside tonight."

"No, I'll only be another few minutes. But thank you!"

I watch her smile graciously, before I turn back toward her husband. He is placing both hands on the sides of the Adirondack chair, and pushing himself to his feet. Standing, he says, "Come with me," and starts slowly out of the gazebo, walking up toward the barn by the house.

"You're not answering my questions!" I tell him quickly, insistently. We can't be through, not yet.

He rubs the temples around his eyes, and then closes them. "On the contrary. I'm about to."

The grass has already become wet with evening dew, as together we stroll in silence up the small hill. I can see that Lucky is staring at us from the porch, a pile of silverware in his hands, and that he wants to join us. For whatever the reasons, however, he knows that he shouldn't, and stays planted on the porch by the house.

When we reach the barn, an immaculate red clapboard structure that might have been pulled whole from the pages of *Vermont Life* magazine, Hilton pauses for a second to catch his breath. He then turns to me and says, "A person can make a lot of mistakes in one lifetime. Especially the kind of person who plays baseball. Professional baseball. Don't you let anybody ever tell you that the kids who play the game professionally today are any worse than the kids who played it professionally twenty or thirty years ago. They're not. So don't you listen when some sports reporter starts running off at the mouth about how corrupt the kids are today, or how spoiled they are. They're no worse today than they were forty years ago. Trust me, I know. Nowadays, the players just get into more expensive kinds of trouble, and the press thinks it's big news."

"And you don't?"

"Baseball players drink too much, they beat their wives. They gamble. They snort cocaine, they ignore their children. They're normal, rotten Joes, just like the rest of us. I don't see the news in any of that."

A thought crosses my mind about Hilton. "Is this about a mistake you once made, Hilton?"

He meets my gaze. "I made my share of mistakes, son. But I spent a lot more time cleaning up after other people's. Baseball players are a careless bunch when they're not playing baseball."

His breathing is hard and labored, and his chest rises and falls underneath his plaid cotton shirt. He reaches for the latch on the barn door, and begins to pull it open, walking away from me as he swings the door free.

Inside I see the Burberrys' red station wagon, and then, as my eyes adjust to the dark of the barn and I am able to scan its contents, I see parked beside it the blue and silver four-by-four pickup that belonged once to a logger named Diamond.

"That's Lucky's father's truck," I observe, verbalizing a fact Hilton obviously knows. "I saw it parked by their trailer, and I saw it parked once at a game."

The older man sits on the trunk's front bumper, puffing slightly, and I sit beside him, my legs suddenly too wobbly to stand on.

"No, this truck never belonged to Lucky Diamond's father," he says, shaking his head. "Trucks weren't exactly his father's style. That's my pickup."

My heart pounds in my ears, and I am unable to hold back any longer, to ask my questions at Hilton's slow, measured pace. "Lucky's father was a baseball player, wasn't he?" I ask, blurting the words out.

When Hilton fails to reply, choosing to stare instead at two small maple trees growing just outside of the barn, I continue, "He was one of those careless types, wasn't he? He was a run-of-the-mill ballplayer who made a run-of-the-mill mistake, and you bailed him—"

"There was nothing run-of-the-mill about Lucky Diamond's father!" Hilton hisses, cutting me off. "That boy's father was Ben Slaughter!"

For a moment the name means nothing to me, and I stare at Hilton, confused.

"Ben Slaughter!" he repeats, his teeth clenched with frustration.

Slowly the name conjures up details, some more precise than others. There was that short but remarkable home run binge, that one week in April. Ten—no, eleven now—eleven years ago. I remember a news clip of one of those home runs disappearing over the "green monster" in left field, the young man jogging around the bases with a smile on his face so bright that I wondered why Fenway Park even bothered with lights. He was a rookie, playing in the majors for the first time in his life, and already the sports magazines and tabloids were touting him as the best Red Sox home run threat since . . . since they traded Babe Ruth to the Yankees.

And then, suddenly, Slaughter was gone, killed when he crashed his sports car into a bridge. And Hilton came to Vermont.

"My God, Hilton. What happened?" I shake my head as the words float wistfully through the barn, hanging between us like mist.

His gaze rolls slowly from the maple trees to me, and his tired, old man's eyes well up with disappointment, regret, despair. He too must remember those home runs, he must remember them in far greater detail than I do. For Hilton, however, there must be other memories as well, memories that from the little I can recall

from the newspaper headlines are all about drunk driving, toxi-
cology reports, and a sports car smashed almost beyond recogni-
tion in Dedham.

"What happened to Ben Slaughter?" Hilton finally says, re-
peating my question ruefully. "It sounds like a book, doesn't it?
Or maybe it's just a sports trivia question: whatever happened to
Ben Slaughter?"

"He died in a car accident, right?"

Hilton sighs. "They said he'd been going ninety-two miles per
hour. A little suburban street at one in the morning, and he's
driving ninety-two miles per hour."

"Was it suicide?"

Hilton scowls at me as if I'm an idiot or insane. "Ben Slaughter? Of course not. He probably thought he would live forever."

One of the Burberrys' cats, a large black and white mouser
with a red collar, runs down the steps from the loft, and races
past us into the driveway. The sun is beginning to set.

"Maybe that's why he was so careless," Hilton continues. "You
were right about that. He was the careless type, and he left behind some . . . some untidy business."

"And you tried to clean it up."

"And I tried to clean it up. It was the sort of thing I did for a lot
of boys over the years."

"No, there's more to it than that."

"Of course there is. Everything Slaughter did, he did in a big
way. Home runs. Diving catches. These throws to home plate
that came in like bullets. It's a shame, but no one ever talks about
his arm anymore. They should, you know. It was a cannon. Anyway, when Slaughter made a mess, he made a big mess."

"He got this Susie McCormick pregnant?"

Hilton frowns. "I don't think I've ever been angrier in my life
than when I heard what had happened. Susie McCormick was
this . . . this baby with a crush on Ben Slaughter as big as any
of his home runs. She met him when he was still in the minors,
and followed him around like a puppy dog. And when she got
pregnant, she decided that she just had to have that child. She
just had to."

The cat strolls back to us, and rubs up against my pants leg,
marking me as his. I reach down and stroke the top of his head.
"Jamie said she was fifteen. Is that true?"

"Definitely. And the single best baseball player our farm system ever produced knocked her . . . got her pregnant. I couldn't believe it, I just couldn't believe it. Of course, that farm system itself was where it happened. Ben didn't play very long in the minors, but he did make most of the stops. Two months in rookie ball, a couple weeks in double A. A little winter ball in Central America, a couple months in Pawtucket. Pawtucket was where it all began."

"Because that's where he met Susie?"

"Yup. Pawtucket. His last stop before Boston." He reaches over and picks up his cat, sitting the animal down on his lap. The cat looks up at Hilton and purrs.

"We paid Ben a hell of a bonus when we signed him," Hilton remembers, almost absentmindedly petting the cat. "We really did. And he chose to invest it with as much stupidity as any man can muster—beginning with that car of his. I probably don't have to tell you this, but it was red. He said he chose red for the Red Sox. I never believed him."

"No?"

"No. He bought red because it was a flashy color. That's all."

It is odd to sit on the bumper of a pickup truck in a barn in Vermont, the sounds of a cat's purr beside me and a thousand peepers just out of sight, and listen to a man named Burberry tell me about a myth named Ben Slaughter.

"Someone . . . some people . . . have told me that he had been drinking at your home. In Dedham."

"That's true. Eunice and I had had a small dinner party for the rookies that evening. We had one almost every year, usually on the first or second off night in April."

I nod, trying to digest as much as I can, feeling for some reason a need to be kind. "I guess he hadn't seemed that drunk when he left your house."

Hilton paws at the dirt in the barn with the toe of his shoe. "Oh, he seemed drunk all right. There was no doubt in my mind that night, or any night since. I knew he was drunk. And that's something I've always lived with, and something I always will."

He cranes his neck and looks away from me. "I never saw a boy with Ben Slaughter's promise," he says. "Not in forty-plus years. He lived his life in a hitting streak."

"Does Lucky know any of this?" I ask softly, slowly. "Any of it at all?"

"He knows that the man who raised him wasn't his father. But I think it's only in the last few days that he has begun to suspect there's a deeper truth."

I wince at the word *truth*. It seems to me now a very strange word.

"So who did raise him? Who was this Diamond who pretended to work for the Red Sox? Was he related to Slaughter?"

"No. Slaughter was an only child. Whatever family he had, lived in California somewhere."

"So who took the boy?"

"Danny McCormick. Susie's older brother. He lived in Boston, which is probably why Susie ended up in New England when she left home. Anyway Danny wanted to raise the boy, he wanted to take care of him. After all, the boy was his nephew. But he needed me to prepare the appropriate paperwork."

"Which you did . . ."

"Which I did."

"Why 'Diamond'? Why isn't the boy named McCormick?"

"Susie didn't have a monopoly on trouble in the McCormick family. Danny got into his share of trouble too. Some small robberies—a convenience store, a gas station—that sort of thing. Neither was especially major. But I still had to provide the adoption services with paperwork that hid Danny's criminal record."

"You gave a little baby to a criminal? God almighty, Hilton, what were you thinking?"

"Danny had a good heart. With a little luck, things might have been different for him."

"He might have been president," I say sarcastically.

"Perhaps," Hilton murmurs, ignoring the tone of my voice. "He was a smart guy. He had a lot of character, a lot of integrity."

"Except for the fact he took off like a bat out of hell when he saw Jeff Grout get smashed by a ton of logs."

"Danny McCormick died this year in the second week in April. Pancreatic cancer. He was diagnosed last winter, about the same time you came to me and said you wanted a team, and gone four months later." He pauses, collecting himself. "But before he died, he too asked me for help. And so I brought Lucky to Vermont."

"Then who was Grout with when he died?" I ask, but before Hilton can respond, I know the answer to this question too. "He really was alone, wasn't he? He wasn't Lucky's father, but he was Lucky's 'old man.' That's what you meant when you said his old man disappeared."

Hilton nods. "Lucky is a very smart, very resourceful eleven-year-old boy. But he's still a boy. He's certainly not prepared to live alone in a trailer in the middle of the woods. Jeff Grout was already logging my land, so I decided to pay him—very well, I assure you—to take the boy in and look out for him until—"

"Until you found him a proper home—"

"Until you, you stupid son of a bitch, figured out that Lucky Diamond should live with you and Harper! Nothing happens in this world without a reason, I've told you that! Nothing! Well, when you came to me asking for a team, I knew in an instant that you and Lucky were a perfect fit: that boy is nothing if he's not love. He's nothing if he's not the son you can cherish the way you cherished Nathaniel!"

I sit there stunned, angry at Hilton for his arrogance, for his belief that he can heal the wounds of bereft fathers and fatherless sons. "You think you can pull all the strings. You think you can stand somewhere behind the scenes like you once did with the Red Sox, and control people. Control their destinies. Well, it's not that simple. You're not negotiating contracts, you're not—"

"I was trying to find a little boy a home," he says, cutting me off. "That's all I was trying to do."

"For God's sake then, Hilton, why don't you and Eunice take the boy in? Hell, he's practically living here now."

He shrugs. "I'm seventy-four years old. Eunice isn't much younger—though she'd like you to believe she is. It doesn't seem fair to bring a boy here who has already lost one set of parents now, does it? Especially when there are younger couples in town . . .

"Besides," he continues, "Eunice doesn't want the headaches of raising a teenage boy, not if she can avoid it. Not now, not at her—not at our—age. As far as she's concerned, the child is simply some stray who belonged to a friend of Jeff Grout in Boston. She doesn't feel the . . . the responsibility . . . for the boy that I feel."

"And you're never going to tell her . . ."

"Not if I can avoid it. I see no reason to subject her to that kind of pressure, not in the few years we have left on this earth together."

Feeling wrung out, I take a deep breath. "You left baseball just after Lucky was born, didn't you?"

"Yes, but that's not how I look at it. As far as I'm concerned, I left baseball just after Ben Slaughter was killed. I was never going to see another swing like Ben Slaughter's, not in my lifetime, and there was no point in hanging around by the batting cage, waiting. So I cleaned up what I could, and then I . . . I left. I gave my notice, said my good-byes, and walked away."

Outside of the barn we can hear footsteps, the sound of the boy approaching. We wait there together, me and the old man, sitting in silence on the bumper of a blue pickup truck.

III.

Chapter 29

L ucky is twelve years older than his sister, but they are nonetheless very close. They might, to the casual observer, be as united by blood as they have been by fate.

A poet once wrote about fathers playing catch with sons, but in the case of Lucky and Catherine Grace—who at eight insists now upon being called Katie—it is brothers and sisters. Lucky has taught her far more about baseball than I ever could, and Catherine will be without question this year the star of the Little League Sprouts. I find it very interesting that Catherine swings a bat much like Nathaniel, swinging from the right side of the plate and holding the bat a tad higher than the textbooks (and Lucky Diamond) recommend.

Alexis and Elsa, who these days do little more than sleep and nap and eat, treat Catherine and Lucky with equal disdain, ignoring each of them unless there's the promise of food or a warm, unmade bed.

When Lucky is home from college for spring break, that week's respite at the end of March, he indulges me. We tramp out to the still-frozen ground of the Havington baseball field, and in the forty- and fifty-degree afternoons he helps me to warm up my arm, to prepare my forty-plus body for the new baseball season. When he returns in May, leaving his books behind him for the summer, he will sometimes help me to coach the Triple-A Tigers. Lucky is now as much a celebrity as he was once a curiosity: he has led the state university to intercollegiate titles two seasons in a row, and when he graduates next year, will in all likelihood be signed by a professional team. Already the bird dogs—the sincere old men in rumpled sports coats who scout for the pros—have begun to mythologize his swing in their own spiral notebooks.

Am I becoming a fixture on the Little League field? Perhaps.

Do the great many fathers and sons I have seen come and go in eight astonishingly short years view me the way I once viewed Hilton? As a man inordinately obsessed with a boy's game? Probably.

And that's fine. The years are short, the summers shorter still. I take from them what pleasure they will give me, trying as best I can to deal with the curveballs that they throw.

And I try not to view those curveballs as part of a grand conspiracy, or plot, or plan.

It was at the very least appropriate, however, that Hilton Burberry died in the fall, when the game that he loved was about to desert him. Once again. It was at the very least appropriate that Mr. Godfrey died in the winter, when the rocking chairs in which he would sit for hours were in hibernation.

And it was at the very least appropriate that Donnie—now Donald—Casey moved to New Mexico with his parents, taken to a climate where day by ninety-degree day his little boy fat melted away, and his heart had a chance to heal.

And through each spring and summer, each season of repetition and ritual and—as she still calls it—"the stuff they do between innings," Harper remains patient with me. More patient and supportive and loving than dreams. Her husband may be viewed as a bit of an eccentric in the village of Havington, a local character with an inordinate interest in Little League baseball, but it is a harmless idiosyncracy.

And it just may be a helpful one. A helpful idiosyncracy indeed.